Once There Was a Villain

By Indy Guerra

For "little me" who always dreamed of being an author,
but was afraid people would think her stories were dumb.
We did it.

Prologue
Borden, First King of the Wildlands

The forest was in upheaval. The land was never meant to be divided like this, all the magic shoved into one corner of the world. Once a beautiful and serene land, now it writhed with turmoil. Magic creatures flooded the territory, fleeing their homes, magic seeped into the trees themselves- causing them to wake, great landslides and earthquakes shifted the landscape. I contemplated the land I now had sole dominion over as I hiked along the river I'd been mapping. This was all Father's fault. He'd abandoned us. He turned his back on his wife and all his descendants down to his great grandchild expected later this year. All because of some prophecy and his own cowardice. Now mother was dead, unable to take the heartbreak. She'd spilled every last drop of her magic into the land, letting the earth itself consume her. Her magic had erupted in the ground, causing mountains to rise up and split the land in two. It was a feat of earth magic, unlike anything I'd ever seen. It was not a fate she deserved and I would do what I could to make sure father regretted every last day of his miserable life.

I stopped as the river came to a wide pool with an island of rock that jutted out in the middle. The engorged river slowed to a gentle trickle that sounded softly in the air. This was the perfect spot. I had tracked this river through the mountain pass and knew that it ran directly into father's land. I swept my hand and a bridge of stone assembled, joining the bank of the river with the island. I crossed it with purpose and drew my sword. I gazed at the ornate weapon bitterly. It had been crafted by my grandfather and passed from generation to generation. I had planned to pass it on to my eldest daughter, but now it would serve a different purpose.

I rubbed the enchanted jewel embedded in its hilt. It was a beautiful emerald green but I knew that would change with what I was about to do. I pulled from my pocket a tiny vial. The steel hilt was cool in my hand as I held the sword and vial away from my body, knowing that the potency of the poison within could kill me in seconds. I hesitated only a moment after popping open the vial. A toxic, acrid smell wafted towards me from the bottle. The consequences of what I was about to do would last for decades, maybe even centuries. But I clenched my jaw and continued. My children would be taught that weak and cowardly rulers deserved to be destroyed. They would hate the so-called King of Gotland as would their children and their children's children. This would only be the first retaliation my line would make. I dripped the inky black substance onto the jewel and watched as it sunk in, absorbed by the magic gem. The black swirled inside the stone, blotting out the green until in its place was a solid black stone, dark as obsidian. I replaced the cork on the empty vial and inspected the tainted blade. I saw my own grim face reflected at me in the inky depths of the enchanted stone. Holding it before my face, I summoned my magic and spoke an enchantment into it, "Let only the hands of they who would restore honor to the Gotland royal line lift this blade from its tomb." With that I plunged the sword into the bed of rock, sealing my spell upon it.

Chapter 1 The Princess

My footsteps fell silently as I ran across the dewy field. I glanced over my shoulder furtively and pulled my navy cloak tighter around my shoulders. The thick wool material kept the chill of the night at bay and prevented the moonlight from revealing the white material of my nightgown underneath. I was panting by the time I'd crossed the distance between the palace and the forest but I didn't stop until I was well within the cover of the trees. Finally, I reached a clearing amongst the dense foliage and paused to catch my breath. My dark hair was spilling out of my hood where I had tucked it, and I brushed it back as I looked around. The moonlight caught in the tiny drops of dew that covered every surface and made them sparkle like stars in the night sky. There were various species of fungi growing along the forest floor and on the bark of the tree trunks that glowed in the dark. It was otherworldly and I breathed in the crisp night air deeply as I took it all in. Feeling more relaxed now that I was beyond the reach of the palace guards' eye, I strolled leisurely through the woods. I paused here and there to admire the glistening flowers that speckled the forest floor. The hem of my gown grew damp with dew as I made my way along. I kneeled down to brush my finger along some little white snowdrops and smiled. This place was my little secret. Father thought there were dangerous magical creatures in the woods, and used them as his personal hunting grounds. No one came here at night and so no one knew the beautiful secrets it hid.

Somewhere in the woods, a snap sounded and I instantly froze. Occasionally I saw deer, rabbits, and foxes out here, none of which would do me harm, but my heart thundered nonetheless. Something was moving slowly through the underbrush and I held my breath in anticipation as it came nearer. It sounded large, a stag perhaps? As I watched, a magnificent white form emerged from the trees. The mare's long, wavy, white mane and tail shone in the moonlight and the entire beast nearly glowed. But what really caught my attention was the opalescent horn that rose up from between its alert ears. A unicorn. It was the purest, most breathtaking beast I'd ever seen. She turned to look at me and my breath caught. Was this one of the dangerous magical creatures father spoke of? Was this creature about to gore me with its wickedly sharp horn? I should've run but I stayed rooted in place. I was enraptured by the impossible animal before me. As she approached with near-silent steps, all I could do was sit perfectly still - frozen in place. She stopped right in front of me and I lifted my head to meet her intelligent gaze. Everything seemed to still for a moment as she considered me and then with a small movement of her head, she tapped her horn against the top of my head. Warmth flooded through me from the point of contact and I exhaled the breath I'd been holding. Then she backed up and continued on her way, disappearing into the forest. I watched her leave, unsure of exactly what had just happened. What was that feeling? I didn't know anything about magical creatures. Until just a moment ago I had no reason to believe unicorns even existed. My moment of reverence was broken as I realized I wasn't sure how much time had passed. Though I wanted to stay and explore longer, I needed to get back before anyone noticed me missing. I couldn't even imagine how my father might respond if he were to discover my secret outings. He'd be livid. I rose from my kneeling position on the ground and made my way back to the palace grounds. I ran across the open field that lay between the palace and the woods and darted into the gardens. On one side of the garden was a tall trellis of honeysuckle that reached all the way to my third floor bedchambers. I climbed it expertly, having done the very same thing almost every night for the last year. The woods were my escape, the only time that nobody was watching me or telling me what to do. I huffed as I heaved myself over the sill of my open window and landed on the floor inside my bedchamber. It seemed there were still a few hours of darkness left so I kicked off my slippers and hung my cloak to dry before climbing into bed. I shivered under the covers a bit in my thin nightgown and tried to push away thoughts of my exciting night and the beautiful unicorn so that I could get some rest. Afterall, tomorrow was a big day. Still, as I drifted off to sleep, visions of the ethereal mare filled my head with wonder, bleeding into my dreams.

Chapter 2 The Witch

I awoke to the feeling of warm sunlight falling on my face. Through the open window I could hear birds singing in the gardens below and the fragrance of honeysuckle flowers floated in. I grinned and stretched my arms high above my head, brushing against the ornate wooden headboard of my four-poster bed. Last night seemed like a dream, but today was going to be the best day ever because today was my sixteenth birthday. Everything was going to be perfect.

I rolled out of bed and rang a little bell at my bedside to call my lady-in-waiting. As an after-thought, I quickly kicked my soiled slippers from the night before under the bed and slipped on another pair of satin slippers just as Eleanor entered from her chamber which was adjacent to mine. She was perfectly punctual. Always there when I needed her, and often there before I knew I'd need her. She already had a pitcher of water in hand and headed straight to the porcelain basin at the other end of my chambers.

"Did you sleep well Lady Vivienne?" she asked as she filled the basin.

"I was too excited to sleep much," I fibbed with a yawn as I followed after her and began washing my face in the cool water.

Eleanor smiled and handed me a cloth, "It's going to be quite the party tonight,"

I patted my face dry and returned her smile, "I sure hope so, I've been planning it for months!"

"Well let's hurry and you can put on your party dress!" she said as she ushered me to the vanity and began brushing through my long, brown hair.

I grinned broadly into the mirror as I watched her work. My excitement was dampened for a moment as I studied her face. Her features were plain, but pretty in an understated way. She was four years older than me and had served me well for the last three years. But she was more than just a lady-in-waiting to me, she was my best friend and I was going to miss her sorely when she left in just three months. Father had rewarded her well for her service to me by approving her betrothal to a handsome young duke. They were to be married in the fall.

"I'm going to miss you," I said softly.

Eleanor looked up in surprise and gave me a soft smile, "I'm going to miss you too. But I'll visit as often as possible and maybe you can come visit me too."

I offered her a half-hearted smile. We both knew that the likelihood of me being allowed to visit her at the Duke's estate was next to none. I had not left the palace grounds even once in my entire life. Father did not allow it. He said that it was too risky. There were witches and warlocks, powerful sorcerers just waiting for an opportunity to curse a young princess such as myself. Father said magic was dangerous and those who wield it even more so. And that was why it had been outlawed in our kingdom of Gotland for the last 150 years. But magic-wielding criminals might still sneak into our lands, said father. Which is why I had to stay within the palace walls where it was safe.

"All done!" Eleanor exclaimed, interrupting my thoughts. "Now let's get you dressed!" She brought over a large box and opened it to reveal the dress that had been designed and sewn for my special day. I lifted it from the box and squealed in excitement. Layers and layers of pale pink tulle and chiffon spilled out as I lifted it and I could hardly contain myself as I took in the sweetheart neckline and long sheer sleeves that would fit loosely and then cinch at the wrists. It was perfect. Just wait till Ronaldo sees me in this I thought to myself. The young Duke was the most handsome and eligible young man in the kingdom and I was certain a formal courtship was in the near future. Perhaps we would even steal away tonight and I would have my first kiss. Yes, today was going to be perfect. Marion entered at that moment and I beamed at my beloved governess.

"How do you like it?" she asked.

"It's perfect!" I gushed. I set it down and bounced over to her, wrapping her in a hug. She stood several inches taller than me, and despite having known her my entire life, she hadn't seemed to age a day. Her face was the sort that made it impossible to guess her age with subtle crinkles by her eyes, and just a few gray hairs hidden amongst her thick, blonde tresses. She smiled at me and hugged me back affectionately, resting her cheek on top of my head.

"I'm glad you like it. The seamstresses worked hard on it. Be sure to thank them." Marion said.

Marion was always making sure I behaved graciously. She said, be gracious, kind, and honest and people will flock to you. She was good at her job, but she made me feel as loved as if she were my own mother.

"I will, thank you, Marion."

She beamed at me in approval and I soaked it in.

I spent the hours preceding the party flouncing around the palace halls in my ball gown, tasting finger foods, and watching the servants decorate the ballroom. The Gotland Palace ballroom was a sight to behold with its huge vaulted ceilings and marble dance floor. On one side of the vaulted ceiling stood a beautiful stained glass window. Ten feet wide and twenty feet tall, it held several depictions of various landmarks across Gotland. Mt.Vale, the Rainy Woods, Runaway River, all set underneath a rising sun. Throughout the room, huge arrangements of pink peonies and greenery adorned every surface and long swathes of pink and white fabric were hung above every doorway. It was beautiful, better than any party I'd seen hosted in this palace. And we had a lot of parties. One for every holiday, every royal birthday, and every major life event. Father looked for every excuse to celebrate. As I walked the halls, basking in the glorious day that was today, I spotted a familiar form down the hall.

"Damien!" I ran towards him with my skirt bunched in my hands.

Damien turned and gave me a grin, "There's my little sister!"

I wrapped my arms around his middle in a warm hug and he planted a kiss on top of my head.

"You look beautiful Vivienne. Is everything coming together as you'd hoped?" he asked, pulling me away by my shoulders.

"Yes, everything is just as I'd imagined." I beamed at him.

Damien ran his fingers through his dark hair in that way that had all the chambermaids swooning and straightened his collar. "Good. I'll see you later at the party, I've got some things to attend to before the celebrations begin."

Ah, Damien. He was always so busy. As crown prince, he had many responsibilities. Politics, governance, delegation, yada yada. I didn't understand most of it and I didn't envy his birthright. Being the second born was so much easier. The only expectations seemed to be: look pretty, be polite, marry well and without complaint. Easy enough.

Damien was good at what he did though. Everyone liked him. He easily won over every man he conversed with, and with his good looks, had every woman gushing. At the age of 21, father was pushing him to pick a suitable bride and though he could have his pick, he for some reason continually delayed making a decision. Perhaps, tonight he'll meet someone who catches his eye, I thought to myself as I waved him goodbye. After all, it was a royal ball. Anything could happen.

Finally, the time for the party arrived and guests spilled into the great room. They were arriving from not only our kingdom, but from some of the neighboring kingdoms as well. My father stood at the foot of the throne, looking every bit the grand king that he was. He was a big man, his belly just starting to get round after years of peace and plenty. His shoulder length dark hair was streaked with silver and topped with an ornate golden crown. He smiled warmly as he welcomed people in, and stroked his well-groomed beard as he scanned the room. I took my place beside my father to take part in the formal greetings. I curtsied and he quickly kissed my hand.

"Happy birthday dear."

"Thank you, Father." I smiled at him and his eyes met mine for a moment before he cleared his throat and turned his attention to the guests. We were soon swept up in a sea of seemingly never-ending curtsies and greetings. This was not my favorite part of these events but as the musicians began playing a familiar sounding waltz, I was rescued from the formalities when a young man asked me to dance. I gladly accepted his invitation and started in on what I knew would be the first of many dances tonight.

A few songs in, Damien snagged me for a dance.

"There's someone I'd like you to dance with." He said cheerfully.

I laughed, "trying to set me up with one of your friends again?"

"You could call it that," he answered playfully. "William Turnpike, he likes you, but he's too shy to ask you to dance."

I wrinkled my nose. "Damien, he's nearly twenty years older than me."

"Fifteen," he corrected me, "and he owns a sizable fleet of merchant ships which makes him one of the wealthiest men in Duthlin."

Duthlin was a neighboring kingdom which bordered the sea. Damien gestured towards William with his eyes and I followed his gaze. William was making polite conversation with another businessman, nodding his round face in agreement with whatever was being said. He was tall and pale, with round cheeks that turned red with the slightest excitement. He was a nice fellow but he was just too, well, old I decided. He wasn't even looking at me. What made Damien think he liked me?

There was an annoying buzzing sensation in my head- like maybe the wine was a bit strong and I shook it off as I turned back to my big brother, "I wouldn't marry William if he owned a herd of unicorns."

Damien tsked in annoyance, "Come on Vivienne, it's just one dance."

I shrugged, "Alright, I'll dance with him,"

"Really?" he asked hopefully.

I smirked. "-if he asks me to." I finished.

I saw Damien's jaw clench but he just gave me a tight smile, "very well." He said and with that the dance was over and I was already being swept away by another hopeful gentleman.

As the music played on and on, I danced with more young men than I could count. Except I had counted and there were 12 of them. My latest dance partner was going on and on about agricultural rights and taxes and, oh jeez, plague. Yuck. I looked around the room, searching for the person I really wanted to dance with- Ronaldo. Why hadn't he asked me to dance yet? Maybe he was just caught up talking or he was running late and had yet to arrive. As I scanned the many faces, many of them watching me, I caught sight of Father. He stood out amongst the crowd with his large stature and fine robes. He was sipping a glass of wine at the foot of the throne and chatting with a beautiful woman who I recognized as Duchess Catherine Weber. She was widowed sometime last year if I recall. Perhaps Father would meet someone special tonight, I thought to myself. My visions of royal wedding grandeur were interrupted though as Damien appeared and began speaking quietly into Father's ear. Father furrowed his brow and rubbed his round tummy anxiously then began nodding in agreement with whatever Damien was saying. Oh bother. Looks like something important had come up and now Father would be busy whispering back and forth with Damien for the rest of the night. I hadn't even gotten to really speak to him yet. It was always like this. Father, spending time with Damien, giving him all the attention. When I tried to speak with Father he always seemed so… bored. Distracted. Even uncomfortable. I had the nagging feeling that he avoided me. But he always gave me whatever I asked for. Dresses, jewelry, ponies, parties. I'd trade it all for his undivided attention. For him to show genuine interest in me. For him to ask about my lessons or my hobbies.

But it didn't matter, I reminded myself. I got plenty of attention from the boys my age, and even the gentlemen older than me. I enticed them with soft smiles and fluttery eyelashes. I laughed at their dumb jokes and hung on their arms. And in return, they paid me compliments and followed me with their eyes wherever I went. They acted like I was the single most important person in the room. And I guess I was.

I turned my eyes away from Father and Damien and their secret little conversations and caught sight of someone much more interesting, Ronaldo. He was surrounded by a group of girls who were practically salivating over him and my face twisted in a pout. I quickly wiped the expression off my face and replaced it with an airy, carefree smile.

Turning back to my dance partner, I interrupted his mind-numbing rant with an excuse about needing a drink and promptly left him on the dance floor, his voice tittering after me. I headed towards a punch bowl, making sure to pass through Ronaldo's line of sight and felt as his gaze snagged on me. He excused himself from the gaggle of girls and moved to intercept me, just as I knew he would.

"Princess Vivienne! You look stunning!"

I gave him an innocent smile and looked him over while batting my eyelashes. He was tall, with light brown hair and a confident smile.

"Ronaldo! I was beginning to think you hadn't come."

He took my hand and bowed down to kiss it, " And miss the biggest party of the season? This is quite the event."

I nodded, feeling quite pleased with myself, "Yes, it is a bit warm in here though. I was just on my way to grab a drink and then I think I'll go get some air."

Ronaldo's eyes lit and he turned to pour me a drink, "Ah! I shall accompany you then!"

Bullseye. I had him. I took his arm and we made our way across the ballroom towards the exit which led to the gardens.

Suddenly a piercing crash sounded overhead and I screamed as a million shards of colored glass rained down around me. I stumbled backward, falling to the ground as I raised my arms up to shield myself. Around me chaos broke out as people screamed and ran to the edges of the room. I lowered my arms to look up at the jagged hole in the center of the stained glass window, then my eyes fell to the sinister form standing before me amidst the broken glass.

Shrouded in a dark cloak with an unnatural wind whirling around her stood a woman. She pulled back her hood to reveal long, dark hair, streaked with gray and a sickly pale face, twisted with rage.

Witch.

Her eyes bore into mine and my stomach dropped to my feet. She began advancing towards me and I scrambled backwards with a gasp.

"Fraud!" she screeched. "Traitor!"

I turned and tried to get to my feet, but with a flash of speed, she snatched my arm and wrenched me towards her. I cried out as her nails dug in painfully, "Let go!"

"Spoiled brat!" she screeched in my face.

Panicked, I looked around for help. I saw Father lying on the ground, watching in horror. Damien stood behind him, stunned.

"Father! Damien!" I cried.

"They can't save you," sneered the witch, "they're all cowards! Just like you!"

I tried to pull away, but her grip only tightened.

"Let me go!" I looked to where Ronaldo had been but he was nowhere to be seen and it seemed he had fled too.

"This is who you surround yourself with?" she accused, "fake friends and politicians? You should be ashamed! A phony princess having a party while the world around her crumbles."

"I don't know what you're talking about, please!" My heart thundered in my chest and tears filled my eyes. But as I looked up into her eyes I saw only anger and insanity. She didn't care what I said right now.

Then she turned her gaze to Father.

"You'll regret your foolishness, king. Perhaps this will teach you a lesson." She raised her fist and Damien leapt forward.

"Wait!" he shouted. But it was too late. She threw down her fist and a swarm of black smoke coiled around us blocking out my vision completely. My stomach lurched and my chest tightened as the air was sucked out of my lungs. And as my mind reeled in the darkness, I had the sense that the worst was yet to come.

Chapter 3 The Tower

My sight rushed back to me and I gasped as air filled my lungs once more. I looked around wildly, trying to process my surroundings. I was on my knees on a thick rug laid over a stone floor. The large room that surrounded me had rounded walls that formed a circle. The witch was nowhere in sight. Where had she gone?

"Hello?" I cried, "Is anyone there?" Only silence answered me. I looked around and realized there was no door in the room, only a huge window with hinged panes. I stumbled to my feet and rushed over to the window, flinging the glass doors open. My heart sank as I took in the sight before me. I was in a tower, the height difficult to determine due to the dense forest of impossibly thick brambles that grew up around the base of the tower and extended out a hundred yards. At the edge of the brambles began a forest of pine trees reaching out as far as the eye could see. I had no idea where I was, but it certainly wasn't the palace grounds. I whipped around and panic began to rise in me. Surely there had to be a way out. I began tearing the room apart. There was a bed, bookshelves, a wood burning stove, and other miscellaneous furniture and chests. I pulled everything back from the walls except the bookcases which stood 15 feet tall and would be impossible to move. When that didn't turn up anything, I began rolling up the thick rug that covered the floor. I was panting with panic and exertion at this point, feeling like a trapped animal. Everything was covered in a layer of dust and my dress was marred with streaks of dark gray where it had rubbed against all the furniture. As I shuffled across the floor on my knees, rolling up the rug, my dress caught and tore. But I didn't care right then. I had to get out of here before the witch came back. I had to get back home.

A distraught sound left my throat as I finished rolling the rug and realized there was no trap door. I stood and spun in a circle, a terrifying reality setting in. I was trapped. Magically transported into an inescapable room. Imprisoned. Walking backward till I hit a wall, I slid down to the ground as another thought occurred to me. No one knew where I was. How could I be rescued if no one knew where I was? I hugged my knees and started to cry, sobbing loudly. How had everything gone so wrong? I didn't deserve this. I hadn't done anything wrong so why was I being punished? I knew Father would look for me but who knew how long that could take? I could be stuck here for days. I buried my face in my dress as the snot and tears ran.

"Poor child." sounded a voice.

My head whipped up, "Who's there?" Silence.

Another voice sounded from up above my head, "Interesting."

I looked around the rafters where the voice came from but didn't see anyone. "Who are you?" A long pause followed.

"We are here to watch over you." The voices sounded small and female, but again I could not see anyone.

"Where are you? Why can't I see you?" I asked.

"We can't tell you." came the voice.

"It would be dangerous for our kind." Agreed another voice. There were three of them as far as I could tell.

"Dangerous? What do you mean?" I asked with a frown. Nothing they said was making any sense.

"We've already said too much." answered one of the voices.

I stood quickly, "What!? You've hardly said anything at all! How do I get out of here?"

"There is no escape." said the first voice.

"Go to sleep, child." said the second voice.

"And wait for the rescuer." finished the third voice.

I scowled and clenched my fists in resistance. Ignoring the useless beings, I continued to double check every nook and cranny, determined to find a way out. I searched and searched, sliding the furniture back and forth across the floor. But my efforts were in vain. I was sealed in with no way out and exhaustion was seeping into my bones. My shoulders sagged in defeat as I considered the words of my apparent babysitters. They had a point. I couldn't find a way out and as the light faded with the setting sun, I had to accept that I would not be going home today. I may as well go to sleep.

"Very well." I sighed. I turned and looked around at the room I had torn apart. Furniture on end, the rug shoved to the side. I set about putting everything back and closed the window doors. Then I turned to the bed and looked down at my dress in puzzlement. I didn't generally dress or undress myself. Eleanor always helped me with that. But the fluffy dress would not be comfortable to sleep in and may not even fit in the small bed, I thought to myself. I could just barely reach the buttons and I spent a good twenty minutes straining to undo every button that ran up my back.

When I finished my arms were aching and I felt the weight of exhaustion from the events of the day sweep through me. I stepped out of my ball gown, leaving me in just my underdress, and climbed into the bed. And as I pulled the covers over myself, not even the lumpy mattress was enough to keep me awake.

Chapter 4 The Mage

I slept a heavy, dreamless sleep and awoke at sunrise. Rubbing my eyes, I swung my legs out of bed.

"She's awake." sounded one of the voices.

"Interesting." said another.

I frowned at the ceiling where their voices carried down from. Were they going to give cryptic commentary on everything I did? Ignoring them, I padded across the room on my bare feet and opened up the window. Looking down, I observed the forest of thorns once more. It created a formidable barrier between my prison tower and the woods beyond. But surely father's knights could cut their way through. Hopefully today, they will find me and take me home before the witch returns, I thought to myself. I sat by the window for a while thinking about everything that had happened before I turned back to the room and called out, “Say, is there any food around here?” There was a long pause.

“I suppose she will need to eat if this is how it’s going to be.” said a voice.

“There are some provisions in the chest by the wood stove,” said another.

I opened the chest and found what mostly looked like dried herbs and wrinkled my nose as the strong scent hit me. At the bottom were a few potatoes and a jar of walnuts. I eyed the walnuts in distaste.

“At this rate, I’m going to starve before they find me.” Nonetheless I opened the jar and munched on a few of the bitter nuts as I took in more details around the room. There was a large basin against one of the walls. Above it, a metal pipe protruded from the wall at a slant. I observed as a few drops of water came from the spout and splashed into the basin. I realized it must be a collection system that channeled water from the roof of the tower. There was a ladle hanging from the basin and I used it to sip from the water that must have been saved from the last rain. Next I turned my attention to what appeared to be a bizarre kind of chamber pot. The pot was secured firmly to the floor with a wooden seat over it that had a hinged lid. I opened it curiously and was surprised to feel a draft when I did so. There was a hole at the bottom of the pot that opened to a tunnel which slanted towards the outer wall so that any waste would be expelled from the tower. Fascinating. I looked around the room again and frowned. It was so dirty. Never in my life had I resided in such a filthy place. The palace horse stalls were cleaner than this. I didn't want my rescuers to see me in such a place. I looked down at my dirty feet poking out from my under-dress. I didn't want anyone to see *me* like this. I glanced towards my ball gown which lay in a heap on the floor. No way would I be able to button that thing back up on my own. I put my hands on my hips in determination. I'd just have to clean this place up and maybe I'd find something suitable to wear while I was at it.

I spotted a broom and got to work sweeping the smooth stone floor. I swept it again and again, dumping the dirt out the window each time. Then I found a cloth that I soaked in the basin and began wiping down every surface in the room. I wasn't used to physical labor like this and I paused frequently to catch my breath. I made a note to better appreciate the many maids who did this kind of work for me.

When I finished I surveyed the room with my hands on my hips feeling quite pleased with myself. It wasn't often that I got to complete tasks like this and feel the sense of pride that came along with those accomplishments. At home I did needlework and lessons, dance class, and horseback riding. But it just wasn't the same as deciding to do something myself and completing it. I went to the window again and frowned. Even if the knights did find this tower, how were they supposed to know I was in here? I glanced back into the room and my eyes landed on the ball gown as an idea formed in my mind. I hurriedly crossed the room to grab the dress and dragged it towards the window. I threw the skirts out the window and wedged the bodice part under one of the glass doors so that the dress hung out the window like a big, fluffy, pink flag. I grinned, even more satisfied with myself for having such a clever idea.

I sat on the ledge by the window for a while, hoping to spot my rescuers on the horizon, but I eventually grew bored. I padded over to the bookshelf and curiously perused the many titles. *100 Ways to Cook Frogs, The Beginner's Guide to Tinctures, Gotland: A History*. Good grief, if I didn't starve, I'd die of boredom. I froze as another title caught my eye. *Magic Theory Vol. 1*. My heart thumped as I pulled the well-worn book from the shelf. This was illegal. This book should not be in Gotland. I glanced around as if someone were about to reprimand me. This felt naughty, it wasn't like me to break the rules. Well, except for sneaking into the forest at night. But nobody knew about that. My curiosity won out though and I dropped to the floor on the rug, placing the book in front of me. I opened it with trepidation and began to read the first chapter.

> *Magic is neither good nor evil, but like humans, is capable of both. It has existed alongside us since the beginning, our gift from Oma, though only the mages can wield it. Mages only exist among the human race and are considered relatively rare with perhaps only one mage for every hundred non-mage. The ability to wield magic*

often runs in families, but it is not unheard of for a mage to be born from non-mage parents. Discerning mage children from non-mage children can be difficult due to the complex nature of the many mage types. A mage's type refers to their core power. All mages are capable of all types of magic with enough practice, but each individual will be especially skilled in one magical type. This type often remains undefined throughout childhood and eventually settles during adolescence or early adulthood as the individual's personality and nature develop. To recognize Mage children, many mage families will perform a discernment ceremony which can help wake up a mage's magical potential. For instructions on performing a discernment ceremony see page 14.

I quickly flipped through the pages, equal parts confused and enraptured by everything I was learning. I had to know more about this forbidden subject. The knowledge called to a deeper yearning in my heart and I read eagerly when I found the page I was seeking.

Performing a Discernment Ceremony:

It is recommended that parents wait to perform a discernment ceremony until a child has reached the age of twelve. Prior to this age a child's mind is not yet sharp enough to maintain the focus necessary for the process.

To begin, you will need a tincture of bloodroot to calm the mind, and sweet nettle salve to dull the senses. Next, lie the child somewhere comfortable in loose fitting clothes and keep the room as quiet as possible with as few witnesses as possible. The rest of the process is up to the child. They must quiet their mind and reach deep inside themselves to find that spark of magic that may or may not live within them. If they are a mage, the feeling will be unmistakable, though each mage reports a slightly different experience. To witnesses, confirmation will only come when the child is able to conjure after the ceremony.

I looked around the room. I wonder if there's any of that tincture or salve somewhere here? I shook my head, was I seriously entertaining such an idea? Magic was banned and for good reason. Magic was the whole reason I was stuck in this predicament. Still, when I thought about potentially wielding magic, it got my heart racing. The idea of it was exciting and scary and it was so ridiculously boring in this tower… I scanned the room again. I mean, the supplies might not even be here, so it couldn't hurt to look. I started going through the contents of one of the many chests. I'm not really looking for the tincture and salve, I told myself. But if I happen to find them…

The first chest I opened was full of clothes. I sorted through them and helped myself to a drab beige dress that looked about my size. It was the sort of thing I supposed commoners would wear- though I wasn't really sure seeing as how I'd never actually seen any of the commoners. In the second chest there were countless jars of unidentifiable substances. Black and green slime sloshed around in them as I rifled through. At the bottom was a wooden box and I pulled it out carefully, the sound of clinking glass alerting me to the content's fragility. I opened it and found it full of tiny, dark brown bottles. I picked one up and read the label. *Lemonweed Tincture.* I eagerly pulled each little bottle from the box until I saw what I had hoped to find, *Bloodroot Tincture.* I placed it alongside the open magic book and excitedly resumed my search. The next chest was full of blankets and bed sheets and I moved on quickly to the next one. This one seemed to contain a physician's supplies. There were bandages, medicines, and an otoscope. I sorted through the medicines, reading the labels as I went. Finally, on a silver tin, I read the words, *Sweet Nettle Salve.* I carried it back over to the book and turned it over in my hands a few times nervously. This was a bad idea. What if it made me sick? What if I got hurt? I looked at the two ingredients before me and frowned. Neither of these were magic potions. In fact, they were rather common remedies that every healer and physician prescribed. So it wasn't like I was using any actual magic, I was just looking for magic. Right? I moved to sit on the edge of the bed and glanced at the ceiling, wondering if the little voices would have anything to say about this. A heavy silence hung around me though and it seemed that they had either decided to let this one play out, or they weren't there. I unscrewed the little tincture bottle and tilted my head back to drip it under my tongue. As the flavor of the drops spread through my mouth I gagged at the bitter, metallic taste. Yuck. I couldn't believe there were people who took this every day to calm their nerves. Next, I opened the tin and scooped out some of the smooth, yellow salve. It tingled on my hands as I spread it over my arms and legs, running my hands up under my dress to get my back, stomach, and chest the best I could. My whole body was tingling now, but as I lay back on the bed, it faded to a dull numbness. I closed my eyes and began to notice the effects of the tincture as my thoughts slowed. It was sort of a nice feeling. Like for a moment it didn't matter that I'd been kidnapped by a witch and imprisoned in an inescapable tower. I frowned at that thought and reminded myself why I was doing this. Right, I've got to search deep inside myself.

I saw myself in my mind's eye. A princess, young, beautiful, rich. Loved by all, but truly known by few. I saw my life till this point play out before me. The passing of my mother when I was a young girl. The confusion I felt during that time. My governess who distracted me from my grief with toys and sweets and endless games. I saw Father grow more distant, the way he looked at me changing as I grew. I saw insecurities. Everyone in my life was either paid to be there or there by obligation. Nobody was there by choice. I saw my failings, naive, sheltered, shallow. I gulped in discomfort as I beheld myself in the most honest light I ever had. I saw my desires; attention, affection, comfort. But beneath those were even deeper desires; connection, adventure, freedom. The last one stood out to me. Freedom. What was keeping me from freedom? In the palace, it was my father's fear of magic. Here in the tower, it was magic itself. So which was it really? Neither. It was the influence of those around me. Pulling me in different directions. Pulling me towards my fate. That was it. I wanted freedom from the influence of others. Freedom to be my own person, to see and understand things for myself. To decide my own destiny. It was my deepest desire.

I suddenly felt a huge release in my chest, like a dam breaking. It seemed my arteries filled with ice as my heart pumped the purest, coldest water through my body. Simultaneously my skin burned like fire was spreading across it and the contrasting sensations were almost unbearable. I gasped and my eyes flew open in alarm, but as I lay there panting, the burning heat and freezing cold faded away. I swung my feet down to the floor and clutched the edge of the bed as I tried to catch my breath. My mind was racing as I looked down at my hands and arms. That hot and cold feeling settled until it was just a faint sensation deep in my bones. It was strangely familiar, like it had been there all my life but I was only just now aware of it.

"She is a mage." spoke one of the voices.

I looked in their direction, "How is this possible?" I asked in a raspy voice.

"Magic has a way of blooming in unexpected places," said another.

"Even when you try to stamp it out." finished the third.

I had no idea what this meant or what it would mean for my future, but one thing was abundantly clear: I was never going to be the same.

Chapter 5 The Flowers

I awoke the next morning from another heavy sleep. It seemed I had blacked out the moment my head hit the pillow and awoke only a moment later, though the heaviness in my limbs told me I'd been asleep for many hours. As I rubbed my face something by the window caught my eye. There was a woven basket sitting on the sill that had definitely not been there before. I crossed the room and peered inside it. There I found a strange variety of things. Dandelions, mushrooms, huckleberries, and some tubers.

"What's this?" I asked the little voices.

"Food." One responded.

"We gathered it for you!" chimed another.

"Oh," I said quietly. Half the things in the basket did not look edible but I supposed not everyone ate the kind of delicious foods I normally ate at home.

“Thank you,” I called up to them, remembering Marion’s insistence to always be gracious. I nibbled on the berries. “Say, won’t you tell me your names?” There was a long pause.

“I am Zenia.”

“I am Hyacinth.”

“I am Amaryllis.”

I sat back against the window frame and eyed my odd breakfast, “Oh, those are all flower names, aren’t they? I miss the palace gardens.” I turned a wistful eye out the window. How long would I have to wait here? What was I going to tell father about this whole being a mage thing? Maybe it would be better if I didn’t tell him. But what then? There was this whole piece of me I was supposed to pretend didn’t exist. I’d have to go the rest of my life never using the magic I was now so keenly aware of. I sighed, everything was so complicated now.

As I thought about my newly discovered magic, I felt it aching in my core, like a muscle that needed to be stretched. I peered up into the rafters anxiously, “Do you know if the witch will be returning?”

“It is unlikely,” responded Zenia. I blew out a breath, feeling somewhat relieved by that, and returned to the magic book I had left open on the floor. I flipped through the pages some more until I came to a page titled: *Chapter Two, Preparing to Wield Magic*. I settled back against the bookcase with the book in my lap as I read with interest.

The first step towards wielding magic is to build a connection with the power that lives at your core. That connection needs to be strengthened and fine tuned. Patiently working through this step will allow a mage to seamlessly summon their magic instantaneously. Building this connection can be done through a series of breathwork practices.

I narrowed my eyes in doubt. Practicing breathing would help me master my magic? That seemed so… simple. I shook my head but read on.

The first and most simple exercise consists of deep belly breathing. With each inhale, latch onto the magic at your core, and with each exhale, push that magic to the surface of the skin. The magic should pulse back and forth, like waves breaking on the beach. Continue this practice until it can be completed with ease on the first breath.

I frowned but closed my eyes in focus and tried to do as the book instructed. I took a deep breath and tried to latch onto the magic in my core. I grasped it for a moment before it slipped away from me and settled back into place. I tried again and the same thing happened. This was more difficult than I thought it'd be. I continued to practice again and again until, with a start, I realized many hours had passed. I stood and stretched, then ate the rest of the contents of the basket. Whereas before I was sure I would not be eating the odd plants I'd been given, I was now hungry enough to pop the dandelions into my mouth with little hesitation. I tried not to think about the strange texture as I chewed- I didn't have much choice, I needed to replenish my energy after the intense mental work I'd done for the last several hours. I shook my head in disbelief at the situation I was in. I was the princess of a kingdom where magic was outlawed- and I was a mage. How ironic. Was I one of those random mages that just popped up without any mage lineage? Or were there mages somewhere in my family tree? What was my type? My core power? Could I master my abilities just by reading books? I had so many questions and no one to ask. My secretive flower friends likely wouldn't be any help.

"Are you guys still there?", I called out.

"I am here." answered one of them, Hyacinth I think.

"Did the witch know I'm a mage?"

"She knew you might be."

"How would she know that?" I asked.

"That is a long story that is not mine to tell," answered Hyacinth.

I pursed my lips in frustration. "Why did she bring me here? I haven't done anything wrong."

"Rhiannon wants revenge."

"Rhiannon?" I asked in surprise. "That's her name? Revenge on who, what have we done?"

"You ask many questions," Hyacinth said in a tired voice, "my sisters will be back soon, I shouldn't be answering you. We're just here to watch over you."

"Well that doesn't help me much." I pouted, but it seemed Hyacinth was done talking to me. I returned to the window, scanning the horizon hopefully. But there were no signs of human activity, just tree-covered hills as far as the eye could see. The daylight was already starting to fade and I had to admit to myself that I wasn't getting rescued today. I turned back to the room and tidied it up before putting myself to bed. Surely tomorrow would be the day, I told myself as my eyelids grew heavy. Tomorrow father's knights would come and take me home.

Chapter 6 The Curse

My rescue did not come the next day, or the one after that. The days started to pass more quickly as I delved into magic theory. I spent hours each day practicing the techniques described in the book. When I wasn't practicing I was cleaning up the room, exploring the contents of the many chests, or eating the odd foraged foods the flowers brought me each day. This went on for several weeks before I was startled to realize I wasn't sure how long I'd been there. I racked my mind, a bit panicked as I counted the days on my fingers. 65. I'd been in the tower for 65 days. I quickly took a small kitchen knife I'd found and marked 65 tallies beside the window. I don't know why it really mattered to me, but it seemed that if I lost track of the days they'd all just blend together and I'd start to lose my mind. I vowed to myself to make a mark each day so I wouldn't lose track of the passage of time.

I'd made 45 more marks beside the window before I mastered the first magic exercise. I could now quickly grasp my magic and bring it to the surface in one breath. Over time it had become second nature. I barely had to think about it and I knew I was ready for something more. The next chapter in the book was titled, *Forging Your Rings*.

Magic is neutral, existing around us without consciousness. Much like the forces of nature, it has no will of its own. This neutrality allows us to guide and shape it but in order to do so we must pass the magic through a series of filters. These will be your rings. Each ring you create and pass your magic through increases the skill and precision of your cast. Failing to create your rings before casting or failing to use an adequate number of rings will result in sloppy, failed casts, or wild, out of control casts. Each ring represents a criteria that the magic passing through it must meet. For example, is it honest, good, true, and just? Other rings mages often use are creativity, compassion, and protection. There are countless rings that can be created and the more rings you pass your magic through, the more accurate your cast will be.

Most mages generally have seven rings at a time. This is a powerful number that results in excellent precision. Not all the rings need to be used in every cast, but using at least three will prevent the cast from running wild and having unintended effects. To forge your rings, bring your magic to your fingertips and then form a ring between your hands while focusing on the criteria or value that suits your purposes. Forging rings will be challenging for beginners and it is recommended to only forge one a day, taking time in between to familiarize yourself with each ring.

Below there was a diagram depicting a mage sitting cross-legged on the floor. They held their hands horizontally, facing each other, and between their hands was a ring of light, maybe four inches in diameter. How curious, I thought to myself. I copied the diagram, eager to try it for myself. I decided protection would be a good first ring. Maybe that would help me not fry myself with some wayward magic. I easily brought the magic from my core and pushed it to my fingertips. Then I focused on pushing the magic into the form of a ring between my hands and to my awe, little tendrils of golden light began pulling away from my fingers and wrapping around to form a circle. Tiny particles of the magic glittered as they spun slowly around the delicate loop.

"Protection.", I spoke aloud to direct the magic. The ring flashed a bit brighter and runes appeared around it, written in the same golden light before the entire image faded away. The visual representation of my ring may have been gone, but I could feel the presence of it in the peripheral of my mind. True to the book, I felt depleted after forging the ring, and though my excitement tempted me to try another, I instead returned to my bed. I could practice with my ring tomorrow, I thought to myself as sleep rushed in, blanketing my mind.

Over the next 12 weeks I continued to forge my rings, taking time between each to practice passing my magic through them. On the day that I made the 194th mark by the window, I had three rings established. A ring of protection, a ring of good, and a ring of creativity. With three rings in place, I was ready to practice my first cast. Beginner casts consisted of manipulating the four elements individually. They were the most basic casts but were crucial to building a foundation that would allow me to perform more intricate casts later on.

I spent every waking moment practicing. As the days grew shorter and the weather colder, the night seemed to stretch on and on. Winter came and went, replaced by spring and then summer. By the 284th day, I was sleeping till midday and going back to bed before sunset. The work of developing my magic seemed to be taking a toll on me as I began sleeping more hours than I was awake. Though with no way to tell the exact time, the days often rushed by and would have all blurred together had I not committed to scoring the wall beside the window each time I woke. I didn't think about my eventual rescue as much anymore. The loneliness was consuming and I preferred to lose myself in the magic, where my focus prevented me from lingering in my darkening thoughts. On the 345th day, I had mastered basic casts in all four elements. Sitting on the window sill, I practiced transitioning from one element to the next. First I rolled a pebble around in a circle, then I formed a sphere of water that hovered above my palm, then I caused a gust of wind to circle me, shifting my hair with it. Then I cast a single flame in the palm of my hand and marveled at the warmth that came from it. Extinguishing the flame, I turned to look out the window where the summer sun beat down on the stone walls. As always, there was no one in sight. I sunk my head down to my knees.

"Do you think they'll find me before my birthday?"

"It is hard to say child," answered Zenia. Her voice was the oldest of the three and the most motherly.

"Maybe if I keep practicing, I could use my magic to escape."

"Perhaps." She answered.

The hopelessness sunk in deeper. It had taken me nearly a year to perform basic casts. To perform the kind of complicated magic it would require to descend from the tower could take years more. Shaking my head, I turned and returned to my bed, eager for sleep to carry away all my worries.

My birthday came and went and the intensity of the sun diminished as the seasons changed again. Sometimes I cried but mostly I just felt dead inside. Nothing mattered anymore. Nothing brought me joy or comfort. It seemed I was destined to rot in this evil tower. The thought sent me spiraling into the darkest regions of my mind. I spent hours staring down at the thorny vines that curled up the side of the tower, wallowing in the impossibility of escape. I laid in bed for days, finding it hard to care about anything really. I just closed my eyes and gave into the numbness that sleep provided me.

When I awoke I found that a thick layer of snow had fallen outside. I squinted out the window as the sun reflected off the snow in a blinding sheen. Shivering a bit, I wrapped a blanket around my shoulders and scored another mark on the wall before setting the blade back down.

"You missed one." came Amaryllis' youthful voice.

"What do you mean?" I asked in confusion.

"You only made one, you need to make two."

I frowned, "But I made one yesterday?"

"Yes, but you slept for two days."

My heart stuttered. "What? Two days? How is that possible?" But the flower didn't answer me. I picked up the knife and made another mark. I suppose I must have pushed myself too much with my magic, I thought. And though the next several days passed as they usually did, on what I thought was the 485th day, Amaryllis corrected me again.

"You missed one again."

"Shhh, don't tell her that." admonished Hyacinth's voice.

"Why?" I asked, "What's going on?"

"Don't worry yourself, child. You are safe," spoke Zenia's voice.

"That's not what I asked, I asked what's going on! Why am I sleeping so long? It's not normal." I said, my voice escalating.

There was a long pause, “Rhiannon never intended for things to be this way.” Zenia said finally.

“You were supposed to be asleep!” Amaryllis chimed in.

I frowned, “What do you mean?”

“Rhiannon left a curse on the tower,” spoke Hyacinth, “to send you into a deep and ageless sleep until someone came to rescue you.”

“But it didn’t work!” exclaimed Amaryllis, “You keep waking up!”

My head spun, “I’m cursed?” I asked, a bit panicked.

“Not you, just the tower. Somehow it’s not working very well on you though.” Said Hyacinth.

“But I don’t want to fall asleep for who knows how long! What if I sleep for years? What if no one ever comes?” I anxiously paced as I turned this information over in my head. “I’m not going to do it,” I announced. “I’ll learn how to break the curse, or I’ll escape, but I’m not going to just lay in here waiting for some rescuer who may never come!” I was shouting now, angry with the flowers who refused to show me their faces. Angry with the witch who sought to punish me. Angry with my father and his knights for not finding me after all this time. Angry with myself for being so powerless to save myself. I glowered out the window, the beautiful view of the snow-covered forest taunting me. I wasn’t going to accept this fate. I’d fight it. I was done having others decide things for me.

Chapter 7 The Plan

Over the next 60 days that passed, I made changes to my daily routine. I never went to bed before the sun set. If I slept late, I'd stay awake until well after the moon had risen. I recommitted to learning magic, spending many hours studying the book of magic and practicing passing my magic back and forth through my rings. I forged a fourth ring, a ring of strengthening. I hoped that it would reflect the strength I was trying to build in myself. Strength enough to withstand the power of the curse.

My magical knowledge was growing steadily. One of my favorite spells caused plants to grow rapidly. I used it to sprout greenery from every crevice along the stone walls that contained me. Moss, vines, and grasses covered the walls now and in some places, there were even little white flowers that bloomed. It brought color into the room that made up my whole world and brought me some small portion of happiness to see the life that I had cultivated. I also cast fires into the little stove that burned with no fuel for hours at a time. They kept the cold at bay and made me a little less miserable as winter dragged on.

Finally, I awoke one morning to find the snow had melted and the forest was alive with bird song. I opened the window and breathed the fresh air deeply.

"How long did I sleep this time?" I asked, feeling the tell-tale heaviness in my limbs.

"Six days." Answered Amaryllis.

I sighed and made the marks. 552 marks covered the wall now. I stared at them glumly as the loneliness crept in again. Though I chatted with the flowers sometimes, I longed for human interaction. To speak to someone face to face. I longed to be touched. To be held. In my mind, I frequently replayed the affectionate touches I had once taken for granted. I sat on the window sill where the sunlight could reach me and wrapped my arms around myself. The view was picturesque, but I felt no joy. I closed my eyes to shut it all out and rested my head against the frame.

"There is no need to suffer, child," spoke Zenia. "Give in to the curse and rest."

I opened my eyes and shook my head, "No. There has to be another way."

I had searched the magic book cover to cover again and again for a way to break the curse, but such magic must have been too advanced to be included in the first volume of magic theory. Without instruction, I had no idea where to even start with something so complex.

I had considered climbing, but I had no skill in such things and my body lacked physical strength especially now that my only sustenance was flowers, berries, and tubers. Besides that, the staggering height and thorny landing were enough to assure me attempting such an escape would likely lead to my death.

I had also thought to grow vines that could be climbed down, but I couldn't seem to grow anything strong enough. My magic wasn't developed enough to do something so specific yet. It all felt very hopeless so I pushed off the window sill and turned my thoughts to the task I had in mind. I wanted to forge another ring. The more rings I had, the more I could refine my magic. And if I couldn't yet find a way out, I really wanted to get some better food. No offense to the flowers, but they just weren't providing enough. The more time that passed, the more I felt I was withering away. My dress hung loosely from my form. My soft, well-fed figure was gone, replaced by a body I didn't recognize. My hair now reached my hips and fell in unkempt waves that had lost their shine. I sat in the center of the room with my legs crossed and quickly formed a ring of golden light between my hands. It was satisfying to see how quickly I could manipulate my magic to do this now. I closed my eyes to focus on the type of ring I wanted to forge. Nourishment. But my mind wandered and I felt anger wash over me. I had never gone hungry a day in my life prior to my imprisonment. I shouldn't have to suffer like this, confined to a single room. I hadn't done anything to deserve this. If I ever saw that wicked witch again, I'd make her regret this. I wanted vengeance. The ring flashed in front of me and my eyes popped open in surprise. Runes appeared around the ring before it faded away.

Oops. I'd forged a ring of vengeance. I contemplated that for a minute, wondering if that might come back to bite me. The book didn't give any examples of bad rings to forge, so perhaps there weren't any? In any case, the deed was done and I didn't have the energy to try and dissolve it- a skill I'd yet to learn. Forging rings didn't take as much of my energy as they used to but still, I felt the tiredness creeping into my bones. I stood and stretched, trying to push the sleepiness away. There were still many hours of daylight left so I needed to keep busy. I had a plan to increase my food supply and step one included creating a bug infestation. Did I want a bug infestation? No. But it was all part of the process. I held my hands in front of me and my rings appeared, forming a circle. Passing my magic through them, I guided it to do as I wanted. The rings all flashed and faded as the spell was completed. I stood still in anticipation and sure enough, from every crack and crevice, insects started to emerge. I squealed in disgust as they all headed straight towards me. Quickly I grabbed the cast iron pot I'd selected for the task and set it before me on the floor.

"Into the pot critters, into the pot!" I directed. They changed course slightly and crawled up and into the pot as

I'd instructed. There were crickets, roaches, centipedes, and spiders. I shivered at all the little legs creeping into the pot. When the last one had made its way in I grabbed the lid and closed it with a clang. I heaved a sigh of relief. Step one complete.

I then went to the open window and began to cast my second spell. This one would be more tricky and I wasn't sure it would work. I finished the spell just as the first birds started to arrive. They flocked to the window sill, quickly filling it with their beady eyes fixed on me expectantly. Summoning them was easy enough, but birds were more intelligent than bugs and wouldn't just do as I asked without anything in return. I cleared my throat, suddenly feeling nervous to address my little audience of birds.

"Right well, I need some soil and grass and things,"

They looked at me blankly and I pulled the pot over on the sill, "For every clump of soil or nesting material you bring me, you can have one of these." I lifted the lid, revealing the swarming pot of bugs and the birds hopped over in interest. I replaced the lid, "Dirt first!" I reminded them. One by one they took off and I left the lid cracked for them before taking a seat on the bed. Over the next several hours the birds flew back and forth, dropping clumps of soil, moss, or dry grass onto the floor and then snatching up a bug. Step two complete. Soon I'd have enough organic material to grow bigger plants that would yield fruit and vegetables. But now the light was fading and I could no longer deny the need for sleep. So I lay my head down, knowing it would likely be several days before I woke again.

Though I knew I'd likely sleep several days, I was not prepared when Amaryllis did her morning duty of informing me how many days had passed and called out, "Twenty-eight!"

I groaned and rubbed my face. This whole 'not giving into the curse' thing was not working out. I was pleased however, to see a sizable pile of dirt sitting inside the window. The birds had done their job well. It seemed they had continued to bring dirt even after the bugs ran out. I walked over to the window and jumped a little in surprise when a raven came and landed on the sill. He looked at me with his little black eyes and cocked his head.

"Hello," I said. He cawed at me and hopped around. "Um, I don't need any more dirt," I told him. Still he looked at me expectantly, hopping impatiently. I came closer and sat on the sill. "You're a very pretty raven," I said. He hopped over to me and pecked at a tiny golden band I wore on my pinky. I'd nearly forgotten it was there. "Oh you like shiny things, hm?" I examined the simple gold band. It wasn't anything special and had no specific significance to me. Just one of many rings from my jewelry collection back home. I shrugged and wiggled it off my pinky. "Well if you like it so much, you can have it." I carefully placed it around his leg and sat back to see what he thought. He hopped around happily, admiring the shiny gold with his beady eyes and I grinned a little. He cawed at me and then took off out the window, flapping his black wings. I watched him go, envying his freedom. If only I had wings to fly away. But there was no such magic. I returned to my original task and knelt beside the materials I'd accumulated. I used my hands to shove the pile of dirt over, spreading it out across the floor. I did this until it lay about four inches deep and covered about a quarter of the room. I didn't care that it was dirty. I wanted more food. I then held my hands over the soil and urged my magic forward. I no longer had to summon an image of my rings to grow plants, the magic came easily enough that I could see the rings in my mind's eye. More complex spells still required me to summon my rings but I was quite happy with my progress for now. I smiled as little green sprouts emerged from the soil growing quickly into plants that bore strawberries, string beans, and cucumbers. Step three complete. Now if I could just formulate such an ingenious plan to escape.

Over the next 65 days, I was only awake for six of them. My little raven friend returned a few times, bringing me various little treasures. Polished river rocks, pretty flowers, and pinecones. I named him Nox and he seemed to like it, hopping happily when I greeted him.

Though I enjoyed his little visits and eating the fresh fruits and vegetables I was now able to grow, I was becoming increasingly worried about the curse. I poured over the magic book again and again. I practiced my magic every day, experimenting with what I was capable of. I couldn't summon enough wind to lift myself off the ground, though I certainly felt lighter. I had tried to form a staircase from the stones that formed the walls, but the tower itself seemed resistant to magical manipulation. I still couldn't form vines thick enough to hold my weight. I was running out of ideas and as the days slipped past me faster and faster I was growing desperate. On the 700th day, I was sleeping for a week at a time at least and I collapsed in tears after scoring the wall.

"I'm going to be here forever!" I sobbed. My breaths came in quick shallow bursts as panic took hold of me. "I want to go home!" I wailed. The flowers were silent. There was nothing to say. They wanted me to give in to the curse. They weren't going to help me escape. I rested my head back against the wall as the snot and tears ran down my face. Looking around the room, I realized how different it looked compared to when I first arrived. It was practically a greenhouse now. A very messy greenhouse, I thought to myself. I had admittedly given up on keeping things tidy. Books were strewn about, soil was tracked everywhere, and linens were spilling out of the chest. I stilled. The linens. A low manic laugh escaped my mouth. It was so simple, it might just work. I could tie the linens together and climb down them, like they did in storybooks I read as a child. I stood and wiped my tears away, a margin of my energy renewed. I had a plan. I was getting out.

Chapter 8 The Fall

The flowers recognized what I was doing of course and said everything they could to deter me.

"It's too dangerous!" said Hyacinth.

"This isn't going to work!" said Amaryllis.

"Just give in to the curse, save yourself the suffering!" pleaded Zenia.

I was determined though and I pointedly ignored them. Making my rope took much longer than I thought it would. I worked, cutting each blanket and sheet in half before tying them end to end. But the curse seemed to sense what my plan was and the sleepiness bogged me down more powerfully than ever before. My fingers fumbled as I worked, my eyelids so heavy I frequently fell asleep atop the linens I labored over. Each time I awoke again, I'd demand to know how long.

"Amaryllis! How many this time?"

"Ten." She responded in a whisper.

I made the marks and counted them over. 730. Two years in this prison.

"Do you know what day it is?" I called out to the flowers. They didn't respond and I glared up at the rafters where they hid from me. Cowards. "It's my birthday!" I spat bitterly. "Not that you care." I turned back to my work and inspected the long length, pulling each knot a little tighter. I tied the last piece of cloth to the end and began dragging the piled up material over to the window.

"Princess please!" cried Amaryllis.

"This is suicide!" exclaimed Hyacinth.

I tied one end of my homemade rope to the leg of the iron stove and threw the window open. I hoisted the pile of material onto the window sill and pushed it over the edge. The ball of material unraveled rapidly as it fell down the great height. It was hard to say how far it really reached, but I didn't really care. I was getting out. Today. And all I really needed was for it to reach far enough that the fall wouldn't kill me.

"Please child," Zenia's voice carried down, "the rescuer will come eventually."

I climbed onto the sill and looked back into the tower one more time. "Goodbye flowers." Then I gripped the sheets and lowered my feet over the edge until they caught against a knot. Beside me hung the tattered remains of the party dress I'd arrived in. No longer the pretty pink I remembered, it had been bleached by the sun and was now an ugly yellowish color. My heart thundered as I hung there a moment just beneath the window. A glance at the forest of thorns so far below sent my head spinning and I gasped for air. There was no going back now, for I surely did not have the strength to pull myself back up over the edge. I instead focused on the sheet right in front of my face and began to lower myself down. The sky above was gray and the wind whipped my skirt around my legs. My descent was painstakingly slow. My arms trembled with exertion and my knuckles gleamed white as I kept a death grip on the sheets. One slip up and that would be the end of me. It was hard to say how far I had gone and how far I had to go without looking down, but it seemed to take ages for me to move from one knot to the next. As my muscles fatigued and my hands grew slick with sweat, it was getting more and more difficult to keep my grip. Almost there, I told myself. Though I had no idea how much further I had to go.

At that moment my hands suddenly slipped and I began sliding down the length of the fabric. My arms flailed and wrapped around the sheet and I was yanked to an abrupt stop as I finally grabbed hold of it. I swung and knocked against the side of the tower as I tried to slow my racing heart, but my brief moment of relief was interrupted by a horrible ripping sound. I looked up sharply in alarm to see the sheet above me splitting through the middle. My sudden stop had pulled at the thin sheet too aggressively. My eyes widened as the material continued to tear. Time seemed to stop for a moment as I realized what was about to happen and before I could formulate my next thought, the fabric gave way and I was free falling down the side of the tower. A piercing scream ripped through me as my arms windmilled through the air. Pure terror blocked out all coherent thought. My body smacked against something hard, knocking the wind out of me and cutting my scream short. I had reached the brambles. Huge branches of thorns ranging in size from the thickness of my thumb to the thickness of my torso flashed by as I turned end over end, smacking against them. The thorns slashed across my body, searing pain erupting from my back, arms, legs, and chest. I had half a thought to protect my face, but too late as I plunged further into the thorns and felt them scrape across my face and eyes. Finally, I tumbled over the last of the thorns and hit the ground a couple feet below with a thud. I couldn't move, I couldn't see. All there was was pain and the warm, wet sensation of blood seeping across my body, pooling beneath me. I gasped and made a strangled noise, my back arching away from the ground in agony. I struggled to inhale as my consciousness faded into the darkness and I wondered if I'd ever wake up this time.

Chapter 9 The Dark

My thoughts flooded back into my mind and I stirred. Pain at the slight movement caused me to still as I tried to recall what was happening. My entire body hurt. It was pain unlike anything I'd ever experienced before. Through it all I was vaguely aware of a small tugging sensation on my face and what felt like two fingers braced against my forehead.

"Don't move, child," said Zenia, her voice closer than ever before.

"Let us finish up," said Amaryllis, her voice coming from down near my legs where I felt the same tugging sensation. I wanted to see them, but only darkness filled my view.

"I can't see," I whispered. They didn't answer and I lifted my hand towards my face.

"Careful! I just finished sewing that arm up!" griped Hyacinth.

I continued anyway, feeling the stitches in my arm pull tight as I bent my arm. I brushed my fingers across my face tenderly, feeling the thick, puckering lines that ran across my eyes and through the right side of my upper lip where Zenia had apparently sewn my wounds shut.

"My eyes," I whimpered, "are they-" I couldn't finish.

"I'm sorry." Was all Zenia replied.

A choked sob escaped my throat. How had it come to this? Why had it come to this? How had I fallen so low in life? Maybe I should have just stayed in the tower and fallen asleep for the next hundred years. Then maybe instead of lying in the dirt, covered in my own blood, I'd be waking up to some dashing knight in shining armor, come to save me from the curse. This was all her fault. Rhiannon. A deep and dreadful anger took hold in my heart. It was dark and desperate, knowing that I'd never be powerful enough to get revenge on the witch who had stolen so much from me.

The flowers insisted I roll on my side, though it was nearly unbearable to do so, in order to sew the wounds on my back. When they were done I just laid there, the sensation of soft fingers brushing across my shoulder and back in an effort to comfort me.

"We have failed in our duty to watch over you," spoke Zenia.

"What are we to do now?" asked Hyacinth.

"We must return her to the land of men," answered Zenia, "she will not survive this land in her current state."

"Then the sooner we go, the better." said Hyacinth, "it will be night soon."

"Come on princess, you've got to get up." encouraged Amaryllis.

"I can't." I cried. It was too much. The pain, the darkness.

"You've got to fight Vivienne," she said, closer to my ear, "Fight like you fought the curse. You can do it."

I sniffled and pushed up onto my hands and knees. Every movement pulled at the many tiny stitches holding my wounds closed. But I rose to my feet despite the pain, because she was right. I had come too far to just lie here and die in the dirt. One of them pulled at my sleeve softly and began guiding me through the forest of thorns. I felt the lightest hand on my shoulder, the touch barely perceptible. Amaryllis spoke softly into my ear, telling me when to duck beneath the low-hanging brambles. Moving through the unfamiliar terrain with no sight was terribly disorienting and I frequently fell to my knees as I stumbled forward. Eventually, the loose soil beneath my feet changed to harder packed earth, covered in moss and pine needles. I must have made it out of the brambles and into the woods, I thought. I walked for hours. I'd stubbed my toes on rocks and tree roots more times than I could count, but I pushed on. There really wasn't any other choice. As the hours passed, the air grew cooler and I wondered if night had fallen. I trembled with cold and exhaustion. Each time I fell it was harder to get back up until finally I collapsed to the forest floor, shivering.

"You must keep going!" said Zenia urgently.

"I'm so tired." I cried.

"You'll die if you stop here," warned Hyacinth, "the creatures in these woods will kill you before sunrise." As if on cue, a howl sounded in the distance.

I clambered to my feet, fear giving me a spurt of energy and the flowers led me on.

Eventually, we came to a stop.

"This is as far as we can go. Stay on this path and someone will find you," said Zenia.

"You're leaving me?" I lamented.

"We cannot leave these woods," said Hyacinth.

"But I can't see, how will I know which way to go?" I cried.

"Here," said Amaryllis, tugging at my sleeve. She pulled my hand out till I felt it brush against the tops of what must have been tall grass. "This grass runs along the path. If you follow it, you'll stay on the path."

"We have to go before Rhiannon realizes what has happened," Hyacinth said urgently.

"Be strong, child. Goodbye," spoke Zenia.

"Do you have to go?" I pleaded pitifully.

"There's no other way," whispered Amaryllis. I felt the lightest brush across my cheek. "Goodbye princess." And then I was alone.

Chapter 10 The Wanderer

I walked, and walked, and walked. My hand skimmed across the tops of the tall grass which guided me along. I walked until I thought I could walk no more and then I walked some more. Each step felt like an impossible thing but my feet continued to fall, one in front of the other against all odds. I felt the warmth of the sun grace upon my skin and then fade again as the day came and went. With the chill of the night I began to shiver uncontrollably. My hands and feet grew numb and my teeth chattered loudly. I thought to summon fire, but with no food or rest, I found my magic totally depleted. It was misery and I cried bitter tears at the deal fate had dealt me. My knees threatened to give out and I fought a vicious battle against myself as the weaker part of me begged for surrender. I could just lie here, I thought to myself. The cold would take me in the night and I would no longer have to suffer so. The thought was tempting, but I fought it back. One foot in front of the other. That was all I could do.

At some point in the endless night, a piercing yowl cut through the air. My heart stuttered in my chest. Some beast was here, in the wilderness with me, but only I was in the dark. A twig snapped behind me and that was all it took to snap my brittle nerves. I took off into the grass, all rational thought leaving me as I fled whatever my imagination thought lay in the darkness. I ran, hobbled really until my lungs were on fire. I gasped for air but I couldn't get enough and finally, as I sunk to my knees, my mind faded into the sweet oblivion of unconsciousness.

When I awoke I thought for a moment that everything had just been a bad dream. I was surrounded by the softest feeling, like a warm fur coat. Surely no such thing existed in the nightmare I'd been living. Then I tried to open my eyes and was brought back to the harsh reality of my blindness. I tentatively extended my hand to feel the soft fur and gasped softly when I felt it twitch. This was no coat. I reached out again and felt the softest velvet ears. A rabbit? I continued to explore with my fingertips and found another and another. There seemed to be a dozen rabbits curled up against me- some even lying on top of me. They had shared their warmth with me when I was in desperate need, but why? I had never seen wild animals behave in such a way. They started to awaken and shift around as I wondered at the phenomenon. I heard the soft thumping as they scratched their little heads and then hopped off. Off to do whatever it is that rabbits do all day.

I sat there in the darkness for a moment wondering, well what now? But my ears perked up to a familiar caw from somewhere in the trees.

"Nox?" I asked hopefully. A flapping of wings sounded and I heard a rustle in front of me as the bird landed. I reached out to touch him, but he had already hopped away and in his stead, I felt the familiar shape of a blackberry. I grabbed it up greedily and popped it in my mouth. Its juice exploded over my tongue with a burst of flavor that I savored with reverence. It had to be one of the last of the season. Nox cawed again and I followed the sound of my only friend in the dark. He led me along, calling to me, and brought me to a small, babbling brook. I knelt and drank deeply from my cupped hands. When I was finished I reached my hand out, "Thank you, Nox." To my surprise, he left his perch in the tree and landed on my hand. Before I could wonder any further, he took off again, leading me on again. I followed him with complete trust and sure enough, when he came to a stop, I felt around and found myself amongst a patch of huckleberry bushes. I ate and ate. It would take hundreds of tiny berries to fill my stomach but I was grateful for whatever I could get.

That night Nox led me to a mossy burrow which I sank into and curled into a tight ball. I began to shiver once more but then the forest animals gathered in my little nest. To one side of me was a doe with her fawn. On the other were rabbits and squirrels, all curling up against me. A few little birds even came down and rested on top of me. We all shared our warmth, staving off the chill of the night. It made no sense to me that these wild animals would help me but I was endlessly grateful.

The next day passed much the same. And the next, and the next. Nox would lead me to whatever food source he could find and I would fumble blindly to eat as much as I could, and then Nox would take me somewhere warm for the night, and the various forest animals would keep me company. It was a strange existence in which I was totally dependent on Nox and the animals of the forest. Each day was spent trying to find enough food to survive and each night was spent trying to stay warm. There was no way for me to remember how many days had passed. I had long since lost count and with the search for food filling my every waking moment, I had stopped caring about the time.

Nox never led me back to the path, though I didn't know why. He was certainly a smart bird and I had no doubt he could. I supposed he thought I belonged out here, with the forest animals. But the days were growing colder, and the food scarcer. The animals were equipped to survive the winter, but I was not. Nox must have known this because one day, he brought to my hand a chunk of bread. I gasped, "Nox! There are people nearby?" He cawed in response and after having spent so many days in his company I interpreted his response to be an excited, "Yes!" I quickly consumed the bread, the small piece feeling more filling than anything I'd eaten since I'd left the tower. "Nox, will you take me to them? I must go home."

He cawed and took off, leading me once more. I followed him and found myself on a road, the worn ruts telling me that humans did indeed pass through this way. "Thank you, Nox," I said. He cawed in response and took off, this time not to lead me, but to send me on my way. And so I set out on the path once more.

Chapter 11 The Slave

I trudged along the path, unsure of how much time had passed. Without seeing the position of the sun or moon, the only clues that morning had come were the birds that began to sing and the slight warmth I felt on my skin. My hand that dragged along the tips of the grass was wet with dew. I wrapped my other arm around myself, shivering from the cold. I could feel the cool air against my bare skin in several places where the thorns had torn my dress and the dress itself was stiff with dried blood. I wasn't sure how well traveled this path was or where it even led. I could only hope that someone would come along and take me with them. Then maybe I could be brought home. Home seemed so far away in my memories. I didn't need the many luxuries I'd left behind. I'd be satisfied with a meal by the fire and some clean clothes. My stomach growled painfully at the thought. I supposed it had been at least a day since I'd eaten. I stilled as I heard something in the distance. My heart sped up in recognition. Horse hooves were clopping along the path some ways behind me. As they drew closer I also recognized the sound of a cart, the wheels squeaking a bit as they turned. I stopped and stood off to the side of the path, not wanting to get run over by the cart.

"What in the blazes?!" exclaimed a man's gruff voice.

I lifted my head in the direction of his voice hopefully.

"Where'd you come from?" he asked.

I opened my mouth, unsure how to answer. "I- I don't know."

Another man's voice spoke up, "What do you think? Take it or leave it?"

"Somebody will want her, grab her."

My heart juddered, "What?" But someone grabbed my wrists and quickly bound them together before lifting me up and setting me in the cart. "Wait! I-" But someone nudged my arm and I flinched away.

"Don't try to oppose them," spoke an elderly man's voice. "Just do as they say."

"Who are they? Where am I?" I asked, frightened.

"We're close to the Wildlands border, headed to Treadmont, the second biggest city in Duthlin. They're going to auction us off there." spoke a woman's voice across from me.

"But I'm not a slave! I'm-"

"You are now," interrupted the old man, "and they don't care who you are or where you came from."

My head spun. Surely if they knew who I was, they'd at least try to hold me for ransom? My father would pay to get me back. But as I thought on this I realized how futile that would be. I had no way to prove who I was. I likely didn't even resemble the young and beautiful princess whose portraits adorned the Gotland palace halls. No one would believe me.

"But who would even purchase me?" I croaked. No one answered me and I wallowed in thoughts of my bleak future. Blind, disfigured, weak, and useless. What kind of work could I be given? Maybe no one would want me, and they'd just let me go? That seemed perhaps a naive hope. For the right price a cheap brothel might purchase me. My stomach churned at the thought and had I anything in my stomach at all I likely would have been sick. I silently promised myself that I would not give in to such a fate. I'd unleash my magic in whatever form it may take and make a run for it if that's what it came to.

We traveled many miles and the soft whisperings of the other inhabitants of the cart let me know there were at least ten other people there. All of them were unsure of what the future had in store for them. I found myself nodding off and jerking awake several times as the motion of the moving cart lulled me to sleep. The others didn't speak to me anymore, though I was sure they were staring at my horrendous, stitched up appearance.

Finally a young boy's voice spoke up, "Where'd you come from? And what happened to your face?"

Someone shushed him but everyone else was quiet in anticipation.

"I- I'm not sure, I think I was in the Wildlands." My voice cracked dryly.

"Well that explains it," exclaimed the old man, "you're lucky to be alive."

I didn't answer. I definitely wasn't feeling lucky. The cart came to a stop and the slavers got off. I heard the others getting off the cart and then heard the sound of splashing water. Someone grabbed my arm and pulled me off the cart. I stood there confused for a moment before gasping in surprise as a bucketful of cold water was dumped over my head.

"This one's going to need a couple bucketfuls. She's filthy." said one of the slavers.

They continued to dump water over my head while I stood there shivering and on the third bucketful, I finally thought to cup my hands together so I could slurp some of the water from them. I ran my hands over my face and arms, slicking the water off my skin. I felt layers of grime coming away, though there was still dried blood clinging to the many tiny stitches all over my body.

"That'll do!" said the slaver, and I was moved to the side. I wrung the water from my hair and skirt a bit but I could tell that we were no longer in the shade of the trees and the sun would dry me soon.

We were loaded back onto the cart and again headed on our way. Soon I began to hear the bustle of the city as we drew nearer. Horse-drawn carts passed us and people crowded the streets. The fabric of my dress became stiff as it dried in the sun and rubbed painfully against my wounds. I did my best not to move too much in order to prevent chafing. The sound of an auctioneer reached my ears and the cart came to its final stop. The people around me started unloading and I too stood and inched my way to the end of the cart. Someone grabbed my arm and I stepped down shakily. Anxiety gripped me as I was led towards the auction. I heard them start the bidding on the next slave while I stood waiting with the others. They sold people off for varying costs. Unable to see who was on the auctioneer's block, I guessed the more able-bodied fetched a higher price. Inevitably it was my turn and I was led up onto the platform where I was directed to step up onto a block for the audience to see. Gasps and chatter broke out from the crowd and I lowered my head in shame. I didn't even know what I looked like now but I could imagine how hideous the thick puckered wounds crossing my face were. Not to mention the rest of my body. I wanted to crawl up into a hole and hide away.

"Starting the bid at ten pence! Do I have ten pence?" yelled the auctioneer, "Anyone?"

My heart pounded. No one was bidding.

"How about five pence? Five pence or she goes to the mines!"

I flinched. Mines? I hadn't even thought of that. I wouldn't survive in the mines. It was deadly dangerous for the average man, let alone a blind girl. Panic welled in me. They were going to cart me off to the mines and I wouldn't last a week.

"Five pence!" came a man's voice from the crowd.

"Sold for five pence to Mr. Alderidge!"

A breath of relief left me. Someone had purchased me, but who? The slavers guided me off the platform and I was handed off to another.

"Alright, Bronson. Let's head home, we've got what we came for." spoke a man's voice.

The one holding my arm, Bronson, guided me through the crowd and then loaded me into a carriage.

The other man, my new owner apparently, spoke again, "What a deal Bronson! Five pence!" He sounded entirely too cheerful about that.

"Are you sure Master Alderidge? That's what you said about the one-legged girl." said Bronson with disdain as he undid the binds around my wrists.

"Yes, and now Mary is doing quite well in the kitchen." Master Alderidge retorted.

I rubbed my wrists and tried to comprehend everything they were saying. It seemed that Master Alderidge was wealthy. The carriage seats were well cushioned and the longer I sat the more aware I became of my own stench.

On cue Alderidge added, "She just needs a good bath and fresh clothes is all."

I pondered on what sort of work they'd expect me to do. I didn't know how to cook or wash laundry. He wouldn't think I was such a bargain once he discovered how useless I was.

The carriage came to a halt and Bronson exited the carriage before turning and lifting me down.

"She's lighter than my little granddaughter!" Bronson exclaimed.

"No worries," replied Alderidge, "Mother Hannah will fatten her up soon enough."

Bronson placed my hand on his arm and guided me as we walked forward to a series of stone steps. I dragged my bare feet, feeling my way as I went. I was certain there was food in my near future and anticipation filled me. But the exertion of climbing the steps was too much. My legs shook and I tried to take another step, but my knees collapsed and I fell painfully onto the steps.

Strong hands gripped my shoulders, pulling me up and Alderidge's voice spoke close to my ear as he gathered me up into his arms, "She's worse than I thought. Quickly, have Mother Hannah meet me in my clinic."

He held me close to his body as he walked quickly and though I knew this was a strange man I'd just met, somehow I felt so safe in his arms. Perhaps it was the fact that I had not been held or embraced in over a year. I craved human touch and in that moment he was giving me exactly what my soul needed. My head lolled back weakly and he shifted me so my face rested against his warm chest.

"Hang in there dear, we'll get you taken care of."

His soothing voice washed over me and though I didn't yet know if I could trust him, I gave in to the exhaustion and lost consciousness.

Chapter 12 The Sorcerer

A delicious savory fragrance filled my nose and I awoke to the growling of my stomach. I swept my hands around trying to determine where I was as the events from the prior day came back to me. My fingertips brushed across cotton sheets and a brick wall. It seemed I was lying on a cot in the corner and I carefully pulled myself up to sit.

"Take it slow hon, you need some food in you." spoke a woman's warm voice. Her footsteps approached and she took me by the hands. She guided me to a table and sat me down before I heard a dish slide in front of me and she pressed a spoon into my hand.

"Think you can manage?" she asked.

I nodded silently. Cupping the bowl with one hand and keeping my face close to the warm contents, I was able to spoon the stew into my mouth with minimal dribbling. Hot broth with beef, potatoes, and carrots filled my mouth and I groaned aloud. It was delicious. I shoveled it in and felt tears drip down my cheeks.

"Don't cry hon, what's wrong?" asked the woman.

I wiped my face, "I haven't had a hot meal in years." I admitted.

"Well that won't do. Here, take some bread too." She pressed a chunk of still-warm bread into my hand and I held it to my nose, just breathing it in for a moment. More tears spilled out as I bit into it and I thanked her with a mouthful of bread.

"They call me Mother Hannah here." The woman said. "What's your name?"

"I'm Vivienne," I said between bites. Despite my hunger, I found it wasn't long before my stomach was uncomfortably full. Years of small, light meals had caused my stomach to shrink. It would take a while for me to adjust to meals that actually met the needs of my body.

"We need to get you washed up," said Mother Hannah. "I've got some water heated up for the tub so come get undressed."

I wasn't too sure about undressing in front of someone I'd just met, but a bath sounded like heaven and I couldn't deny I was in dire need of washing. She guided me over the stone floor and began unbuttoning what was left of my dress. As I pulled my underdress down over my shoulders I heard her take in a sharp breath. I crossed my arms over my bare chest, feeling awfully vulnerable and Mother Hannah quickly put her warm hands on my upper arms and guided me into the tub. I sat uncomfortably in the water, but when the kind woman added a pot of hot water I sighed as the warmth flooded over my sore body. She handed me a cloth and a bar of soap and let me wash myself as she poured water over my back and hair. Layers of grime lifted off my skin, leaving me soft and smooth aside from my wounds. Mother Hannah began to wash my hair, her hands working soap into the length of it. She worked at it for a while and then stopped and placed a hand on my shoulder.

"Dear, I hate to say this, but I think we have to cut your hair."

I swallowed and didn't answer.

"It's full of sap and plants and it's just one big mat." She said in dismay.

I nodded jerkily. "Very well." My hair had always been a point of pride for me. It was dark and shiny and long. But I had felt the weight of the mass of hair on my back, reaching well past my hips, and knew she must be right. It had not been brushed since long before I'd fallen from the tower. Mother Hannah left and returned quickly, placing her hand back on my hair.

"I'll save as much as I can and it will grow back eventually, dear," she said in a reassuring tone. I nodded again, afraid if I said anything I might start crying again. I heard the sound of the shears working to cut through the thick mat of hair. It took a moment and then suddenly my head was lighter than it'd ever been. Mother Hannah lathered soap in my remaining hair and then rinsed it before ushering me out of the tub. She was drying me off before I could say anything and I felt a bit like a child again, being dried off by my governess. When she was done she stepped away for a moment and I was left standing in the middle of the room, naked and shivering. Then she came back and pulled a dress on over my head. She buttoned it expertly and then sat me back at the table.

"Let me just even out this hair now," she said. I sat still as she trimmed the tips of my wet hair. When she was done I reached up and felt the tips with my fingers. It stopped about an inch above my shoulders. It was unspeakably short by the Gotland court standards. But what did that really matter anyway? I heard the clank of a bowl in front of me and eagerly reached for the food again. Just then a door opened and footsteps entered.

"Ah, perfect. Thank you, Mother," spoke Alderidge.

"She'll be needing light duties till she regains her strength. I've got to head back to the main house." She moved towards the door where Alderidge stood and I heard her whisper urgently to him for a moment. "Do you think you can heal her?" was all I heard Mother Hannah ask.

My ears perked up. Heal me?

"I'm feeling optimistic," he answered as Mother Hannah left, "but first we need to discuss some things."

I heard him sit across from me at the table and I lowered my food.

"What's your name?"

"Vivienne," I answered.

"Vivienne, who did this to you? Who was your last master? This sort of treatment of slaves is illegal in Duthlin. I'll need to report them."

I paused. This was not the line of questioning I was expecting. "I was not a slave prior to the day you purchased me." I said quietly.

Alderidge cleared his throat, "I see. Then who is responsible for your injuries?"

I swallowed thickly, visions of brambles filling my head. "Does it really matter?" I croaked. I heard the irritated tapping of his fingers against the tabletop.

"Very well!" He announced abruptly. "I'd like to try and restore your sight, what do you say?"

"You can do that?" I asked in disbelief.

"You're in the presence of the best healing mage in Duthlin!" he boasted. "I don't think I'll be able to do much for your scars at this point, but if anyone can heal your eyes, it's me."

I raised my eyebrows a bit. "Okay." I nodded. If he could give me back my sight, maybe I could find an opportunity to escape back to Gotland. Otherwise, I may be stuck here, working as a slave for the rest of my life.

"First, I need you to agree to six months of servitude."

My brow furrowed in confusion, "I don't understand. You purchased me."

"Yes," said Alderidge, "but we run things a little differently here. First, we don't brand slaves in this household. I choose the cheapest slaves, I do my best to get them back to health in return for six months of servitude. At the end of those six months, you have a choice. You can choose to stay, not as a slave but as a servant in my household or you may choose to leave and I will release you from your servitude. If you stay as a servant you will have the opportunity to apply for citizenship and may leave at any time, with reasonable notice of course."

I cocked my head in interest, "Don't you lose money that way? And what's to stop them from just running away after you heal them?"

Alderidge chuckled, "You're a clever one, aren't you? I have them give me their word that they'll stay. If they go back on their word and run away, it's all the same to me. I don't want dishonest servants in my home anyway. Most choose to stay; not just for the six months, but after that as well. They are well-fed, housed, and able to attain citizenship. Thus I acquire honest, happy servants who work hard because they choose to be here. Any money lost is worth not having to engage in the nasty business of disciplining slaves or chasing them down when they run away."

"Fascinating," I said thoughtfully. "I agree to your terms. Six months of servitude in return for my sight." It was a good deal. No branding, no punishments. Six months of hearty food and a dry bed while I regained my strength to return to Gotland. And I'd be able to see again. The thought had my heart swelling with hope. Maybe things were looking up for me.

"Excellent!" Alderidge exclaimed and I jumped a little as he slapped his hands on the table top. "It's going to take a few sessions so we'll start immediately!" He began clearing the table and I fought the urge to snatch my bowl back from him. There'll be more food later, I reminded myself.

"Alright, hop on up." He said, patting the table.

I stood, a bit unsure and felt the height of the table. The weakness in my arms and legs said there would be no 'hopping' happening right now.

Alderidge seemed to realize this and moved towards me, "Right, I'll just help you then."

His hands gripped my waist and I sucked in a breath in surprise. Instinctually I grabbed his forearms to steady myself as he lifted me to sit on the table. We both quickly removed our hands and he moved to the head of the table, dragging a chair with him.

"Okay, now lay back." He instructed.

I did as he said and found that he had placed a folded blanket at the end of the table for me to lie my head on.

"Try to relax. Embrace the magic and it'll be much easier for me." He said softly, his voice close behind my head.

I took a steadying breath and tried to relax. As much as I could anyway, lying on a table in a strange man's house so he could do magic on my face. He placed his fingertips on my temples and a moment later I felt the warmth of his magic swirling around in my head. It was a wonderful feeling. Every ache faded away and I sighed in relief. I felt my own magic stir, wanting to rise up to meet his, but I kept it in check. If he found out I was a mage, he'd have a lot of questions that I wasn't yet sure how to answer. So for now I just melted under the influence of his magic and hoped my sight would return.

Chapter 13 The Light

Over the next several days, Alderidge and I did an hour-long healing session each morning. After each session, he'd tie a clean bandage around my eyes.

"I don't want you using your eyes throughout the day," he had said. "You can open them for a bit after each session to see how things are progressing, but trying to use them too soon may further injure them."

So I wore the bandage as he'd instructed and rested my eyes. Mother Hannah assisted me with bathing and provided me with clean clothes to wear. She brought me three meals a day. Each of them exquisitely delicious. When I wasn't eating or doing healing sessions, Mother Hannah brought me simple tasks to do. Preparing dried herbs, peeling hard boiled eggs, and shelling peas. Anything that could be done seated and with only my hands to guide me. In the evening a young maid from the kitchen would take me for walks around the grounds. She had a bubbly, fun personality and introduced herself as Kate.

"You're going to love it here! The other girls can't wait to meet you!" she said excitedly.

"Do you like working here?" I asked curiously as we walked arm in arm.

"Oh yes! I feel quite lucky to be here. You see, I was about to be purchased by the brothel madam, but Master Alderidge out-bid her! He's very kind, and handsome too!" she giggled.

I smiled for the first time in what felt like forever. It was hard not to. Her energy was contagious and I found great joy in our daily walks.

"Kate, do they make you do this? You don't have to walk with me if you don't want to."

"Oh no, Vivienne! I volunteered! I said you needed fresh air and a bit of light exercise. I enjoy walking with you, it's quite pleasant really." she assured me.

I smiled again. It felt nice to be in the company of someone who genuinely wanted to be there.

A couple of sessions in, Alderidge decided to remove the stitches in my face. He worked with a tiny pair of scissors and tweezers pulling each little thread out. I could feel his soft breaths on my face as he leaned close over me.

"These stitches are like nothing I've ever seen, who did them?" He asked.

"I'm not entirely sure," I admitted.

"You don't know who stitched you up?" He asked incredulously.

"Well I couldn't exactly see them…"

Alderidge cleared his throat, "Ah, right. Well in any case, they're ready to come out. Try opening your eyes now."

I sat up and blinked my eyes open, looking around. "I see shadows, just darker and lighter areas really."

"That's good. If we hadn't seen any progress by now I might've thought they were beyond repair, but since you're seeing some changes I think progress will happen a bit more quickly now." He tied the bandage over my eyes as always. "Let's go ahead and remove the rest of your stitches."

I didn't move. All my stitches? They were practically everywhere. My back, my ribs, across my collarbone, both arms, both legs, including one particular wound that reached quite high up my thigh… "I have quite a lot of them… I'd have to undress…" I said hesitantly.

"Oh! I apologize, I didn't think about that. Let me get Mother, perhaps I can teach her to do it."

He sounded a bit flustered and my mouth twitched. "It's okay, Mother Hannah is a busy woman is she not? If we just do one section at a time, and someone was to help with some drapes for the ones on my back, I think we can manage."

"Alright then, where would you like me to start?" he agreed.

I reached back and unbuttoned the first button on my dress to loosen the neckline and pulled it down just enough to reveal the length of the wound across my collarbone. He shifted and set to work pulling out the delicate stitches. I could feel his breath against my neck as he leaned in close, immersed in the task. I focused on taking long, slow breaths. I didn't want him to think I was anxious at his proximity. Later, Alderidge fetched Kate who helped me undress and draped blankets over me to preserve my modesty as he removed the stitches from my back and ribs. I was glad to have Kate there as her presence alleviated some of the awkwardness of the situation. She helped me dress again, then took her leave. I sat on the table and hiked my skirt up to uncover the last wound on my leg. Alderidge sat in front of me and started at my knee where the wound began and worked his way up. I fidgeted restlessly and tried not to imagine what he looked like. Kate said he was very handsome. But that was Kate's opinion. Perhaps he was actually very plain, or maybe he was ugly. The curiosity was eating at me.

"Does it hurt much?" he asked quietly.

I cocked my head to the side. "Not too badly. It's gotten much better since we started our sessions." I felt his hands brushing against my thigh as he neared the end of the wound and hoped he couldn't see me blushing.

"All done." He said.

I pushed my skirt back down as he put his things away and headed out the door.

"Same time tomorrow!" He called over his shoulder.

"I'll be here!" I called back.

Over the next several sessions the shadows in my vision gradually grew darker, the light areas grew brighter. Color crept back in till everything was a blur of fuzzy colors. And then one day, after a healing session, Alderidge took the bandage off my eyes, and as I blinked a few times everything came into focus. Crystal clear, in a way I had only hoped for and before my eyes was the young, concerned face of Alderidge peering down at me where I lay on the table. Handsome indeed, his skin was several shades darker than my own and he had black hair that curled a bit and hung just past his jaw, though most of it was tucked behind his ear. I looked up into his brown eyes, taking in his dark stubble and strong, slightly hooked nose. A wide smile broke out on my face and his eyes widened in surprise.

"I can see you." I proclaimed. I sat up abruptly and he swung his head back to avoid getting smacked in the face. I ran to the door and flung it open before running out onto the estate grounds. I hiked my skirts up to run faster and stopped in the middle of an expansive green lawn with well-kept landscaping that showcased a variety of flowers in yellows, pinks, reds, and blues. I spun around, taking it all in. The gleam of golden sunlight that shone through the leaves of the oak trees, the cloud-dotted blue sky, and the contrast of the huge red brick home that stood amongst it all. As I turned, I spotted Alderidge running to catch up with me. He wore a navy vest over a white dress shirt with the sleeves rolled up, exposing his dark forearms. A breeze blew strands of hair across my face and I grinned at him.

"Thank you." I breathed, tears pricking my eyes.

He stuffed his hands in his pant pockets and grinned back at me, his eyes meeting mine.

"What did I say? Best healer in Duthlin."

Chapter 14 The Estate

With my vision restored, I moved out of the adjacent cottage that Alderidge called his clinic, and into the servant's quarters with the other girls. They welcomed me with open arms, not seeming to mind my scarred face. They were an odd bunch, the servant girls. There were a few girls with scarred backs from previous owners, there was Mary with the peg leg, and Alice with her round, pregnant belly. Alderidge had done his best to try and save Mary's infected leg though it was beyond saving by the time she came to him. He'd healed the whipped girl's wounds. He'd purchased Alice, knowing she was with child and wanting to keep mother and baby together. The girls were grateful for a second chance at life and were absolutely devoted to him. All the staff were really. From the butler down to the stable boys. All had been rescued by him in one way or another. Many had been there for several years and told stories about those before them who had earned citizenship. Some had left to return to family, some got married, and others opened shops in town and would come back to visit their friends at the estate. They worked diligently, seeming to enjoy their work. I reflected on the slaves and servants who worked in the palace and didn't recall any such vigor from them. Gotland didn't have many slaves as far as I knew. At least that's what Damien had said. Something about if they had more slaves they could produce cheaper crops but the price of slaves was too high and… I had stopped listening at some point. I was naive and indifferent to what went on around me. I wondered if Eleanor felt such devotion to me. Or the chambermaids. Or the kitchen staff. Did they care about me at all? Why would they? They had nothing but the next day's work to look forward to.

While Bronson served as butler, it was Mother Hannah who ran the household. All the staff respected and loved her. That was how she came to be called Mother Hannah. She was a middle-aged woman with warm, brown skin and hair that had just started to gray. She wore strange but beautiful gowns she called sarees. The girls said Alderidge had brought her back with him when he returned from studying abroad in the northern country of Alana. She had shown me around the estate and asked about my previous work experience. I didn't have any of course so I gave vague answers. Cleaning, gardening, keeping books. All things I had technically done during my time in the tower. It all sounded rather useless now but Mother Hannah perked up as I spoke.

"You can read?"

I nodded and she looked at me thoughtfully.

"I need someone to clean and organize the master's study. Can you do that?"

I nodded more fiercely. "I can alphabetize or sort books however he'd like." I wanted to feel useful during my time here and this was something I felt I could do well. Mother Hannah seemed to like that answer and took me to Alderidge's study. When she opened the door I was greeted by a grand study featuring a large wooden desk surrounded by bookshelves full of thick tomes. Behind the desk was a window overlooking the grounds. The desk had piles of books and loose papers piled on it.

"Master Alderidge is usually a very clean person, but he has too much to manage and can't keep up with the mess," said Mother Hannah, looking around the room. "Your duty every evening will be to empty the waste bin, shelve any books that aren't in use, and dust all surfaces."

I nodded and started immediately. I picked up a stack of books and Mother Hannah left me to my work. The books were organized by topic it seemed, unlike the alphabetical system the palace librarian used. I supposed that made more sense and would make things easier to find. But as I became immersed in the work I decided to take it a step further and alphabetize each category. When all the books were properly shelved I looked at all the loose papers that littered the desk. It seemed to be mostly financial records. There were receipts, tax documents, and a large ledger with balances marked in it. I shuffled through the papers and began sorting them. Receipts, tax documents, and miscellaneous into separate piles. Then I organized each pile by date, putting the oldest ones at the top as they most likely needed to be dealt with first. As I finished up I heard footsteps at the door and looked up to see Alderidge's surprised face. He was wearing his usual dress clothes with the sleeves rolled up. He had a mug of tea in hand and a newspaper tucked under his arm.

"What have you done with my desk?"

I straightened sharply, "I was just organizing it." I realized I had gone beyond what Mother Hannah had asked of me and wondered if I had gone too far as Alderidge walked swiftly over to the desk to see what I had done. I stepped back in trepidation, wondering what he was thinking as he rifled through the stacks I had made, taking in what I'd done. Slowly he started nodding.

"This is good." was all he said before sitting and pulling himself up to the desk. I hesitated and he continued, "You can continue your work. So long as you're quiet it won't bother me."

I felt awkward but set about dusting the bookshelves in silence. Every now and then I glanced at him out of the corner of my eye as he referenced receipts and wrote in the book. His handsome face was focused intently on his work. His eyebrows furrowed and he rested his bare forearms on the desk. He seemed to be recording every earning and expenditure in the ledger. At some point,

I watched for too long from the side of his desk and his eyes snapped up to meet mine. I jumped and turned back to the shelf, embarrassment coloring my cheeks.

"Curious one aren't you?"

He didn't sound annoyed but I glanced back and apologized quickly.

"That's all right. I'm afraid I'm not doing anything of much interest though. Just finances."

Curiosity got the best of me and I turned back to him, "Do you record every single transaction?"

He raised his eyebrows, "Of course. If you don't know where your money is, you don't really have the money."

"Seems like it would take a long time, running all the numbers."

He sighed heavily. "Yes, it is very time consuming and very boring."

"Is that why you're three months behind?"

His eyes snapped up to me again, this time his eyes a bit narrowed and I sucked in a breath.

"Sorry! I just mean to say, it seems you could use some help." I explained quickly.

"Yes," he said slowly, "unfortunately, none of my staff know arithmetic."

I blinked at him a couple of times then looked away and bit my cheek.

"You know arithmetic?!" he asked, standing abruptly.

I nodded hesitantly and he looked me up and down.

"You've had an education. It's not common for slaves to have had an education," he said quizzically.

I didn't want him to know who I was. In six months we could go our separate ways and I could return home. If he found out who I was, who's to say he wouldn't hold me for ransom? Or maybe he knew Rhiannon and would return me to her. He was a mage after all. Alderidge seemed kind, but I hadn't known him long and I didn't trust him yet.

I looked down at my feet then glanced up at him again, "Like I said, I wasn't a slave prior to the day we met."

He nodded slowly though his eyes were a bit suspicious and then to my surprise, he gestured for me to sit in his seat. I looked at him quickly but did as he bid. He pushed the chair in and leaned against it casually.

"All right, let's see what you've got."

I swallowed nervously but straightened up and took the pen in hand. Alderidge watched over my shoulder as I worked, his eyes closely following everything I wrote. This went on for a half hour or so before Alderidge finally spoke.

"You're pretty good at this."

I blushed a bit and smiled a little to myself. "I had a good teacher," I said, thinking fondly of my governess.

"I'd like you to spend some time on these records in the afternoon before dinner each day. I'll let Mother know." Alderidge instructed.

I nodded, "Yes sir."

Working as a servant in the Alderidge household was going to look a lot different than I expected.

Chapter 15 The Servant

Having lived much of my life in royal comfort, I never would have thought I could feel such happiness working as a servant. In the mornings I dressed and got ready with the other girls, donning the navy blue dress and white pinafore that made up my uniform. The girls would all help each other with pinning their hair back into simple, low buns and then we'd hurry down to start breakfast. The other servant girls had become like sisters to me and we worked well together. We'd chat and laugh as we set the table and prepared breakfast for all the staff.

A small part of me wondered if maybe I could just stay here forever. I could live amongst these girls I considered family, laughing, working, and playing. I'd never have to go back to being confined to the palace walls. Never have to face the certain scrutiny that would accompany my now scarred face. All those pretentious, judging eyes. Here, they didn't care. We all had scars and no one hid them. No one was ashamed. It was a level of acceptance I'd never experienced before. The thought of staying was tempting. But I missed Father and Damien, Eleanor and Marion. Surely they missed me. They were probably still looking for me, not knowing what had become of me. The thought stirred up guilt and I pushed it away. I would keep my word and do my six months of service. Then I would return and… then what? Go back to living my life as a sheltered princess? Hiding my magic from everybody? Oh, my magic. It ached inside me, dying to stretch and play. I kept it locked down, only casting little spells when no one was around to see. Heating a kettle with fire from my palm, or growing flowers in the window boxes on the servant's quarters. It wasn't enough. I wanted to test my limits, to learn and grow my abilities. It seemed there was no possible future where I got to both live with all my loved ones and be true to myself.

One evening, as I was tidying up the study, a certain title caught my eye. *Magic Theory, Vol. 2.* My heart pounded and I glanced at the door furtively. Alderidge had already looked over my bookwork for the day and headed down to dinner. I studied the row of books and found that he had volumes one, two, and three. Why was I surprised? Of course he'd have these, he was a mage, I thought to myself. I pulled the middle book from the shelf and flipped it open. Excitement coursed through me. Maybe I could teach myself some more. I couldn't just take it though, what if he noticed it missing? I was the only other one who spent any time in his study. I decided to just read a chapter and then maybe later I could find some privacy to practice what I'd read. I hungrily consumed the information on the pages, soaking it all in. My magic hummed beneath the surface of my skin, longing to be used. I glanced at the clock on the wall and realized I was out of time. I had to be on time for dinner or I'd be missed. I snapped the book shut and returned it to the shelf before hurrying down the stairs to dinner.

That night, after all the girls had fallen asleep, I slipped out of bed with my blanket wrapped around my shoulders and silently made my way out and around the back of the estate. There was a garden shed that stood a ways away from the main house and I headed towards it. I ducked inside and closed the door behind me. There was a bit of magic I'd read about today that I wanted to try. In the book, it explained that learning more about your core power and mastering it was necessary to become a skilled mage. I hadn't a clue what my core power may be but luckily the book had detailed a spell that would determine whether or not a mage's core power had even settled yet. I seemed to be a bit of a late bloomer considering other mages awakened their powers at twelve so I figured there was a chance my core power hadn't even settled yet.

I sat on a wooden crate in the shed and rubbed my hands together. The autumn air was chilly and my breath came out in little white puffs. I summoned my rings and passed my magic through them, trying to focus on refining it down to its core. The golden light swirled in little tendrils around my fingertips. Now, if I did it right, and my magic had settled, it should- suddenly the golden magic flashed brilliantly and the little tendrils of gold turned pure white. The magic shone brightly enough to illuminate the entire shed. Whereas the golden magic usually flitted around softly, the movement of this magic was harsher, stronger. It was less wispy, and more like a beam of light as it circled around my hands. I stared in awe. It felt amazing, the strongest magic I'd ever conjured. Whatever it was, this was my core power. I played with it for a while, wondering about its nature before closing my fists and banishing it back to my core. I needed to get back to the servant's quarters and get some sleep. Otherwise, I'd be tired tomorrow and the others would notice. I swung the door open and darted back across the grounds. As I rounded the corner of the main house I ran right into something firm and stumbled backwards. I looked up and gasped as I found myself looking into the face of none other than Alderidge himself. His eyes were wide in surprise for a moment and then he narrowed them at me.

"What are you doing out here in the middle of the night?"

"I… Well I-" I had no explanation but as I stuttered, footsteps sounded from the direction I'd come and we both looked to see a young man round the corner with a lantern. His mouth popped open in surprise and I recognized him as one of the stable hands.

"Patrick?" Alderidge exclaimed. He looked back and forth between us and when I looked at Patrick, he was looking back and forth between Alderidge and I. I could see that both of them were forming a similar idea and I flushed in embarrassment.

"No, I-" I turned back and forth between them, not knowing who I needed to be explaining myself to.

Alderidge cleared his throat awkwardly. "Well, we best all be getting off to bed."

Patrick bobbed his head up and down, looking like he'd just seen something he wasn't supposed to. "Yes sir." Then he turned on his heel and headed back the way he'd come, towards the stables. I ducked my head and stepped around Alderidge but his words made me stop.

"Vivienne."

I turned back to him and we locked eyes.

"You ought not to be running around with boys in the night." he admonished.

I bristled and glared at him, but I didn't dare talk back so I just turned my back sharply and hurried back to bed.

Chapter 16 The Master

I hardly saw Master Alderidge after that, and that was just as well. I was a terrible liar and I feared if he looked at me too long, he'd see all the secrets I was keeping. His eyes had a way of making one feel that way. He'd come by the study sometimes in the evening to look over my work but other than that, he was always working. I felt a bit put off after our encounter in the night. He had chastised me, yet I hadn't done anything against the house rules. Besides, he was walking around at night too. What was he doing up? And why did he so easily assume I was fooling around with the stable hand? I didn't even know him! I was a princess for heaven's sake! I could count the number of people allowed to reprimand me on one hand. And he certainly wasn't one of them. Though I supposed he was now. I was a servant in his household, and he was the master. I didn't much appreciate that fact. I belonged to no one. I grumbled as I washed the windows, my brow furrowing in irritation.

Suddenly something snapped against my buttock and I shrieked in surprise. I whipped around, rubbing the sting in my behind to find Kate holding a rag and laughing her head off. Another girl, Bethany, ran around the corner with her rag all twisted up and snapped it at Kate who shrieked and started twisting her rag up again. They were supposed to be washing the windows in the next room, but it seemed they'd gotten distracted. I laughed as they chased each other around the hall and then twisted my own towel up and took after them. We chased each other around, dodging attacks and giggling like children.

"Oh my, what a ruckus."

We all turned sharply to see Alderidge leaning against the wall looking all too casual with a mug of tea. The other girls straightened and tucked their hands behind their backs meekly.

"I hate to interrupt, but Vivienne, I need you for a moment in the study," Alderidge said, hiding a smirk behind his mug as he sipped.

Drats. I balled up the rag and followed him as he turned and led the way to the study. I fidgeted as we fell in step.

"Good to see you're getting along with the other girls." He said smugly.

I flushed, embarrassed. "Yes, well they straighten right up when you come around."

"Ahh, not out of fear of course! They all love me." He said confidently before taking another sip.

"Yes," I agreed, "It's quite the little harem you've got going here."

Tea sprayed out of Alderidge's mouth and he coughed loudly. I didn't wait for him to recover but stepped ahead with a smirk of my own. I reached the study first and schooled my expression before holding the door for him. He looked at me crossly, dabbing his mouth, but I didn't meet his eyes. I may be a servant but I certainly wasn't subservient. Alderidge crossed the room and stood by his seat. He studied me for a minute and I felt warm under his gaze. He seemed to be second-guessing whatever he had brought me here for, but after a long pause, he gestured for me to take his seat. I did so and he reached around me to pull a ledger over.

"You've been doing well with the books so I thought we might take it a step further." He flipped open the ledger and continued, "I'm preparing healing potions for my next business trip and need to know how many to prepare and how to price them. This ledger contains last year's earnings as well as the cost of production for each potion. I need you to look through it and come up with numbers for this season."

I studied the ledger with interest and nodded. "When would you like it finished?" I asked.

"Preferably by the end of the week."

I nodded again. Should be easy enough.

A couple hours into it I had decided it was certainly not, 'easy enough'. Alderidge seemed to have two different price scales. One for his normal, everyday sales, and one for these quarterly business trips. Whoever he was selling to on these business trips was paying three times the cost of normal sales. And they were buying a lot. Cumulatively, potion sales from his quarterly business trips alone were double that of all his other sales combined. I rubbed my eyes as the numbers swirled around my head and decided to come back to it again tomorrow.

When I entered the servant's quarters, the other girls pounced on me.

"Did we get you in trouble?" asked Kate.

"No," I said with a yawn, "He just wanted me to do more bookwork."

"Oh, come on, is that all?" Bethany asked, hunting for more.

"What do you mean?" I asked in confusion.

"Patrick says he saw you two sneaking around together!" exclaimed Alice. She was in her rocking chair, rubbing her full-term belly.

"Oh it's a secret romance!" shouted Mary, flinging her arms up. The room descended into giggles and I blushed bright red.

"Hang on girls, you've got it all backwards." I tried to explain. But it was like trying to preach to squirrels. They were all running around, dancing and giggling. I shook my head in exasperation. The girls were not going to believe me anyway.

"What about you Alice?" I diverted, "Since when were you and Patrick so chummy?"

It was Alice's turn to blush as everybody turned and looked at her.

"We've been chatting for a while. I think," she turned a deeper red, "I think he wants to get married."

The room exploded with shrieks. The girls were jumping up and down, and someone was crying. I smiled widely. It seemed nobody would be sleeping for a while.

The next morning, after all the morning chores were done, I headed over to the study to get an early start on the work Alderidge had given me to do. As I came to the closed door, I paused. Voices were speaking inside. Alderidge and another man conversed in an urgent tone.

"What does she want now Smith?" Alderidge asked.

"She's summoning us all to the Wildlands." said the other man.

"What for?" Alderidge asked.

"She won't say. But if we don't go, it'll be bad. You know how Rhiannon gets."

I froze. My ears rang and my heart pounded. In my mind I was back at the party, the witch looming over me. My chest rose and fell quickly. He knew her. Was working with her somehow. My body told me to run, but my feet stayed rooted in place. No, no, no. This couldn't be happening. I put a hand over my heart and tried to fight through the fear. I needed to think rationally. Alderidge didn't know who I was. I was hiding in plain sight. He didn't seem like the kind of person who would work with Rhiannon, so maybe there was more to this.

"Very well. Let her know I'll be there."

They bid farewell and footsteps sounded towards the door. I jumped back in a panic. I didn't want to be caught eavesdropping. I silently ran back down the hall a ways and then turned and walked towards the door slowly so that when the other man emerged from the study, it appeared as though I was just now approaching. He was clad in a worn coat and his hair was a graying brown. He looked at me briefly then went on his way, tugging his coat closed around his wide belly. I peeked into the open study cautiously. Alderidge was sitting in his chair, slumped back. With his elbow resting on the arm of the chair, he was holding his face in his hand. I considered him for a moment. How could this man, who tried to help so many people, be connected in any way to Rhiannon?

"You seem distressed," I said quietly.

He turned his head just enough to peer at me with one eye before rubbing his face and laying his head back against the chair. He sighed deeply.

"Every time I think I'm free, someone throws another chain around my neck," he muttered.

I tilted my head in curiosity. "What do you mean by that?"

He gave me a sad, half smile and sat up. "No worries dear. I'll find my way out. I always do." He offered me his seat like usual and I took it.

Leaning casually against the chair with his confident demeanor back in place he asked, "How's Patrick?"

I looked up over my shoulder at him and glared. "I wouldn't know."

"Ah, over so soon?" He didn't sound in the least bit sad.

"Can't be over if it never began." I retorted.

"Really? Well that's a shame, Patrick is a good fellow."

"Yes," I agreed, "I'm sure he and Alice will be quite happy together."

"Alice?" he asked, sounding confused.

"Mhm." I said smugly.

"I suppose they would make a handsome couple." He said thoughtfully.

I peered up at him, wondering if he intended to make light conversation the entire time I worked, and he caught my eye.

"Right then, let me know when you've got those numbers all worked out," he said briskly. "I'll mostly be in the clinic for the next few days."

He left swiftly and once the door closed, I raised my hand and let my magic twirl around my fingers. With all this bookwork to do, I was often left alone in the study. This gave me time to read the magic book and practice a bit in private. I stared at the little golden tendrils in focus and they changed into that potent white magic. Alderidge seemed like a good man. But the books told me he had secrets and now I knew he was somehow connected to Rhiannon. He wasn't to be trusted.

Chapter 17 The Family

I finished the budget Alderidge had requested a few days later and made my way around the main house to the attached clinic. The door was open and I paused there to observe what was happening inside. An elderly man sat in a chair with what appeared to be his family members standing around the room. Alderidge was kneeling beside him with his hand over the old man's chest. His yellow healing magic was swirling around, much more gently than my own core power. I watched in fascination as the yellow light faded away and Alderidge stepped back.

"How's that feel?" he asked.

"Amazing!" exclaimed the old man. The family broke out in relieved grins and Alderidge clapped the man on the back.

"No more horse racing for you! You've got a few winters left in you, best not to cut them short!" Alderidge admonished jokingly. They exchanged money and handshakes and I stepped aside as the family left. Alderidge was putting some things away, his hair falling into his face as he closed a chest. I watched for a moment, my eyes drawn to his arms, his shoulders, his back, his- I averted my eyes and mentally shook myself. I came here for a reason, I reminded myself.

"Must be nice, helping people feel better," I commented.

"Pays good too," Alderidge replied with a cheeky grin.

I barked a laugh, "That it does." I handed over a new ledger. This one is full of recommended prices, and quantities for his healing potions. "Where do you go to sell the potions?" I asked quizzically.

He flipped it open to read through. "Oh, here and there." He said vaguely.

I frowned at him.

"This looks good, and you finished quickly too. Unfortunately, I'll have to postpone my business trip. Another matter has come up that I must attend to. I'll be leaving in the morning." His brow was furrowed as he snapped the ledger shut.

I chewed my cheek. He was going to see Rhiannon.

"Do you have to go?"

He looked at me surprised and I realized how that sounded. "I just mean, it seems you don't really want to go." I looked up at him through my lashes, hoping that I was right. That he didn't want to meet with Rhiannon. That he'd stay and not go near her.

He fiddled with the ledger. "I won't be gone long. Just for the day."

My heart sank. Didn't he know she was evil? What she was capable of? What she had already done? I fisted my hands. I could tell him. Tell him how she'd kidnapped me and locked me away. Cursed me to sleep forever. I could tell him these scars were all her fault. That her curse didn't work and I was left to waste away in isolation. I could tell him about all the suffering she'd caused me. But Alderidge wouldn't meet my eyes. I swallowed my feelings of betrayal down. Maybe he was in on it; maybe he knew all about the poor princess she'd taken, and just didn't know it was me. I turned and walked out. I wasn't going to reveal myself. Not yet. Maybe not ever.

The next morning the estate continued its usual routine despite Alderidge's absence. We cooked, cleaned, and washed laundry. We filled in for Alice who had stayed behind in the servant's quarters. The local midwives had been summoned early in the morning since it seemed the baby would be arriving sometime today. The girls chattered and giggled in excitement but my thoughts were filled with a certain sorcerer. What did Rhiannon want? Why was he agreeing to meet with her? What if she gave him some horrid task to do? What if she hurt him? I chewed my lip anxiously as I worked and wished the day would pass faster.

In the evening as I sat to eat dinner with the girls, Bethany came running in.

"Master Alderidge is back!" she exclaimed. "And he's in a mighty foul mood. He didn't even greet me when I welcomed him back." She said with a pout.

"Maybe he'd like his tea?" Kate suggested.

"Yes!" Agreed Mary, "You should bring it to him Vivienne!"

I looked at her, startled and she winked at me.

"Yes! Go on Vivienne!" the girls encouraged me.

"What? No, what if he wants to be left alone?" I protested.

"Master Alderidge loves his tea. He's always drinking it," said Kate.

"Yeah, he can't be mad at you for bringing him tea!" said Mary, bouncing on her seat.

The girls continued to push and prod me. "We'll let you know when Alice is getting real close so you don't miss it, go on!" said Bethany.

"Alright, alright." I relented. I stocked the tea tray in the kitchen and headed over to the study. I stepped down the hall slowly to prevent the dishes from sliding on the tray. The other girls were much better at this kind of thing. But I'd never served tea. It had always been served to me.

When I reached the open study door I came to a halt. Alderidge was sitting in his desk chair, elbows on the desktop, with his head in his hands. Mother Hannah was beside him. She had her hands on his shoulders and was comforting him quietly. I got the distinct impression that something terrible had happened. I tried to back away but Mother Hannah caught sight of me standing in the doorway with the tea tray and gestured for me to enter. I hesitantly entered the room and placed the tray on the desk as quietly as possible. I felt like I was intruding and would have liked to leave then, but custom dictated that I should serve the tea as well. My heart hurt for him and I wondered what was causing him such grief.

"The girls thought you might like some tea," I practically whispered.

He nodded silently. Mother Hannah patted him on the back and whispered something in his ear. Then she gave me a sad smile and left. I poured the tea and added honey the way he always had it. He preferred the honey over the white sugar I'd grown up using. Alderidge kept his face in his hands, his hair falling over his fingers. I didn't know what to do. I wasn't good at comforting people. I didn't know how to react to people's emotions. I thought of how Marion had treated me after my mother passed. Sometimes she'd just sit beside my bed so I wouldn't have to be alone. I swallowed my discomfort and pulled a chair over to sit beside him. He didn't react so I took a deep breath and placed a hand on his shoulder. I leaned in to try and see his face.

"What can I do?" I asked in a hushed voice.

He lifted his head a bit but didn't meet my eyes. "Nothing," he said thickly. "There's nothing you can do." But then he turned and to my surprise, rested his forehead against my shoulder. I sat rigidly, not knowing how to respond. My instincts said to hold him. But formalities said this was already inappropriate. I raised my other hand and gently placed it on the back of his head. He seemed to hold his breath for a moment but as I slowly started combing the back of his hair with my fingertips, he let out a deep sigh and his tension seemed to melt away. He kept his hands in his lap and we stayed like that for a little while. Although I wondered about his sadness, I also felt a spark of guilt for enjoying this closeness. His hair, so close to my face, smelled like oranges and cinnamon. The skin on the back of his neck was warm against my fingertips and I studied his olive skin against my own, pale hand. I thought I heard a soft sound and glanced toward the doorway before jumping back an inch in surprise. Alderidge pulled back to see what I was looking at. Kate was standing there, trying to catch her breath and looking between us quickly.

"Sorry, I- I didn't mean to interrupt-" she stuttered.

I stood abruptly, "What is it?" My voice cracked awkwardly and I fought back a grimace.

"Alice is about to have the baby, thought you'd want to be there." Kate gasped.

I stepped around the desk and hurried after her without looking at Alderidge although I was keenly aware that he stood and followed us. We ran up the stairs of the servants' quarters and I heard Alice's groans from the sleeping chamber. Kate ducked into the room and I followed before turning swiftly to face Alderidge.

"Sorry, Master Alderidge." I said, beginning to close the door. "This is lady's business."

Alderidge opened his mouth in protest but the midwife's voice carried from inside the room, "No men!"

I smirked a little at his expression and closed the door in his face.

The birth was not as imminent as Kate had thought, but a few hours later, when Alice was propped up in bed with a tiny baby girl asleep on her chest, I opened the door again. I smiled softly at the two men who sat in wait against the wall. There was Alderidge, idly spinning yellow healing magic between his fingers, and next to him was Patrick. He was wringing his hat nervously and stood quickly when the door opened.

"Can I see her?" Patrick asked.

I whispered to Kate who crossed the room and whispered to Alice. Alice looked up and nodded with a smile so I opened the door wider to let him enter. I leaned against the wall next to the door and Alderidge came and leaned against the doorway.

"I figured I'd wait close by, just in case." He explained.

I nodded and together we watched as Patrick knelt at Alice's bedside to meet her baby. He may not have fathered her, but as he looked at the little one his face was filled with adoration. He brushed his fingers softly against her little pink head and turned to kiss Alice on her forehead. The moment was sacred. It was an honor to be there and everyone in the room was quiet in reverence. Patrick cupped Alice's cheek and grinned at her. I sighed out loud and Alderidge looked at me. He watched me watching them.

"What are you thinking?" he asked softly.

"I hope someday somebody will look at me the way Patrick looks at Alice," I answered quietly. I felt a bit embarrassed after saying it and looked to see his reaction. But Alderidge had already turned back to the ongoing scene. His lips were pressed together and his eyes were dark. I opened my mouth, wanting to ask him what had happened but he quickly lifted off the doorframe and left. Rhiannon had done something. I was sure of it and I felt in some way responsible. I should have warned him, I thought. But whatever had happened was done and like Alderidge had said, there was nothing I could do about it.

Chapter 18 The Return

Over the next couple of days Alderidge made himself scarce. It was hard to tell if he was just busy preparing healing potions for his upcoming trip, or if he was avoiding me. Whatever the case, the moment of closeness we had shared when he returned from seeing Rhiannon appeared to be over. I told myself that I didn't really care if he avoided me, because it made it easier to practice magic without being caught. My progress was slow. It was difficult to find privacy and time to play with my newfound core power. Eventually though, I was able to concentrate the bright white magic into rings of runes that glowed in my palms. It seemed the only way to determine the nature of the magic was to experiment with it. This seemed potentially dangerous to me. What if I was a fire mage and started a house fire? Besides, I was extra busy now, helping cover Alice's duties.

The day before Alderidge was due to leave on his business trip, I was in the study doing my duties when I heard a tap at the window. I glanced over and gasped in surprise at the sight of a certain feathered friend.

"Nox!" I exclaimed. I crossed the room and threw the window open. Nox hopped around happily and then flew to land on my arm. I grinned at him happily and offered him a tea biscuit Alderidge had left behind on the morning tray. Nox pecked at it and seemed to enjoy it.

"What in the world?"

I jumped and whipped my head to the door where Alderidge stood, mouth agape. My mouth popped open in a little surprised "o" and I glanced back at Nox who seemed entirely unbothered as he ate the biscuit.

"Ah, sorry, I thought you were done with the tray," I said in a high voice.

Alderidge sputtered, "What? No- that's not- what is-?"

Nox cawed and took flight, swooping out the window. I watched him go and then turned quickly back to Alderidge with wide eyes and my hands held behind my back in the perfect picture of innocence. Alderidge looked at me in bewilderment, "How-?"

"I've got kitchen duty!" I suddenly exclaimed, making a beeline for the exit.

"Kitchen duty?" he asked in bewilderment as I rushed past him. "There was a bird! In my study! What-?"

But I was already at the end of the hall and didn't stop to explain. What would I say? 'Oh, that's my bird friend who used to visit me when I was locked in Rhiannon's tower. You know, that evil witch you're working with?' Nope. Better to do as he'd been doing and make myself scarce.

When the day came for Alderidge to leave on his business trip, the stable boys helped pack crates of potions onto a horse-drawn cart while the girls and I packed food and tucked it in amongst the crates. Mother Hannah kissed the sorcerer on the head and he gave her a quick hug before climbing onto the cart. He rode out down the long path and just like that, he was gone.

"Does anyone know where he goes?" I asked as we returned to our daily duties.

Bethany shrugged, "Everyone is just happy to be here. We don't ask too many questions."

That seemed to be the general attitude in the Alderidge household. It was a life so good, most slaves couldn't hope for better. I turned my attention back to my cleaning duties. Usually Alice was the one to clear the master's breakfast table but I was taking over the task now. I cleared the dishes onto a tray and reached for the newspaper Alderidge had left beside his plate when I froze. My eyes widened in recognition of the name on the front page. Father. I set the tray aside and unfolded the paper to read the headline.

Gotland King Welcomes New Heir

What? My heart raced as I read the article.

More than a year after the disappearance of both his children, King Edward Hawthorne has welcomed a baby boy with his new wife, Queen Catherine. It's been a hard two and a half years for Gotland's monarch following the disappearance of Princess Vivienne, soon followed by the disappearance of the Crown Prince, Damien. Months of searching were fruitless and the widowed king was forced to assume the worst and declare his children deceased. Things seem to be looking up for the royal family with the much celebrated arrival of a new heir just nine months after the royal wedding. The happy parents will be celebrating the new prince with a grand party this week.

My head spun. Deceased? Damien? Gone? I sank to the floor, dropping the newspaper beside me. How could this be? He'd given up. He wasn't still looking for me. Everyone thought I was dead. What about Damien? Had Rhiannon taken him too? Was he locked up somewhere?

"Vivienne, are you alright?" came Mary's concerned voice.

I looked at her, dazed.

Mary hurried over and took my arms. "Go lie down for a while Vivienne. I'll finish this up."

I nodded blankly as she guided me all the way back to my bed. I was vaguely aware of Alice giving me a questioning look from her bed across the room but I wrapped myself in my covers and turned away from her. I didn't want to talk right now. I was still trying to wrap my head around this. All this time I thought they'd still be looking for me. I thought I could keep my word to work at the estate and then I'd return and be welcomed back with open arms. But no. Father had given up. Moved on. He had a new family. A new heir. What had become of Damien? I lay there for a while, feeling dizzy and overwhelmed until my thoughts cleared a bit and I came to a decision. I had to return.

I whipped the blankets off and stood abruptly. Alice jumped a little and looked at me in surprise. I started grabbing the few things I owned. A winter cloak, a comb, and a satchel. Then I removed my pinafore and draped it on the bed.

"Vivienne, what's going on?" asked Alice in a concerned voice.

I looked at her and pain crossed my face. I hated to leave the girls on such short notice. I knew they'd worry for me. "My family- my brother needs help. I'll come back. I'm not sure when, but I'll come back." I promised.

She looked at me wide-eyed but before she could ask any more questions I was gone, racing down the steps and across the grounds to the stables.

"Vivienne? What are you doing here?" asked Patrick.

"Master Alderidge left something behind," I lied. "I've got to catch up to him. Could you saddle a horse for me?"

Patrick nodded enthusiastically and got to work. "Do you know how to ride? I could take it for you."

"I'm a fine rider," I said quickly. It was true. I'd had many riding lessons back home and knew my way around a horse.

Patrick finished quickly and I stepped up into the saddle.

"Take good care of her. I'll be back, promise." My voice cracked and he looked at me in confusion, but I took off before any tears could fall. I was going home.

Chapter 19 The Villain

I traveled all day that day, rarely stopping for rest. By nightfall, I was at the border between Duthlin and Gotland, though I only knew it thanks to a merchant passing by. I had spent many hours studying geography, but I'd never been to any of the locations I'd studied. My book smarts didn't do me much good on the road. I debated stopping to camp overnight but I hadn't brought much with me. It'd be a long, cold night, sleeping on the ground in the autumn weather. Winter was just around the corner and I was not prepared for it. Instead I decided to walk on through the night. I pitied the horse but promised when I arrived I'd let her rest as long as she liked.

In the wee hours of the morning I passed through the expansive farmlands of Gotland. As a youth, I'd been taught that Gotland was made prosperous by its rich, fertile land. But as I passed farm after farm and field after field, I found myself a bit underwhelmed. I reminded myself that most of the harvests would be over by now. Still, the tiny homes that were scattered here and there seemed destitute. I reached the inner city at midday and found it none the better. The streets were lined with beggars. Filth ran down the cobblestones in streams. I watched as a group of men loaded a linen-wrapped body onto a cart beside two others. It was then that I noticed the sickness that ran rampant. The grayish hue of the beggars. The way the merchants coughed wetly between transactions. Plague. There was a plague in Gotland. I stopped at a well to draw water for the horse and caught the eye of an old maid.

"How long has it been like this?" I asked her.

She scrunched her eyebrows at me. "What'r you talkin' about?"

"The plague. How long has it been here?"

"Longer than I've been alive. Though this last year has been the worst."

I gaped at her. How could this be? A plague in Gotland for decades? And I'd never heard about it. My mind spun and a memory surfaced. A young man at my birthday party, urgently trying to tell me something. But I hadn't listened. I didn't care. But what about Father? Surely he would know about this. Why hadn't he done anything? Surely there was magic that could purge this sickness? I looked around in horror. This was my home. These were my people. And they were suffering. Had been suffering for a long time. While I was planning parties and eating fancy foods, they were dying in the streets. I thought I might be sick and steadied myself against the mare. I needed to speak to Father. Things were not right here. These people needed help. If Alderidge could restore sight to my damaged eyes, there had to be magic that could rid my kingdom of plague. I mounted my horse and continued on my way to the palace which sat at the other end of the inner city. I wished that I had learned healing magic. My healing abilities would not be near as potent as that of Alderidge since healing was his core power, but maybe I could help a little. Traveling through the city was slow. The streets became increasingly crowded as I drew nearer to the palace walls. My heart ached as I saw them in the distance. Those walls once contained my whole world. I had dreamed of traveling to the northern country of Alana where the sun heated the land almost all year. I'd dreamed of standing on the beach on the western coast of Duthlin. I'd never seen the ocean. So many things I'd wanted to see, but I never could have imagined the nightmare just beyond the walls I so desperately wanted to escape.

As I approached the outer wall I stopped close to a small structure, hiding in the shadow it cast with my hood pulled low. I wasn't ready to be seen yet. I'd come here in such a hurry, I hadn't really thought this all through. What if the guards at the gate didn't recognize me? I thought back to the last time I'd looked in a mirror at the estate. I'd lost the round youthfulness of my face. My scars were now just pink lines across my face but they still drew attention. I didn't want to be some crazy lady outside the gate, claiming to be the long-lost princess. They'd lock me up for that. Or they'd try. I'd use my magic to fight back. But then I'd definitely be locked up. Magic was still illegal. I frowned as I considered my options. As I watched, carriages began arriving. The guards let them pass into the palace grounds one by one, speaking with the driver of each one first. The party was tonight I realized. These were party guests. I narrowed my eyes as I observed the procession of carriages. They weren't taking the main road through the inner city. There were Gotland knights on horseback, guiding them around the worst part of the city. The path was longer but they'd avoid the slums I'd just passed through. This was how they were keeping it quiet I realized. Guests were guided through the upper class part of the city where lords and ladies resided on their estates. They only saw the wealthier district and thus, news of the plague would for the most part stay out of the news in the other kingdoms. I didn't understand this. All this secrecy to maintain the image that everything was fine in Gotland. But it wasn't. Gotland needed help.

The long line of carriages continued for hours on their slow crawl through the gates. The sun began to set and I put the mare away in the nearest shelter. Now was the time for me to make my move. I walked along the wall and crouched by a bare, leafless tree fifty yards or so from the front gate. I summoned a flame in the palm of my hand and coaxed it towards the bark of the tree. I urged it to grow rapidly and then ran quickly back to the growing shadows.

Just as I intended, the knights and guards stationed around the gate hurried over to see what was happening. In their absence I snuck around the carriages and sat on the back of one which had already passed the guard's inspection, pulling myself up as it rolled forward. The carriage paused in the courtyard that lay before the front entrance and the esteemed guests exited. I stayed in place and allowed myself to be carried around back where they would be keeping the horses. This way I could hop off without drawing attention to myself. I made my way to a side entrance used mostly by the servants, though I had used it many times as a child to sneak out of the castle. I followed the familiar passages, making my way to the grand ballroom. But I wasn't ready to reveal myself just yet, so I paused under the arch that stood over one of the grand staircases leading down into the ballroom. I watched as guests spilled into the room in their fine clothing. Silk and ribbon, gold and diamonds adorning every inch of them. My eyes narrowed as I thought of the people just outside the walls living in squalor. There were more guards stationed around the room than I'd ever seen at any of our parties before. I supposed that had a lot to do with a certain witch kidnapping a certain princess. A figure entered the room and my stomach clenched as I recognized my Father. His arm was wrapped around his new wife who was holding their tiny child. She placed the baby in an ornate bassinet beside the thrones before she and my father took their places in the grand seats. Guests came by, bringing gifts and congratulating them. Father's chest was puffed out in pride and he smiled at his bride. Deep sadness surfaced in my chest. No one seemed to care that I was gone. Father had certainly moved on. I had come here to see him, but I couldn't seem to move my legs. I suddenly felt very small and forgotten, hiding here. I was home, but it didn't feel like it.

Father stood with a goblet of wine to address the crowd.

"Welcome!" his voice bellowed out. The chattering voices quieted down to hear him speak. "We thank you all for joining us to celebrate the birth of our son and heir, Prince Edward the Second!"

Applause rang out and he continued his speech. A richly dressed couple entered at the top of the staircase and I shrank back against the drapery to avoid their attention.

"Can you believe this is the 8th party he's thrown since the royal children disappeared?" whispered the woman.

My heart sank.

The man shook his head in disapproval. "He got engaged just three months after. He certainly didn't waste any time getting a new heir."

My stomach turned with unease and I thought I might be sick. He'd been throwing parties just like he always did. As if Damien and I had never existed. Damien was out there somewhere and nobody was looking for him. Not to mention the unspeakable state of the rest of the kingdom. He was pretending none of it existed, I realized. No plague, no missing children. Just him in his castle with his perfect little family. Anger boiled up in me. How could he? I'd always looked up to him. Imagined him as this benevolent and wise ruler. His speech droned on and on, drawing laughter and applause from the crowd and I couldn't take it anymore. I descended the stairs with purpose, my path leading me straight to the throne.

He was still speaking, "Gotland has never seen such prosperity-"

"LIES!" I shouted.

All heads turned to me as I stormed forward. "You lie!" I shouted again, anger radiating from me. Party guests backed away, parting the crowd for me. Father's eyes widened in surprise and then fear.

"Guards!" He ordered.

Rage ripped through me and my magic lashed out, forming golden rings five feet in diameter that circled me. Screams broke out and Catherine clutched the baby to her chest, eyes wide in fear. The guards didn't dare come any closer with my magic circling me.

"Who are you? What do you want?" Father demanded.

A low, dangerous laugh escaped me. "What? Don't you recognize your own daughter?" With that I extinguished the magic rings and dropped my hood back, revealing my face. Gasps sounded from the crowd and hushed chatter spread throughout the room.

Father's face morphed into recognition. "Vivienne?"

"You never came for me!" I accused, pointing my finger at him.

His mouth gaped open and he stuttered over his words, "We tried, for three months we tried. But we didn't have the resources, and the thorns, you have to understand."

Everything in me stilled. "The thorns?" I said, my voice wooden.

The king seemed to realize his mistake and shrank back even further.

"You found me," I stated, my heart breaking a little more. "You knew where I was, and you left me there."

"We couldn't get through, there was no way to get to you!" he claimed.

But that wasn't true. There were powerful mages in every other part of the world. All he had to do was ask for help. But he was prideful, stubborn, and afraid. I had paid the price for these failings, but no more.

"You sit here throwing lavish parties while your people suffer," my voice cracked, "while your family suffers."

He had his hands raised in surrender now, backing away from me. My power was growing within me till I couldn't contain it. My hair whipped around in a wind I didn't consciously summon. The rings of golden light broke forth again, circling me erratically. My thoughts were wild and out of control. My rage was overflowing and with it my power.

"You are not fit to rule," I shouted over the growing wind as hot, angry tears streamed down my cheeks, "so I will remove you from the throne!"

He backed into the throne and fell to the floor. I tried to summon my rings to harness the overwhelming power flowing from me, but suddenly the golden rings flared white and my core power took over, obliterating the rings meant to direct my magic. The white rings were blinding as they spun around me. The power within them thrumming audibly. Every guest had fallen to the floor now, the king shielding his face from the brightness of my power. It was all too much. The rage, the heartbreak, the pain. It suddenly ripped out of me in a terrible scream. Simultaneously my magic exploded around me and everything was enveloped in the blinding white fury of my core power.

Chapter 20 The Wards

I wasn't sure how much time had passed, but when my vision returned after the blazing flare of light, I found myself on my knees, head lolled back looking at the ceiling. I lifted my head to look around. The ballroom was blanketed in the slumped forms of party guests. In front of me the king and queen were also lying at the base of the thrones.

My heart pounded. Were they dead? Did I kill them with my magic? My heart rate steadied as I spotted their rising and falling chests. They were asleep. All of them were asleep. A flicker of movement caught my eye and I rose to my feet to see.

Marion.

I ran over and kneeled beside her.

"Marion?"

Her eyes flickered open drowsily. "Oh Vivienne," she sighed, sadness in her eyes.

"I didn't mean for this to happen." I whimpered.

"Shhh," She hushed me, "you must activate the wards. Below the dungeon. Protect the kingdom. Find your brother." Her eyes were falling shut, unable to stay open.

"Wait, Marion-"

"I'm sorry," she whispered, "I'm sorry I never told you. I'm sorry I couldn't do more."

"What? What do you mean? Marion?"

But she had already fallen asleep. Unable to rouse. Cursed by my magic. I stood and a sob escaped me. I didn't mean to do this. I just wanted… revenge. I just wanted revenge. And now I had it. So why did it still hurt so much? I stumbled around the room in a daze, coming to stand over the queen. She was still clutching her baby though her arms were loose around him. I reached out with trembling hands and lifted him into my arms. Gazing down at his face, more tears dripped down my cheeks. He hadn't done anything to deserve this. An innocent child. I walked to the bassinet and laid him down, studying his tiny features. I was no better than Rhiannon. Taking out my rage on those who had nothing to do with my suffering. I didn't know how to undo this. I didn't even know how I had done this in the first place. I'd never wielded power of this magnitude. My thoughts were interrupted by the sound of footsteps echoing from across the grand room. I turned slowly and recognized the man immediately.

Alderidge.

"What have you done?" he asked breathlessly.

I didn't answer, frozen at the side of the bassinet.

He stormed across the room, headed straight for me. Halfway across he suddenly recognized me.

"Vivienne?"

I still didn't answer, unsure of what to say.

"What have you done?!" He was yelling now and continued on his path to the foot of the throne. "You've cursed the entire kingdom! How did you do this?"

My heart stalled. The entire kingdom? How was that possible? Marion's words echoed in my mind. Activate the wards. Protect the kingdom. Find your brother. I turned from him wordlessly and walked swiftly from the room. He followed, calling after me.

"You must lift this curse! You've endangered the whole kingdom!"

"I know," I called back, not stopping.

"Not to mention you've effectively killed my entire business!"

I paused, "What?"

Alderidge threw his arms up in exasperation, "How do you think I make all that money? Gotland citizens are my biggest customers!"

I narrowed my eyes at him. "You've been selling magic potions on the black market, haven't you? That's illegal in Gotland."

"So is cursing the entire kingdom!" he shouted.

I frowned and turned my back to him. I needed to get beneath the dungeon. I wasn't aware that anything even existed beneath the dungeon. Alderidge was hot on my heels, barraging me with questions.

"What did you do to all those people? Who are you really?"

I stopped abruptly and whirled around to face him. He barely had enough time to stop without running into me. I gave him a hard look and then noticed where we were standing. I turned to look sadly at the massive oil painting hung on the wall beside us. It was a life-size family portrait depicting Father, Mother, Damien, and me. I was only six at the time but I still remembered standing all dressed up, with Mother's hand on my shoulder. Her long, dark blonde hair tickled the top of my head. Alderidge turned to follow my gaze and his mouth gaped open. Twelve years may have passed since the completion of the painting, but standing so close to it the resemblance was unmistakable.

I continued on my path leaving him to stare at the painting a minute longer before he followed after me again.

"You're the missing princess. Princess Vivienne Hawthorne. How did you end up at my estate?"

I frowned. I didn't really have anything to lose at this point. He was much more skilled at magic than me and seeing as how I had so little control over my own magic, he could easily overpower me if he wanted to. "I have your friend Rhiannon to thank for that," I answered bitterly.

Suddenly he caught my shoulder and spun me around, pinning me down with his dark eyes. "Rhiannon cursed you?"

I gave him a once over. Was that concern I heard? "Not exactly," I answered carefully.

He looked a bit relieved, his shoulders dropping an inch.

"What, she didn't tell you all about it at your little meeting?" I asked snidely.

Alderidge's eyes widened a bit in surprise. "You knew I was meeting her?"

I shrugged and continued down a flight of stairs as if I didn't really care. But I did care. I wanted to trust him. He seemed to put two and two together because he called out to me again. I ignored him and hurried down the spiraling stairs. The air grew cooler as we descended below ground level.

"Vivienne!" He caught my shoulder again but he had too much momentum coming down the stairs and stumbled for just a second, pushing me against the stairwell wall. He stopped himself with a hand on the wall beside my head. My eyes widened at the sudden proximity, his face mere inches from my own. His eyes were intense, begging me to listen.

"Whatever she did to you, I had nothing to do with it. I didn't know anything about it. She's evil Vivienne, please don't lump me in with her."

I searched his eyes for the lie, but only found sincerity. Though I wasn't a hundred percent certain, I nodded slowly and he backed up.

"Sorry, I didn't mean to push you."

I nodded silently again.

"Can you please lift the curse now?" he pleaded.

I chewed my cheek nervously and averted my eyes. "I don't know how," I admitted.

"What do you mean you don't know how? What did you do?" he demanded.

"I didn't mean to," the tears were threatening to break free again. "I tried to reign it in but it just- I lost control."

"Lost control?" He suddenly waved his hand in front of me and I gasped as my magic tugged and my golden rings appeared between us. All of them were shattered. Except one. Vengeance.

"How did this happen? How could you be so irresponsible?" He accused me. "Didn't your mentor teach you better?"

I shook my head in denial, "I didn't- I didn't have a mentor. I taught myself."

"Taught yourself?" He repeated dumbly.

"Look, magic is illegal in Gotland. I didn't even know I was a mage until I was 16. There was no one to teach me so I just… read books." I finished lamely.

Alderidge ran his hands down his face and let out a slow breath. "Okay, if you lost control, the curse probably took the form of your core power."

I nodded in agreement, recalling the piercing white light of my core power.

"So, what's your core power?"

I looked at him like a stunned deer and shook my head.

"You don't know. Of course." he rubbed his face again. "What is your plan here exactly?"

"I need to activate the wards first."

He nodded, "Yes that would be a good place to start. Alright, lead on." He gestured down the stairs and we resumed our descent. The dungeon was dark and dank. The cells stood empty- Gotland had a jail in the inner city so the dungeon was rarely used anymore. Scanning the abandoned space, I spotted what appeared to be an arched doorway that had been walled off. Square stones filled the passage, sealed together with mortar.

"I don't suppose you could break through this?" I questioned Alderidge.

He considered the barricaded door with a dubious look and then planted his palm in the center of it. His seven rings appeared as he focused on the task. Dust fell from the stones and cracks appeared, crawling out from his hand. After a minute progress slowed and then Alderidge pulled his hand back, extinguishing his rings. He wiped his forehead, a bit out of breath.

"You didn't finish," I said with a frown.

"Thank you, Princess, I can see that." He replied sarcastically. "Stone isn't exactly my forte. You want to give it a go?"

I shook my head. "I don't have much control, what if I bring the whole castle down on us?"

"Not even you are that powerful, Princess. Besides, you know the best way to learn control?"

I blinked at him blankly.

"Practice." He finished.

I lowered my eyebrows at him and placed my own hand on the cracked stones.

"I only have one ring left." I reminded him.

"A skilled mage can do a lot with one ring."

"But the book said I need-"

"Forget the book!" He exclaimed, "This is why you need a mentor!"

I bit down on the retort I wanted to throw at him and stared the door down in focus. Golden magic snaked out from my hand, twisting erratically. Without my rings to guide it, it struggled to find form.

"Don't fight it. Follow it. Keep it on a leash, but don't force it. What would your magic do without guidance?" Alderidge spoke in a low voice, close behind me.

I loosened my ineffective grip on the magic, allowing it a little more freedom. Green tendrils emerged from between the stones, growing and expanding into roots that pushed the stones apart. They tumbled down and I stepped back to avoid them. Before us appeared a jagged opening, just large enough for us to duck into. Beyond the doorway was another spiraling staircase that disappeared into the pitch black underbelly of the castle.

Alderidge lit a single flame in his palm and I followed suit. The little fires gave us enough light to make our way through the dark. The staircase ended at an open, circular chamber. In the center was a cylindrical pedestal, a little over a yard in diameter. Runes circled it and I studied them curiously.

"Why would a kingdom that has outlawed magic have magic wards to protect it?" I murmured.

"My guess is it hasn't always been illegal," Alderidge replied. "At some point, one of your ancestors commissioned a powerful sorcerer to create this. These wards are very old and very powerful."

I considered his words. Gotland used to employ mages. What had happened since then? Why had the royal family turned so vehemently against magic?

"I think it requires a member of the royal family to activate it," Alderidge said.

I nodded and placed my hand in the center of the runes. I pushed a little magic into the ancient stone and the magic of the wards latched on to it. The runes lit up with golden light that pulsed, blowing our hair back. I felt it in my bones as the power expanded to cover the entire kingdom in its protective shield. The pulsing settled and I drew my hand back with wide eyes.

"Whoever created this ward was a very powerful Protection mage. Not just a mage, but a sorcerer." Alderidge said reverently.

"What's the difference?" I asked.

He frowned and shook his head at me. "You have a lot to learn. I can teach you. I'll be your mentor."

It was my turn to shake my head. "I don't have time for that. I have to find my brother."

"Don't you think breaking this curse is a little more pressing?"

"Damien is missing, he could be in trouble. Besides, even if I could break the curse, I don't know that I would. The king isn't fit to rule. Damien must return and take the throne."

Alderidge rubbed his face again. "Well, do you have any idea where he is?"

I bit my cheek.

"Of course not." He said, sounding unimpressed. "Alright, let's go." He started back up the stairs and I followed after.

"Where are we going?"

He didn't stop to look back at me, still climbing the stairs. "I've heard about a Clarity mage on the west coast of Duthlin. She can probably at least give us a place to start."

"What's a Clarity mage?"

"A Clarity mage sees the truth of things. The present, the past, and sometimes the future," he answered.

"So she could see the truth of where Damien is?" I asked in wonder.

"Hopefully."

"But the coast of Duthlin is at least five days ride."

"Good, it will give you some time to work on your magic. You're a danger to yourself without proper mentorship."

I pursed my lips in a pout. I thought I'd done pretty good up until this point, all things considered. Except for the whole 'cursing the entire kingdom' part.

Chapter 21 The Mentor

After leaving the palace grounds, I took Alderidge to where I'd hidden the horse away.

"See? She's right here," I said, patting her on the flank.

"I can't believe you stole my horse," Alderidge said disapprovingly.

"I was going to bring her back," I said, patting her again. I looked at her more closely and then turned to Alderidge, biting my cheek.

"What?"

"Umm, she's asleep," I answered reluctantly.

He rubbed his face and muttered something under his breath. Why did he look so good even when he was annoyed with me?

"Well, I suppose the animals had to sleep too. Otherwise, the rats would start eating people," he said finally.

I looked at him appalled and he chuckled.

"Let's find somewhere to stay the night, and I guess we'll start walking in the morning." He suggested.

I nodded. I hadn't slept in about 36 hours. The physical toll of riding so far combined with the emotionally draining events of the last two days had me feeling hollowed out. I looked back at the palace and considered returning to my own chambers but decided against it. I didn't want to sleep in my childhood bedroom while almost everybody I'd ever known lay cursed in the other room. We instead picked an inn in the nicer section of town. We simply walked past the sleeping innkeeper and picked out some empty rooms before falling fast asleep.

I awoke to Alderidge banging on the door.

"Rise and shine Princess! We have a Prince to rescue and a kingdom to save, let's go!"

I swung out of bed and sat with my head in my hands for a moment. The memory of last night didn't seem real. Had I really crashed that party and unleashed my magic on everyone? I needed to make things right. I needed to find Damien. He could help the people of Gotland. And I needed to master my magic so I could lift the curse. I laced up my shoes and washed my mouth out in a basin of water. I missed the indoor plumbing in the Alderidge estate. It seemed that Gotland was so behind in so many advancements that had been made in Duthlin. I peered into the mirror above the basin. My shoulder length hair was disheveled and dark circles hung under my eyes. I sighed and brushed my fingers through my hair a bit before leaving the room and heading downstairs.

Alderidge had helped himself to a heapful of food and had brewed some tea. I sat across from him and grabbed a piece of bread.

"We should gather some supplies and then head for the border. My cart and horse are stashed just over the border. We can use my horse to ride further into Duthlin until we can get a second horse."

I nodded. It seemed Alderidge had thought this all through. "Why are you helping me?" I asked quietly.

He chewed thoughtfully. "For one thing, my business is going to take a huge hit if I can't sell my potions in Gotland."

I frowned at him.

"But also, I do have a conscience, believe it or not. I feel some level of responsibility for you, and I'm a sucker for a damsel in distress."

I choked on the bread and coughed, "I'm not-"

"Alright! Let's be on our way!" he interrupted. He rose up and exited the inn leaving me to scramble after him.

As we walked through the ghost town that had once been a marketplace, we gathered supplies. We each filled packs with dry goods, canteens, and bedrolls.

"Shouldn't we leave some coin?" I asked.

"Do you have any money?" he asked with an eyebrow raised.

I shook my head no and he shrugged in return and continued filling his pack.

"It's not like they'll be needing it right now anyway," Alderidge said.

I frowned. He had a point. If I didn't return with the rightful ruler and lift this curse- all this stuff really wouldn't do them any good.

We began the long walk through the inner city, passing by the sick, sleeping forms of dozens of beggars.

"I've never been to the inner city. I didn't know it was this bad." Alderidge commented.

"Neither did I," I said quietly.

He shot me a curious look but didn't pry any further.

Once we were clear of the city and into the more rural farmlands, he brought up another topic.

"Let's talk about your magic."

I nodded, not knowing where to start.

"You said you didn't know you were a mage until you were sixteen. Did you not ever experience your magic in any way before that?"

"I don't think so."

"So you're a late bloomer," he surmised. "How long have you been practicing magic then?"

"Ever since I found out. So, a little over two years." I answered.

Alderidge paused, "Wait, you're only eighteen?"

"Yes?" I answered in a confused tone. "Why?"

He brushed his hair back without looking at me. "Nothing, I just thought you were older."

"Well how old are you?" I asked.

"Twenty-two."

"Oh. Well how on earth are you running such a successful business at twenty-two?" I asked a bit incredulously.

He gave me a self-satisfied grin. "I've been running the estate since I was seventeen, turns out I have a knack for it."

I tried to ignore the feeling in my stomach when he smiled at me and he continued,

"We're getting off track though. Do you have any clues as to what your core power might be?"

I shook my head. "I don't even really know what all the core powers are."

"It's hard to say how many there are. I can think of maybe twenty off the top of my head, but there are new ones discovered all the time."

"New ones?" I asked in wonder.

"Well, I don't know that there's ever *new* magic. But there's not even always a mage of every type alive at any given point in time. My theory is that the new types being 'discovered' aren't really new at all. They're just old ones that no one has seen in a while." he explained.

"Fascinating." I breathed.

"Yes," he agreed "but that may make it difficult to figure out what you are."

"Won't I need to forge new rings?" I asked.

"Yes, you will need new rings. Your core power doesn't require any rings, but most other things do. We can work on that when we make camp."

We walked for most of the day, passing by gray field after gray field. The air was bitterly cold and smelled like snow, though none had fallen yet. When the sun had begun to set, we stopped and made camp. Alderidge started a fire and we set up our two little tents near it.

"Before we start with new rings, we ought to dissolve that vengeance ring. What in the world possessed you to make such a thing?" he asked.

"It was an accident," I said defensively.

"That seems to be the trend with you."

I scowled at him.

"Summon your ring and then I'll guide you through dissolving it."

I pouted a bit and asked, "How did you know it was a vengeance ring anyway?"

"I can read some runes," he replied. "It is a tedious language that few bother to take the time to learn, but once you've mastered your core ability like I have, rune reading is the next step in magic education. Now go on."

I did as he said and the golden ring appeared before me.

"Alright, now in your mind you need to dismiss the need for this ring and allow the magic to dissolve into its raw form."

I closed my eyes to focus. I don't need vengeance. I don't need vengeance. I don't need vengeance. But as I thought about it, my father came to mind. The cowardly king who abandoned me in the Wildlands to an unknown fate. Maybe the others didn't deserve to be cursed, but he did. Then I thought of that wicked witch, Rhiannon. She punished me for something I didn't do. She had caused me so much suffering. I was just a young girl when she locked me away. If I could curse her too I would. Golden magic flashed in front of me and Alderidge made a sound of exasperation.

"You didn't dissolve it, you reinforced it!"

The now-brighter ring faded as I drew my magic back in.

"Maybe I still need it," I said stubbornly.

Alderidge shook his head. "What am I going to do with you?"

He sounded genuinely stressed and I pressed my lips together, feeling a touch guilty.

"Can we move on?" I pressed.

Alderidge rubbed his face. "Yes," he conceded, "let's try forging another ring. Something good this time please?"

I chewed my lip thoughtfully before raising my hand and summoning my magic again. It formed a circle and I spoke my intentions into it, "Strength."

The ring flashed and runes appeared around it, signaling its completion.

Alderidge nodded in approval. "You did that well."

I smiled a bit at the praise and stifled a yawn.

"We should sleep," I said. Alderidge nodded and we each crawled into our small little tents. I curled up into a ball in my bed roll and spread my heavy winter cloak over the top. The night was cold and though we had observed not so much as a goosebump on those who had been cursed, there was no such luck for us. We'd just have to bear with it while on this unexpected journey.

Chapter 22 The Ravine

I awoke in the morning to find several inches of snow blanketing the ground. We dusted it off the tents and packed them away before continuing on our path. We ate as we walked as it was too cold to stay still for long and we both agreed to not take the time to build a fire. We occasionally cast small fires in our hands to warm them, but to keep them going all the time would be too draining. The land was bleak and the trek was dull.

"Tell me about this brother of yours?" Alderidge asked.

"He's smart, charming, and popular with the ladies. He's been involved in politics and governance for years already. Everybody likes him. He just has a way with people." I answered, a bit out of breath from our pace.

"Sounds like prime king material. Tell me about your relationship with him. I never had siblings, I don't know what that's like." Alderidge inquired.

"Well, I was his baby sister. He doted on me. He got annoyed with me. The last couple of years before I… left, he was always busy. We didn't really spend time together anymore."

Alderidge nodded, considering my words.

"So who do you get your magic from?" He asked.

I shook my head. "Not sure. Father was terrified of magic. You should have seen his face when I… well anyway, definitely not him. And he never would have married a mage. So I'm thinking either it skipped a generation, or I'm one of those odd mages that just pops up randomly. Kind of ironic, all things considered."

Alderidge exhaled and nodded.

"What about you?" I asked. "Is the Alderidge family a line of mages?"

"Yes, the Alderidge family has had quite a few mages in their line. Father was an Earth mage."

I glanced over at him. "Have they since passed?"

"Yes. Some sort of carriage accident I'm told. I was studying abroad in Alana where my mother was born when it happened. Took several weeks for the news to reach me, but I came to Duthlin straight away and took up running the estate."

"I'm sorry, that must have been a lot for a seventeen year old," I condoled.

"It was… unfortunate. Though I must say the estate is doing much better under my management. The Alderidge's were nearly bankrupt. I had to dig them out of debt."

I raised my eyebrows a bit. It seemed Alderidge possessed financial wisdom his parents had not.

"You lost a parent too, did you not?" He asked.

"Yes, my mother. I was very young, I don't remember much about it. They said she was sick." It was odd to talk to someone about it. During my life in the castle, everyone knew so there was no one to tell. The conversation felt strangely intimate, though I supposed if we were going to be traveling together, it was inevitable that we'd be getting to know each other better.

That night when we made camp, Alderidge pushed me to forge another ring. I chose protection and completed the ring just as smoothly as the last.

"At this rate, you'll have a solid seven rings long before we reach the coast," Alderidge commented.

"Then maybe you can teach me something new?" I asked.

He smiled at me with those dark eyes and my chest squeezed.

"Yes, we can start working on something new soon." He answered.

When it came time to set up our tents, my cold fingers fumbled with the ropes. I cursed quietly in frustration as the canvas of my tent crumpled, the supports uncooperative in my numb grasp. Alderidge on the other hand seemed to have done this plenty in the past and was already done with his. He stepped over to help me and reached for the rope I was struggling with. He instead closed his hand around my own and I froze instantly, jumping a fraction of an inch. He snatched his hand back and raised it in surrender.

"Sorry! I didn't mean to make you uncomfortable." he apologized quickly.

I winced internally. "No, sorry. I wasn't-" I smoothed my hair back, trying to find words. "I was alone for a long time. There was no…" I waved my hands around trying to articulate my thoughts, "touching." I finished. "So I'm just not really used to it anymore."

I met his gaze hesitantly and found him considering me with wide, curious eyes. There didn't seem to be any judgment there, just kindness, and maybe a little pity.

"It's not that it feels bad!" I rushed to explain. "I like it, touching I mean. It's just-"

Alderidge was raising an eyebrow now, one side of his mouth curling up as he watched me. My face flushed hot and I opened my mouth to try and explain further but he stopped me with a raised hand.

"It's okay." was all he said. And then he turned back to the tent and showed me how to do it again. I listened to him, feeling warm despite the snow and when it was finished I offered a quiet thank you.

That night as I lay in the tiny tent I reflected on our conversations throughout the day and let out a breath. I'd never stumbled over my words or blushed the way he seemed to make me. It was downright embarrassing and I pushed the thoughts away and gave into sleep.

The next day there was a fresh coat of snow and more still falling. We had camped at the treeline of the forest which lay between Gotland and Duthlin. Somewhere in the midst of the forest was the border and beyond that would be Alderidge's horse and cart. We had trudged through the woods for a while when we came to a ravine that ran through the forest. It was maybe 40 feet deep and the sides sloped steeply down to its valley. I grimaced at the height but Alderidge seemed pleased.

"This means we're on the right path. If we follow alongside the ravine, we'll reach my cart sometime tomorrow."

"We've got to stay next to it?" I asked, eyeing the depth dubiously.

"Yes, it'll lead us right there." He said, seemingly oblivious to my doubts.

We walked on through the snow and I made sure to stay several feet away from the edge. As the hours passed, my nervousness lessened somewhat and I relaxed into the monotonous hike.

Suddenly ahead of me Alderidge slipped and fell on his rear, sliding a bit towards the edge. I gasped and leapt forward but he had already caught himself. He let out a laugh that was far too lighthearted for my liking.

"That was a close one!" He exclaimed, still not seeming very bothered.

I shook my head as I caught up to him. "You could've fallen down the ravine." I reminded him.

Alderidge brushed himself off nonchalantly. "If that happened I'd just climb back up. It's not that steep."

I shook my head again and we continued on our way, though I noticed Alderidge did stay a little further from the edge than before.

A few minutes later as we trudged along, I suddenly felt the snow under my feet give way. I gasped as the snow tumbled down the side of the ravine and I lost my balance, tumbling down with it. Before I knew what was happening I was flying end over end down the embankment, a scream escaping my lips. For just a moment I was free falling and my stomach lurched before I again impacted the soft snow that cushioned my fall.

"VIVIENNNNE!!!"

I looked back up the embankment to see Alderidge making his way down towards me, mostly just sliding on his rear through the snow. He came to a stop just a few feet below me, his jaw-length hair wild from his quick descent.

"Are you okay? Are you hurt anywhere?" He asked, concern on his face.

I shook my head no, unable to speak. My heart was racing, I couldn't catch my breath, and my limbs shook.

Seeing that I was okay, Alderidge let out a relieved breath and then threw his head back with a laugh. "You should have seen yourself! Your legs were straight up in the air!"

I choked out a laugh which turned into a sob and I slapped my hands over my face as hot tears started rolling down my face.

Alderidge was on his knees before me in an instant. "Vivienne? What's wrong? Are you hurt?"

I made an ugly gasping sound and my shoulders shook as I sobbed again. "I just- I was falling. Again." I choked out.

He grabbed my shoulders, pulling me into his chest and I made no effort to resist.

"I haven't been around heights since I fell and I just-" I hiccuped another sob into his chest, "didn't realize how scary it would be." I continued sniffling and hiccuping for a minute as I fought to catch my breath and Alderidge just held me tightly. I knew what I was saying wasn't making any sense, but he didn't ask. He just kept his arms around me with his chin on top of my head till my breathing slowed. Finally, I pulled away and wiped my face in shame.

"Sorry," I muttered, sniffing again.

Alderidge shook his head and wiped a tear from my cheek with his thumb. The gesture was so gentle I fought off another round of tears.

"Let's get back up there," Alderidge said quietly.

He grabbed my arms and helped pull me to my feet. We then trudged back up the embankment, spending half the time on all fours to gain purchase in the powdery snow. Here and there Alderidge would grab my arm to steady me until we made it to the top, out of breath.

"Shall we call it a day?" Alderidge asked.

I nodded, feeling a bit defeated. We went a little ways into the trees away from the ravine and picked a spot to make camp. We built a fire first, working together to gather fallen branches. As I carried an armful over to our spot, I noticed a sharp pain in my wrist. I dropped the sticks and rubbed my wrist with a grimace. Something was definitely wrong with it.

Alderidge eyed me. "So you did hurt yourself."

"I think so," I admitted. "I didn't notice it before, but it's quite sore now."

"Let me see." he gestured for me to come over as he pulled his gloves off.

I offered him my wrist and he took it in his hand, using the other to pull my glove free. He then ran his fingers across the bare skin of my forearm, with tiny tendrils of yellow magic spun between each finger. I held very still and noticed how dark his skin looked against the snowy backdrop.

"It's sprained. It'll be a quick fix." He said after a moment. Then his healing magic wrapped around my arm, some of it sinking into my skin. It was warm and soothing, quickly melting away the sharp pain in my wrist. I peered up at him through my lashes as he focused on the task. His eyes were trained on my arm so I took a moment to appreciate his strong, dark brows, the set of his jaw, and the dark stubble that shadowed it.

"There, should be good." He said and looked up from our hands to meet my gaze. We were frozen like that for a moment, my arm held lightly in his hands. He swallowed thickly and it suddenly occurred to me that I'd just had a meltdown and my eyes and nose were probably bright red from crying. I broke eye contact, self-consciously and he released my arm.

I flexed my wrist. "Thank you," I said.

He handed me my glove and nodded before turning to finish with the fire.

When camp was all set up, we sat by the fire to eat our supper. It was quiet between us for a while, though it wasn't a terrible silence.

"Will you tell me?" Spoke Alderidge.

I looked up at him in question.

"About what happened when you went missing?" he clarified.

I looked back into the fire and let out a heavy sigh before nodding. "Rhiannon broke into the castle. She came and stole me away on my sixteenth birthday." I started.

Alderidge leaned forward in interest.

"Somehow she transported me into this tower. There was no way to escape. No doors, no stairs. Just a tall, tall tower in a forest of thorns. She left me there. She had cursed the tower to make me fall into an endless, ageless sleep. Like the curse I cast on Gotland." I admitted. "But it didn't work right. I kept waking up, alone in that tower. The sleep kept getting longer and longer. I was afraid one day I'd never wake up. That no one would ever find me. I stayed there for Two. Years." My voice cracked a bit. "I couldn't take it anymore. I couldn't give in to the curse. So I tried to climb down." I swallowed dryly. "And I fell." I wrapped my arms around myself and tried to breathe through the tightness in my chest. After a moment I stole a glance at Alderidge. His eyes were wide with a mixture of emotions. Mostly horror. I looked away quickly.

"You spent two years all by yourself?" he asked in disbelief.

"Well, the flowers were there. They were…Well I don't know what they were. They spoke to me, but I never saw them. They're the ones who tended to me, after I fell."

Alderidge rubbed his chin thoughtfully. "It sounds a bit like pixies."

"Pixies? I didn't know there was such a thing." I responded in surprise.

"Yes, they can camouflage themselves. They're small, maybe only six inches tall. There used to be lots of them in Duthlin but now they're nearly impossible to find." He explained.

I thought back on every interaction with the flowers. It did all seem to match up. It would explain why they hadn't just carried me out of the forest of thorns. It also explained the odd meals they brought me.

"Why did she take you?" Alderidge asked.

I sighed. "I don't know. She was angry at the king for some reason. I am finding more and more that I really know very little about anything. The world, my home, my family. I'd just been living in ignorant bliss. Did you know I'd never left the palace grounds before the day Rhiannon kidnapped me?" I let out a bitter laugh and shook my head. "What a foolish girl I was."

"That's not entirely your fault. It seems you were quite sheltered." Alderidge said quietly.

"No," I agreed, "but if I hadn't been so self-absorbed, I would have asked more questions. I would have been more curious. More concerned." I stared into the fire. "I'm trying to make things better," I said quietly.

Alderidge was studying me with curious, thoughtful eyes.

"You are not how I thought you'd be," he commented.

I wasn't sure what he meant by that, but before I could ask he spoke again.

"We should sleep. If we really push, we can cross the border tomorrow evening."

I nodded in agreement. The emotional toll of the day was catching up with me and I needed to sleep. We both rose to go to bed, but I paused.

"Alderidge?"

He turned to me.

"Thank you. For helping me."

Our eyes met for a moment, the flames reflecting in his dark eyes. A half smile flickered across his face.

"Don't thank me just yet."

Chapter 23 The Border

We rose early the next morning and ate as we walked. There was a silence between us that I wasn't sure how to breach. I'd told him about the single most traumatic event in my life and now I felt vulnerable. I realized I really didn't know much about this man and there was one question that was eating at me.

"What happened when you went to see Rhiannon? Are you working with her somehow?" I asked out of the blue.

Alderidge looked at me, then looked away with a pained expression. "It's a bit complicated. I have to explain a few things first." he started.

I frowned at him. "Right. She just ruined my life is all, but sure- explain away."

He grimaced. "I can promise you I want nothing to do with her. But the rest is…"

the people I love without sacrificing my conscience to Rhiannon." His face was pained and conflicted, and a thought suddenly occurred to me.

"She's looking for me, isn't she?"

He looked into my eyes with a tortured expression and I took a step back.

"She asked you to look for me, to bring me to her?" My heart was racing and I took a couple more steps back, but Alderidge didn't move.

"Is that what this is?" I accused, "You're taking me to her?"

"No," he said finally. "I wasn't sure what I was going to do. I was trying to convince myself that maybe she wouldn't hurt you, but after what you told me last night…" he shook his head.

"How could you even consider taking me to her!" I yelled.

"She's going to hurt me, Vivienne. She already has. She hasn't found the people I've hidden from her, but it's only a matter of time. I didn't know how else to protect them," he pleaded.

I ran my fingers through my hair in distress. I wanted to trust him. I wanted to trust him so badly. But trust was a brittle thing, and mine was wearing thin.

"So what now?" I demanded. "You said you're not taking me to her so what are you doing?"

"We're going to find the Clarity mage," he answered.

"Why? Aren't your people still at risk?"

"Yes," he answered softly. "And they always will be with Rhiannon in power."

I tried to take a deep breath to slow my heart.

"So why are you here? How does this help them?"

"I think you can help me," Alderidge said.

I blinked at him in surprise and then narrowed my eyes at him in suspicion. "Me? Why?"

"I have a hunch," he started, a gleam in his eye. "That somehow you're important in all of this. I'm not sure how, but I think the clarity mage can help us figure it out."

"How do I know you won't change your mind?" I asked warily.

"Because I need you," he answered. I blinked in surprise and he swallowed before continuing, "If you are what I think you are, you may be the key to stopping her."

"And what is it you think I am?"

His dark eyes bore into mine. "Salvation."

I shook my head slowly as I considered him, seeing him in a new light. He was wealthy, powerful, high-born. Now he stood before me, vulnerable, at the mercy of Rhiannon. I clenched and unclenched my fists in indecision.

"I give you my word, I will not betray your trust," he pleaded.

It's not like I had much of a choice. I needed to find that clarity mage and thus, I needed Alderidge to lead me there. I dropped my shoulders in surrender and whipped my cloak around me in a huff.

"That's not much to go on," I grumbled. But I turned and continued walking in the direction we were supposed to be going.

"Says the one who broke our agreement," Alderidge replied with a cheeky grin that broke through the tension.

I clicked my tongue. "I was going to come back…"

"To finish your six months of service?"

"Well, no," I admitted.

Alderidge shook his head in mock disapproval. "I thought you liked it there?" he said, a bit pouty.

"I did," I answered honestly. "But, well I needed to return. I didn't know the state of things." I frowned at the thought.

Alderidge nodded in contemplation. "I suppose I'd probably be in trouble with the King of Gotland if he found out I purchased his daughter for five pence and had her washing the windows."

I shook my head ruefully and fought the grin trying to come out.

"I ought to have you arrested for that." I agreed and he barked a laugh.

We continued to hike through the snow for hours, an agreement of careful trust hanging silently between us. Suddenly Alderidge stopped.

"Do you hear that?" he asked.

I listened for a moment. "I hear birds singing?"

"You put all the birds to sleep in Gotland," Alderidge said with an amused look. "Which means we must be near the border."

I lit up at the thought of not having to walk anymore and we pushed on with renewed energy. Eventually we spotted an odd mirage ahead of us. It was like we were looking through a warped glass window and I studied it curiously as we approached.

"It must be the wards," Alderidge said.

I nodded but didn't move to cross it.

"Do you think it'll let us back in?" I asked.

Alderidge raised his eyebrows in surprise. "You know, I hadn't thought about it. You're the one who activated it, so I would think you could pass back through. I probably can't though."

I nodded. It made sense, but as I stepped across the border and felt the wards wash over me, I still felt nervous. Once on the other side, I reached a hand out tentatively and then breathed a sigh of relief as it passed back through the ward. Alderidge reached his own hand out and pressed it against the impenetrable wall that formed the ward. He'd been right.

"Well, guess I won't be visiting Gotland again for a while." he chimed.

We continued on our path and Alderidge let out three short whistles. An excited whinny answered him from a little ways ahead of us and from the underbrush emerged a huge black horse. He trotted over and greeted Alderidge like an overgrown puppy and the corner of my mouth curled up.

"He just waited here for you?" I asked in disbelief.

"Well I did leave him in a very nice pasture near a stream. But yes, Cyrus is a loyal friend." He showered the beast with affection and then gestured for me to come over. I approached and Cyrus regarded me with curiosity. I gave him a gentle pet and he shoved his nose against my neck, rifling around under my hair. I giggled and inched away.

"He likes you. That's good or else you'd be walking the rest of the way." Alderidge said in approval.

"What?"

"Cyrus doesn't let just anyone ride him. He's very particular. That's why I got such a good deal on him." he said with a grin.

I gave him a disapproving look which just made him smile bigger. Alderidge led us through the trees to a clearing where a small creek flowed by. The cart sat there too and he rifled through it, picking some things out.

"Let's make camp here. It's a good spot." Alderidge suggested.

I nodded and we quickly pitched our tents. By the end of this journey I was going to be quite seasoned in this camping thing, I thought to myself.

Chapter 24 The Pupil

In the morning Alderidge began putting packs on Cyrus' back and I frowned.

"Aren't we going to take the cart?" I asked.

Alderidge shook his head. "The fastest way to the coast is too narrow and bumpy for the cart. It'll be faster for us to just ride Cyrus. Come hand me your pack." He waved me over and I complied. I eyed the horse and chewed my cheek. I had not anticipated sharing a horse with Alderidge.

"I didn't bring a saddle because I didn't think I'd be riding him so we'll have to ride bareback," Alderidge said, more to himself than to me. He finished packing everything up and turned to me expectantly. "Alright, front or back?" he asked.

I looked at him bewildered. "I've never ridden bareback," I said hesitantly.

"Hm, let's try in front then." Alderidge decided. I looked around, searching the clearing for a log or something. No way was I going to be able to climb onto the back of this beast unaided. I could use the cart... But then Alderidge stepped behind me and put his hands around my waist. I sucked in a breath of surprise and straightened.

"Ready?" he asked.

He didn't wait for a reply before hoisting me up towards Cyrus' back. I clambered over clumsily and let out a huff of exertion as I finally righted myself. Satisfied that I was in place, Alderidge planted his hands on Cyrus' back behind me. He let out a low "Hup!" as he propelled himself up and swung his leg over. I had to admit I was a tad bit impressed, but the thought was interrupted by him scooting into place right behind me. Heat flushed through me and I stiffened. Though we weren't right up against each other, his legs were touching mine and if I leaned back at all, I'd be leaning on his chest. His hands reached out and he lifted my hood up over my head in a gentle gesture.

"Let me know if you get too cold." he said in a low voice near my ear.

I shivered, but it had nothing to do with the cold. I cleared my throat and nodded quickly.

Alderidge then reached around me and took the reins. I could feel the muscles in Cyrus' back shifting as he walked and I marveled at his size and strength. I was grateful for the heat he gave off. Despite my skirts being pulled up a bit, exposing my thick wool stockings, I was warmer now than I had been walking. Though that was partially due to a certain sorcerer sitting close behind me. Thanks to our trusty steed, we were able to talk more easily without being so out of breath. Alderidge urged me to forge another ring and I chose to do endurance.

"How did you do that thing? Back at the castle, when you exposed my rings?" I asked, recalling how he'd tugged on my magic and caused my rings to manifest.

Alderidge cleared his throat. "Ah, well, that's actually a rather insulting and invasive thing to do to someone. It's generally frowned upon amongst mages."

"Oh."

"In my defense, you had just cursed an entire kingdom." Alderidge supplied.

"In *my* defense, I was imprisoned, scarred, and sold while my father was throwing parties with his new little family, and he deserved it," I retorted.

There was a long pause, but I couldn't see his face so it was impossible to know what he was thinking.

"Well, are you going to show me or what?" I asked impatiently.

He let out a long sigh. "Very well." He released the reins with his right hand. "I can't help but feel like a bad mentor for showing you this. Shouldn't we be working on something more… constructive?"

"Just show me," I said in an exasperated tone.

"Alright, you grasp your hand like this to snag their magic and then you spread your hand like this to display their rings." He made a quick motion like he was snatching a gnat from the air and then spread his fingers out and waved his hand like he was wiping a window.

I turned to look at him the best I could. "Like this?" I did the motion quickly and to my surprise felt it snag on his magic. His seven rings appeared and my lips popped open in surprise.

"Hey!" he exclaimed.

"Sorry! Guess we're even now," I said with a shrug.

I could feel him shaking his head in disapproval as I turned around and the rings faded away.

"You ought not to go around doing that to people or you'll quickly be making enemies," he warned.

I nodded understanding. "Right, got it."

"Well, what do you want to learn next? I've never had a student before, I'm not really sure where to start."

"Show me healing magic." I urged.

"Ah, that is my specialty and a very useful skill." he agreed. "You won't be able to heal nearly as well or as fast as I can since it's not your core, but all mages are capable of simple healing spells."

He handed me the reins and began shuffling with his hands behind my back. When he reached back around me, his left hand was bleeding from a gauge in the palm.

I gasped, "What did you do?"

"This way you can practice," he answered.

"You didn't have to do that!" I protested, taking his hand in mine.

Alderidge chuckled. "Don't worry about me princess. Waiting till I'm bleeding out on the floor is not a good time to try and learn healing magic. This way is much better. Now, summon your magic, pass it through all your rings, and then picture it weaving into the tissues of my hand. The idea is to help my body do what it already knows how to. You're just going to lend it some magic to speed up the process."

I pressed my lips together in disfavor but took a breath to steady myself and called on my magic. Following Alderidge's instructions, I let my magic wrap around his hand. The wound began to close and I realized it was much smaller than it had originally appeared. The blood dripping from his hand had caused it to look much deeper. I squinted in concentration and gripped his hand harder, willing it to heal.

"Don't fight with it," warned Alderidge, "work with it. Hold your magic with a loose grip, the way you'd hold reins."

I nodded and relinquished some of the tension I was holding in my body. As I did, the healing seemed to speed up slightly. Finally, the wound closed and the bleeding stopped. There was still a scab though and I frowned at it.

"Well done!" Alderidge praised me.

"But there's still a scab," I said, "what if it scars?"

Alderidge flexed his hand and examined it. "My body will do the rest, and I'm not worried about scars. I think they add character."

I scowled. "High price to pay for character," I mumbled to myself.

"Do your scars bother you?" Alderidge asked curiously as he replaced his glove and took the reins again.

"Well, yes," I said. "They're everywhere. I can't hide them. People look at me with either pity or fear. Or disgust. This one makes my lip pull up-"

"I didn't mean if you like them, I meant do they hurt or restrict your movement at all?" he interrupted.

"Oh. Um, I feel some of them pull sometimes when I move, but they don't hurt anymore."

"Then you shouldn't worry about them," Alderidge said bluntly.

I scowled. "That's easy for you to say with your stupid, flawless face."

Alderidge barked a laugh. "Flawless?"

I could practically hear the smirk on his face. I rolled my eyes. "Look, for most of my life my value has rested squarely on my marriage potential so forgive me if I'm a little bitter about being totally disfigured!" My voice had risen more than I intended and it warbled as I blinked back tears.

Alderidge was quiet for a moment. "I'm sorry, that was insensitive for me to say."

I swallowed thickly and blinked rapidly, trying to clear my eyes.

I felt him lean in closer and he spoke in a low voice, "If it counts for anything, I don't think the scars have hurt your marriage potential at all."

Warmth crept into my face and I bit my cheek. This sorcerer was going to be the death of me.

Chapter 25 The Wolf

Alderidge continued to give me magic lessons as we traveled. I forged more rings and was able to direct my magic more precisely. Though he had me use my core power on inanimate objects to try to discover what it was, nothing happened to the rocks and sticks I used. It was a mystery and it seemed the only way to solve it would be to keep experimenting. I was hesitant to try on anything living but Alderidge convinced me to just try plants first. Again, there were no observable changes to the shrubbery and trees I tried to cast magic at.

We talked about the various core powers, ruling out all the elemental powers. So far, Alderidge didn't have many ideas as to what my core power could be. He said I could be a sleep mage. Which would explain the curse I'd cast. But he also explained that some core powers could put people into a temporary sleep while the magic worked on them.

"For example, it would be possible for me to put someone into a dormant state- a magically induced coma- in order to preserve their life while my healing magic lived within them. It would be an impressive feat. It's something I've never done and something I hope to never have to do." he explained.

I had learned so much about magic and yet there was still so much I didn't know.

Suddenly in the distance, we heard the howl of a wolf. We all stiffened, Cyrus included. He snorted and stamped his foot nervously.

"Maybe it's just one wolf?" Alderidge mused.

A second howl sounded from another direction.

Alderidge clicked his tongue. "No such luck." He drove Cyrus forward into a run and we both leaned forward into the wind. We began to hear barks and howls closing in behind us. I wrapped my hands in Cyrus' mane and tried to steal a glance behind us, but Alderidge's arm was in the way. Alderidge pushed Cyrus on, increasing his speed, but the sound of the wolves was getting closer.

"What do we do?" I yelled. "Can we fight them with magic?" I asked.

"I'm not particularly skilled in combat magic!" he called back. "And there are quite a few of them!"

My heart raced. The wolf pack was gaining on us and the closest thing I had to a weapon was a pocketknife. That and my wild, mystery magic that may or may not put them to sleep. Suddenly the wolves were all around us, baring their gleaming fangs at us. Alderidge's chest was pressed to my back as I peered over his arm at the beasts hunting us down. One of the wolves nipped at Cyrus' leg and another cut in front of him. The great black horse whinnied in fear and reared up away from the wolves. Without a saddle or stirrups, Alderidge and I were thrown from the horse's back, down into the snow. I landed squarely on top of my mentor, his body somewhat cushioning my fall. I clambered off of him and turned to see him gasping for air- my weight having knocked the wind out of him. Sensing a moment of weakness, a large gray wolf lunged towards him, and before I could even think, I threw myself between them.

"NO!" I screamed with my hands stretched out. Golden magic turned bright white in my hands, arcing out like the sweep of a sword. It lashed out towards the wolf and knocked it back onto its side. My chest heaved as I tried to catch my breath and I stared in surprise at what I'd done. The wolf got back up and with its packmates began closing in again. I backed up and my legs bumped into Alderidge who had risen up though he was still clutching his chest.

"Any chance you could do that again?" he wheezed as he stood with me, back to back.

I looked at my hands again, wondering how I had done that and if I could replicate it, but then I noticed a change in the wolves' demeanor.

Alderidge raised his hands, preparing to wield his magic, but I stopped him.

"Wait!"

The wolves were no longer growling and baring their teeth.

Alderidge held perfectly still with his hands outstretched. "Vivienne?"

"They're not attacking anymore," I breathed in disbelief.

The pack of eight or so wolves just stood there, looking at us with curiosity. Then they ducked their heads and padded away, following their alpha.

Alderidge and I watched them go as they disappeared into the snowy woods.

"Okaaay, what just happened?" Alderidge asked.

I shook my head and looked at him wide-eyed. "I don't know. I was hoping you could tell me."

Alderidge ran his gloved hand over the top of his head. "You concentrated your core power for one thing," he said. "It's a form of combat magic and I certainly didn't teach you it, so where did you learn it?"

"I didn't learn it, it just happened." I insisted.

Alderidge shook his head and considered me warily. Then he turned and collected Cyrus who was still anxiously tossing his head.

"Alderidge?"

He wiped his face and turned back to me. "You really ought not to call me that."

I frowned in confusion.

"You're not my maid anymore. In fact, I am quite outranked by you, and you did just save me from getting my throat ripped out by a hungry wolf. Plus, I don't much like the family name to begin with so just call me by my first name."

I blinked at him blankly as I realized I wasn't sure I remembered his first name. "Harris?"

"What? No!" Alderidge protested. "You don't even know my first name?!"

"Henry?"

"No! For goodness sake, we've been traveling together for days!"

I furrowed my brows. "Harry?"

"Stop guessing!"

I grinned mischievously. "Howard?"

"Oh you think it's funny do you?"

I smiled bigger. "Horace?"

He shook his head in exasperation. "Just get on the horse," he commanded in defeat.

I pinched my lips together to suppress my smile and approached the horse. Alderidge lifted me up and I swung my leg over with much more grace this time.

I looked down at my mentor with a playful grin. "Come on Hemsley."

His mouth popped open in surprise and then he shook his head ruefully. "What a naughty little princess."

Chapter 26 The Market

Hemsley and I discussed what happened with the wolves at length over the next day.

"Do you think my core power could have something to do with animals?" I asked.

Hemsley nodded. "It's possible. Animals do seem to like you for some reason. But…"

"But what?" I prodded.

"It just doesn't make any sense. A fauna mage generally has a sort of gentle nature to their power. Yours is not a gentle thing at all. It's precise, despite your lack of control. It's impossibly strong despite your lack of apprenticeship. And it doesn't behave like any other core ability I've seen before." He shook his head in befuddlement.

"Maybe the clarity mage can help me figure that out too." I contemplated.

Hemsley nodded. "Perhaps."

As we rode we came upon a more well-traveled path.

"This road will lead us to Treadmont. I can send word to the estate that I'll be away a while longer and we can pick up another horse and some saddles." Hemsley said.

I nodded. I had come to somewhat enjoy the closeness of sharing a horse. His body blocked the wind on my back and his voice was soft and warm by my ear. But we would make better time if Cyrus wasn't so burdened down, and the saddle would be much more comfortable. Every night we stretched and rubbed our behinds by the fire before going to bed. The hours of riding each day left us awfully sore.

As we approached the city, the sounds of bustling people reached us. I took a steadying breath. The last time I had been here was to be auctioned off at the slave market. Now I would see the city for myself with my restored vision. Once in the city, our pace slowed- impeded by the crowded streets.

"Does this bring back any memories?" I asked.

"Of course, the day I bought a slave straight out of a horror novel," Hemsley teased.

I gasped in offense. "Why you-"

"Now, now, you didn't see you," Hemsley defended himself. "You looked like someone had tried to butcher you and sew you back together. Dried blood everywhere, blind, thin as a rake. Your hair looked like a rat's nest-"

"Alright! I get it!" I said crossly.

"Mother Hannah did well though, hm? You've rounded out, your hair is growing back, you even started smiling. I might even go as far as to say you seemed happy at the estate..."

I turned to look at him out of the corner of my eye. "I didn't know you were paying so much attention."

Hemsley's eyebrows shot up. "Right well, it's all about return on investment."

"Ah, yes." I scoffed with a shake of my head.

We rode in silence for a moment. "I was happy," I added softly.

"Really? A princess happy to wash windows and keep books?" Hemsley asked curiously.

I shrugged. "I love those girls. They accept me as I am, broken as I may be. There were times that I thought, maybe I could just stay."

"Why'd you leave?" he asked.

I sighed heavily. "I didn't realize everyone thought I was dead. I thought they were still looking for me. I had planned to keep my word and complete my six months of servitude. It was the least I could do in return for my sight. But when I discovered that my loved ones thought I was dead, and my brother was missing…" I shook my head, "I had to go back."

Hemsley was quiet so I continued. "I wish there were a way for me to have everything I want."

Hemsley chuckled, "Don't we all?"

I smiled sadly. "There's no going back for me. Not now. The crimes I've committed in Gotland will ensure I never have a place in the palace again. I once worried that when I returned as a princess, the worst I'd face was the judgment of the court for my appearance and having to hide my magic. I guess I don't have to worry about that anymore."

"You could-" Hemsley cleared his throat, "you could return to Alderidge estate."

I whipped around to look at him in surprise. His eyes met mine and I stared into his open face. He was serious. He was inviting me back when all this was over. I swallowed thickly and turned back to the road.

"I think I'd like that," I said softly. "I suppose you do need help with the books," I added cheekily.

Hemsley huffed a laugh and leaned into me, resting his chin on top of my head. His arms wrapped around me, pinning my arms to my sides. I stiffened for a moment and then realized he was hugging me. Oh. I released the tension in my shoulders and blushed scarlet.

"You wouldn't return as a maid." he said, releasing me from his arms. "You'd return as my apprentice."

I nodded, excited by the idea. Learning more magic, mastering my powers. It stirred a desire in my heart I hadn't known was there.

Cyrus trotted through the city till we came to a post office at which point Hemsley hopped off and went inside for a bit to send word to the estate. He returned quickly and we continued on to a market selling livestock. We dismounted and walked through the market, looking for a suitable horse.

"This mare here looks good," Hemsley said as he inspected a horse.

I nodded, but then something caught my eye further down. I hurried over, leaving Hemsley behind. It was a white mare who looked as though she'd seen better days. Something drew me to her. The sadness in her eyes, a familiarity. I rested my hand on her head and she regarded me with tired eyes. I brushed her forelock aside as I petted her and I suddenly froze. Beneath her shaggy hair was an unmistakable nub. A unicorn. Her horn had been removed, likely by poachers. She was not the one I'd met before, I was sure. This one was younger, though she'd clearly seen her fair share of hardship. I let the hair fall back over the tell-tale sign of her true nature just as a scraggly old man spotted me and walked over.

"I can't believe she's letting you touch her. She doesn't let anyone touch her," he said in surprise.

Hemsley approached at that moment. "Vivienne, we need a horse that's actually rideable."

"She'll let me ride her," I said, somehow feeling it to be true.

"Vivienne…"

"She's the one, I'm sure of it." I insisted.

Hemsley gave me a skeptical look.

"Pleeeease," I pushed. I felt like a child begging for a pony but I didn't care.

Hemsley sighed and rubbed his face, mumbling something about a spoiled princess. "Alright, how much for the unrideable horse?" He asked in defeat.

I grinned at the mare and she showed me some interest.

Hemsley exchanged a small amount of coin with the man and I happily opened the stall and led the white creature out of the market. While Hemsley went to purchase some saddles, I took the mare to a well where I began washing her. I used a small amount of fire magic to dry her as I went, the same way Hemsley had taught me to warm my hands. When Hemsley returned with two saddles, her white coat was gleaming like the snow.

"Well she certainly looks a lot better. But how do you know she'll let you ride her?" he inquired.

I gave him a secretive smile. "She's never been ridden before," I said.

"A horse that's never been ridden? You think that's the best choice right now?" Hemsley asked, crossing his arms in disapproval.

"She's not a horse," I whispered slyly, "she's a unicorn."

Hemsley looked at me as though I myself had just sprouted a horn. "Viv-"

"Shhh, look!" I revealed the nub hidden beneath her hair and he came closer to inspect it.

"Hmm." He didn't seem totally convinced. "How can you be sure?"

I petted her fondly. "Because I've met one before," I revealed.

Hemsley looked at me incredulously. "You've met a unicorn?"

I nodded. "There are woods backing the Gotland palace, I met one there."

Hemsley rubbed his jaw thoughtfully. "Unicorns originate from Duthlin, but they've become increasingly difficult to find. Legend says they bestow magical blessings to those they deem worthy."

I stared off, recalling that night in the woods. The unicorn who had touched me on the top of my head with the length of her horn. The warmth that had spread through me…

"Oh," I said, looking at him wide eyed in realization.

He took in my expression and jumped towards me. "You've had a unicorn blessing??"

I nodded. "I think so."

"What was it like?" he asked eagerly

"It was sort of warm and serene," I answered thoughtfully.

"And what did the blessing do?" he asked in excitement.

He really was a bit of a nerd, I realized with a half grin.

"I don't know," I said truthfully. "What do they normally do?"

He shook his head, "We don't know. They're pretty rare. Unicorns are very particular about who they choose. Generally, young maidens, pure of heart, innocent. That kind of thing."

"Oh," I said, scratching my head awkwardly. "I suppose maybe that did describe me back then." I frowned. That bothered me for some reason. Perhaps I had been given a blessing and had since lost it due to my crimes. Now I might never know what it had been.

"Well if you figure out what it is, I'm awfully curious to know."

I nodded absentmindedly, as I saddled my new ride.

"What are you going to call her?" Hemsley asked.

I smiled softly. "Celeste."

"Pretty," he commented.

I grinned at him. "Celeste and Cyrus, isn't it kind of cute?"

He chuckled while saddling Cyrus. "Cute isn't the kind of word usually used to describe Cyrus, but sure."

I had to agree. He was huge, powerful, intimidating. But Celeste, she gave off a different impression. She seemed sad, lonely, maybe even defeated. But I could tell that she still had some fight left in her. And I hoped that one day, despite everything she'd lost, she could run free with her head held high once again.

Chapter 27 The Springs

Celeste did better than I had anticipated. After a while, I removed the bridle and bit as it seemed to agitate her more than anything. She responded well to oral commands though all she really had to do was walk alongside Cyrus.

"How's it going over there?" Hemsley asked, eyeing Celeste.

"She's not used to belonging to anyone," I answered. "But she's cooperating well enough."

"Sounds familiar," Hemsley muttered and I narrowed my eyes at him.

I decided not to make any retort and noticed him perk up in recognition of something further down the path.

"The hot springs are this way!" He exclaimed.

"What?"

"Water, heated by the earth. It creates pools of hot water you can bathe in. I've never been but I hear it's fantastic," he explained.

"You want to stop to take a bath?"

"I don't know if you noticed Princess, but we smell awful."

I grimaced. He was right. We hadn't bathed in over a week. "I suppose it might be worth the delay…" I agreed.

He grinned in triumph and coaxed Cyrus into a trot. We stopped where the dirt ended and rock began. Ahead of us was a gorgeous series of pools, one spilling into the next before eventually leading off into a creek. The trickling sound of little waterfalls filled the air and bright green ferns grew between the pools. The serene view was indeed inviting. We both dismounted and I pressed my hand to the earth, pushing my magic down. Thick grass grew up filling a circle six feet in diameter around me. The horses bobbed their heads and helped themselves. Hemsley was already hanging his coat alongside his cloak on a tree. He excitedly removed his vest and gloves and then started untucking his shirt.

My eyes widened. "You're just going to undress in front of me?" I asked incredulously.

"If you don't want to see, don't look," he responded with a wicked grin.

My face went bright red and I scowled at him, but he didn't stop so I awkwardly turned around. I clenched and unclenched my hands, looking out into the trees. This was totally inappropriate.

"Are you gonna get in?" Hemsley called.

"No!"

"Aw, come on Viv. There's nothing to see here, I left my underclothes on. You can have your own pool and keep your undergarments on. I'll even look away till you're in," he assured me.

I turned around cautiously and saw him soaking in the nearest pool, chest bare. Another wave of heat flooded my face and I averted my eyes.

"I promise I'll be a gentleman. Don't worry about me," he said.

I met his eyes and nodded. "Okay, but you've got to look away till I'm in," I insisted.

He gave me a huge grin and quickly pivoted around the pool so his back was to me. I slowly removed my gloves and cloak and then unbuttoned the front of my dress. I cast frequent glances over to where Hemsley was lounging. I didn't think he'd peek, but I couldn't help myself. I unlaced my shoes and noted the stench of my thick wool stockings. I pulled those off too and hung them over the edge of another pool. They needed a good washing, but this would have to do and I could dry them with my magic. Now just in my bloomers and underdress I stepped cautiously into one of the pools. The water was blissfully hot with steam rising into the winter air. I stepped further in, the water reaching up to my knees, but just as I did so, I realized the rocks were coated with slick algae. My foot slipped and I threw my hands back to try and catch myself. I let out a short squeal as I fell and then felt my hand crunch painfully against the rocks before my head went completely under the water. The pool was not so deep and I quickly stood up and gasped for air, clutching my hand to my chest. Hands gripped my shoulders and I opened my eyes to see Hemsley standing right before me.

"Are you okay?" he asked in concern.

I looked down at my hand and whimpered as I saw that my ring finger was definitely pointing in the wrong direction.

"Let me see," Hemsley commanded, gently taking my hand. He wrapped his healing magic around it and as the pain faded, I looked up at him from under my wet lashes. His face was a mask of concentration and concern. His hair hung around his face, little droplets of water dripping from the ends. He looked up to meet my eyes and I realized he was done healing my hand.

"Thank you," I breathed. But I didn't pull my hand away. I didn't want to. His hands were warm and big around my own. He moved his hands, wrapping them around mine in a way that was more affectionate and had nothing to do with his healing magic. I had my other hand in a fist against my chest to keep it from wandering out to him. He didn't move away, but instead seemed to lean in closer. I leaned in closer too, his deep brown eyes drawing me in. Moisture gleamed on the angles of his face, highlighting the structure of his jaw and cheekbones. We looked into each other's eyes for a moment that I swore was going to be ingrained in my brain for the rest of my life. His eyes darted to my lips for a fraction of a second and my heart squeezed at the implication of that look. I felt breathless and my stomach fluttered, wondering what was going to happen next, but then he flinched painfully and took a step back.

"You sure fall a lot," he said in a forced playful tone. He looked away, off into the trees.

"Yeah," I replied dumbly.

He climbed out and returned to his pool wordlessly, leaving me still standing waist-deep in the water. What just happened? I realized I still had my hand out where he'd been holding it and I mentally shook myself. Out of the corner of my eye, I saw that Hemsley had sat himself not quite with his back to me, but angled away nonetheless. I silently washed myself, trying to process what had happened. Had I imagined it? Misinterpreted it? Was I so starved for affection that I saw it in places where it did not exist? I sat down in the pool, feeling glum and confused.

"Want to see a trick?" Hemsley called.

I turned with a raised eyebrow and he reached out with an orb of water floating in his hand. As I watched, it froze, forming a perfect sphere of ice which he tossed to me. I caught it and inspected it curiously. My eyes flicked back up to Hemsley where he had shifted to face me with his forearms resting on the rock and his chin on his hands. I looked at the ice ball with a half smile. Hemsley was my mentor, my ally, and maybe even my friend. That was enough. There was no need for me to wish for more. I did not want to fail to appreciate what I already had.

"Teach me," I said and he smiled that crooked smile that made me doubt everything I'd just told myself.

Chapter 28 The Prophecy

Turning water to ice was the beginning of a new chapter in my magic knowledge. Hemsley taught me as we rode across Duthlin, headed for the coastal town of Port Trim, where the Clarity mage supposedly resided. According to Hemsley, any element could shift forms. Water was the easiest. It could shift from ice, to liquid, to vapor with relatively little effort. Fire could change from sparks to flames to currents of white hot energy that cracked like lightning. Earth was more difficult. It was stubborn, but it could change from the finest sand to the densest rock. From there, the form of rock or metal could be morphed into different shapes. Hemsley said Earth mages could forge swords with their earth magic alone. Air was difficult for different reasons. It was difficult to grasp, impossible to contain. My mentor spoke of Air mages who could separate the different parts of the air making it thinner, and more difficult to breathe. Such things were advanced and likely only attainable by those who held an elemental power as their core.

"Each core ability has cousin powers though," Hemsley expanded, "For example, my healing power is more closely related to water magic, and protection magic is more closely related to earth magic. Each type of magic belongs in a class, but those classes overlap. It's less about boxes and more about a family tree with everything interconnecting."

"So could my affinity for a certain element point us toward identifying my core power?" I asked.

"Yes! If it's a known ability that is."

I nodded thoughtfully while trying to make the rock in my palm dissolve into sand.

"Whatever it is, I don't think it's related to earth," I commented in frustration.

Hemsley chuckled. "That makes two of us."

Finally, the rock crumbled into pea-sized chunks. Not the fine sand I was going for, but it was progress.

"Try water," Hemsley suggested.

I nodded and raised a hand in a claw, palm up. Water droplets formed at my fingertips and ran down into my palm until I held a tiny pool of water. The water flowed up and formed an orb that hovered above my palm. I froze it solid and it dropped into my hand. I gripped the ice and it instantly melted back to liquid.

"Now try evaporating it. It's a little more tricky, you'll have to introduce heat, but not fire. Any mage can evaporate water with fire, but it takes more skill to cause the water particles to disperse without it," Hemsley urged me.

I nodded and drew the water up into an orb again. I focused on pulling the particles apart and the orb split into a dozen fine rings of water circling each other. The rings grew larger around and became finer and finer. They spun faster and faster, growing warmer and then the water evaporated into a puff of vapor that dispersed immediately into the air.

"Impressive," Hemsley commented with a cocked brow. "I'd say you have an affinity for water. It may be one of the easier elements to manipulate, but that was still pretty advanced."

I grinned at the praise. "So my core power may be related to water magic?"

He nodded and I pondered on that. There was this whole piece of me that was still a mystery. I ached to know more about myself and my magic. It felt like there were holes in my being. I'd lost my identity when Rhiannon took me. Lost my family. Lost my place at home. But there was this piece of myself I could still claim and I wanted it. Badly.

As we traveled, the trees grew thinner and eventually fell away. The land we crossed now was covered in sandy dunes and tall grasses. The air smelled strange. Like fish and salt.

As we crested another dune, a small coastal town was revealed before us. There were dozens of wooden structures, houses, stores, and shacks. Docks reached out into the water and in the distance, fishing boats bobbed in the ocean. My breath caught at the sight of the ocean. The vastness of it was hard for my mind to grasp. It seemed to go on forever. The wind blew through my hair, icily cold and the sound of birds squawking sounded in the distance. And the waves, I could hear them crashing against the rocky shore even from my position above the town.

"Wow," I breathed.

Hemsley stared out at the ocean too, taking in the scene.

"It's beautiful isn't it?" he said.

I nodded, "I've never seen the ocean."

"What? They don't have these in Gotland?" he joked.

I laughed and shook my head. "It's amazing."

He smiled and we stood there a while, watching the rhythmic movement of the ocean.

"You know," I contemplated, "I wouldn't be here if I'd never been kidnapped. I'd have gone my whole life living within Gotland, never seeing what the rest of the world has to offer. I'd have grown old and died never seeing the ocean."

Hemsley looked at me curiously.

"I'm still angry. I'm still hurt. But," I paused, "maybe it's not all bad."

He was quiet and turned back to the ocean, thinking his own thoughts and the silence between us was peaceful and calm.

In the town, Hemsley asked a few people for directions and we wandered around for a while, trying to make sense of the odd little town. Finally, we came to a three story building on the outskirts. A sign stood out front that read: Aberdine's Children's Home. I frowned.

"Are we in the right place?" I questioned.

Hemsley shrugged and dismounted so I followed suit. We climbed the steps of the broken down front porch and I knocked on the front door. There was no answer, but the sound of children's voices carried to us from around the back of the house so we headed that way. Behind the house was some sort of play yard where children were running and playing. They were bundled in threadbare coats and mittens, their cheeks chapped red from the cold wind. But they ran and screamed and laughed nonetheless. There were maybe a dozen of them, playing with old balls and fighting with sticks.

"Who are you?"

I looked down to see a young child missing both front teeth with snot dripping down his face. We exchanged a look and Hemsley cleared his throat.

"I'm Hemsley, this is Vivienne. We're looking for the Clarity mage."

"You gonna have to talk to Grandma Aberdine," said the child, pointing at the back door of the house.

Hemsley tipped his head and we followed the boy's directions. Hemsley opened the creaky back door for me and I stepped inside. I could hear voices down the hall and we followed them into the kitchen. There we found an elderly woman sitting on a stool, peeling potatoes. A young girl was chopping them at the counter and they looked up as we entered.

"Hello," Hemsley said, "sorry to intrude. I'm told I've got to speak with Grandma Aberdine."

The old woman nodded her head. "That's me. You here to take home a child?"

I shook my head hard with wide eyes, "No ma'am."

Hemsley chuckled, "I'm afraid not. We're actually looking for a Clarity mage. I heard a rumor they resided here."

Grandma Aberdine narrowed her eyes at us. "Well you heard wrong. There's no mages here."

My shoulders slumped in disappointment. "Do you know where we might find them?"

"No," Grandma Aberdine said.

"Wait, please we've come a long way. We can pay money. We need to find them," Hemsley pleaded.

The woman stared us down with suspicious eyes. "What do you want with a Clarity mage anyway?"

We exchanged a look, trying to decide how much to reveal, but if this woman was the Clarity mage she'd know if we were lying. I shrugged and stepped forward.

"I am Vivienne Hawthorne, princess of Gotland. My brother is missing, we need him to take the throne in order to save the people of Gotland. We've come to ask the Clarity mage for assistance in finding him."

The room was silent for a minute. Grandma Aberdine just stared at us and the girl cutting potatoes came and placed an empty bowl in front of her before standing beside the seated woman with a hand on her shoulder.

"I am that mage," said the girl.

We exchanged a surprised look and considered the girl. She was maybe twelve or thirteen, thin as a rail, with wispy white blonde hair. Her eyes were a piercing, icy blue and though her admission was initially surprising, looking into her eyes revealed a depth of power there.

"Will you help us find my brother?" I asked.

"I will cast my sight about, and see what I can see," she stated. "Come and sit," she instructed.

We looked around and saw no chairs so we knelt on the kitchen floor.

She came and knelt before me, so close our knees touched. I found myself leaning back a little, somehow intimidated by the tiny mage.

"Are you prepared to know the truth?" she asked me.

Her gaze was so intense, I hesitated. "Yes," I breathed.

"Where there are many secrets, there are many truths to be told. If that is the case for you, it may be that my magic calls forth truths yet to come to pass. You may hear things you don't understand, things you don't like. The truth can be ugly. Are you sure you want to know where your brother is?"

"I have to find him," I said determinedly.

"Very well." She held her hands out, palms up. "Give me your hands."

I did as she said and placed my hands in hers. Her thin, pale fingers were cold against mine and I shivered.

Golden magic spread out and circled around our joined hands. After a moment it turned pale blue and more rings appeared circling the mage's head. They crisscrossed, spinning in front of her eyes like the rings of a planet. Here and there between the rings, her piercing eyes peered out at me. And then she spoke.

"You are a princess fallen from grace,
Loved by a mage still locked in a tower,
Treasured by a slave risen through the ranks,
Betrayed by a traitor risen to power.
Recover the gift given without thanks,
Master the ancient magic unleashed,
Heed the ally with secrets to keep
Free the boy now become beast."

Her fingers were gripping mine now, her voice commanding.

"One will die, two will fall, and three will rule. Kingdoms will fall, armies will march, balance must be restored."

Her hands were crushing mine now and I couldn't pull away.

"Breathe dear," came Grandma Aberdine's calming voice. "Focus. Find the prince."

The mage breathed deeply and loosened her grip. She cocked her head as if she'd seen something odd.

"The journey ahead is long and perilous, but I see the prince."

The magic dispersed and she released my hands. "What was all that? Where is my brother?" I asked breathlessly.

"There were too many secrets, too many truths fighting to get out. I can't see them all clearly, but all have either already happened or will in the future."

I exchanged another wide eyed look with Hemsley who looked equally disturbed.

"As for the prince, he is in Alana."

My mind raced. Alana? How was that possible? Why would he be there?

"And," she added, "you won't find him without me."

"Without you? You mean, you've got to come with us?" I asked.

She nodded but Hemsley was already shaking his head.

"Hang on just a second. Did you not just say it was going to be a long and perilous journey?" he protested. "We can't bring a child! Why can't you just tell us exactly where he is?"

"There are limits to my power," she said. "Alana is far away, my vision can only reach so far. Take me with you and I will guide you to him. Leave me and you will fail. I have seen it." She spoke decisively and Hemsley and

I looked at each other, an entire conversation passing silently between us.

"We've got to find him," I said in a hushed voice. "Without a good and benevolent king, Gotland will waste away."

Hemsley groaned and rubbed his face. "Fine."

Chapter 29 The Wildlands

The young mage packed her few belongings and bid goodbye to the other children who waved as we rode away. She sat behind me, waving back at them until they were out of sight. I glanced back and saw tears streaming down her face silently.

"You don't have to do this," I whispered.

She wiped her face and set her jaw. "This is the way things must be."

"You'll have to forgive me," Hemsley called over to us from his horse, "I haven't asked your name."

"Chloe," she said. "Just Chloe."

"We're grateful to have your help Chloe," said Hemsley. "How long have your powers been awakened?"

"Since two winters ago," she replied.

"And have you had any training in that time?" Hemsley asked.

"No, I never sought a mentor. When my core ability emerged I had a vision. In that vision, I saw that I needed to wait. There were those who would like to profit from my power so we kept it secret, Grandma and I. I knew that there was a greater purpose for my gift. And then you came, and now I see."

"If it was kept secret, how did rumor get out that a Clarity mage even existed?" I asked curiously.

"People in town started to talk when Grandma would urge them not to go fishing on certain days, or to not drink from the latest shipment of wine. Or when nobody could shortchange or lie to her anymore. Nobody suspected the child at her side."

"I see," I said quietly.

"We should stop in town and buy compasses," Chloe said, changing the subject.

"No worries," replied Hemsley, "I have a compass."

"No," said Chloe, shaking her head. "We each will need one."

"Okaaay." Hemsley scratched his head and threw me a look to which I shrugged. If the little mage with creepy vision powers said we needed more compasses, we should probably get more compasses.

At Chloe's instruction, we stopped in town and Hemsley purchased two more compasses so that we each had one to carry on our person. When we reached the outskirts of town, Hemsley drew to a stop.

"I have a confession," he stated.

I raised a quizzical eyebrow at him and he pulled out a small velvet pouch.

"I have a small amount of travel dust." He paused as though that was supposed to mean something to us.

"And that is??" I asked impatiently.

"Well, it's magic dust that lets you travel great distances," he explained.

I recalled the dust Rhiannon had thrown that had whisked me away to the tower. I narrowed my eyes at him. "Do you mean to say, that we didn't need to trek through the snow for days? We could have just magically transported here?"

"Not exactly," Hemsley defended himself, "Rhiannon gave it to me for the purpose of recapturing you. She's enchanted it so that it can only take us to the Wildlands."

"Why would we go to the Wildlands?" Chloe asked curiously. "Wouldn't the fastest way to Alana be to cross through Got- oh, nevermind I see. Since when did Gotland have magical wards?"

I grinned, "It's kind of nice not having to catch you up on everything. I'm the only one who can pass through the wards so we've got to go around. This travel dust should more than compensate for the lost time though."

Hemsley nodded. "The only thing is it's a bit… unpredictable."

I pinched my lips together, unimpressed.

"It may take us right to the border, or it may drop us somewhere in the Wildlands which can get a bit… wild."

"As long as it doesn't dump us into the lap of Rhiannon, I don't care," I said.

Chloe peered around me. "Who is this Rhiannon?"

"Can't you just figure that out with your powers?" Hemsley asked.

Chloe shrugged nonchalantly, "I'm tired."

Fair enough.

"Rhiannon is the witch who kidnapped me from my home and locked me away for two years before I escaped. She also has an entire society of the world's most powerful sorcerers under her thumb, including our very own Hemsley here," I supplied

"Hey!" said Hemsley defensively. "I haven't dropped you off at her door, have I?"

"No, but you were thinking about it," I accused.

"Only because she's taken something from me I'd really like to have returned," he argued.

"Right, this thing you keep vaguely describing that must be really important," I said, feeling increasingly annoyed.

Hemsley opened his mouth to argue back but Chloe interrupted, "Alright, I get the picture. Let's just go."

Hemsley clamped his mouth shut and I looked away from him in irritation. Why did it have to be like this? One moment we're barely allies who don't really trust each other and the next we're face to face and I'm sure he's going to kiss me. So which is it? Why won't he tell me what Rhiannon did? Why did he pull away in the hot springs? I sighed and rubbed my face. "She's right, we should go."

Hemsley waved us closer and took a fistful of the dust.

"I'd recommend taking a deep breath," I said to Chloe and then Hemsley threw the dust over us, and just like last time, everything was enveloped in darkness.

Light rushed back to us and suddenly we were under the forest canopy, birds chirping in the distance. There was no snow here, in fact it felt considerably warmer than it had a moment ago in Duthlin. The serene forest felt strangely familiar and I rubbed my chest anxiously, trying to slow my heart.

"Are you okay?" asked Hemsley, peering over at me.

I bit down on the feelings in my chest and nodded jerkily. "I've been here before, though it's the first time I'm actually seeing it."

"My magic feels differently here," Chloe said quietly.

Hemsley nodded. "The Wildlands are saturated in magic. Your magic may feel like a single flame in a dark room at home, but here it is but one flame in a wildfire."

His words were ominous and I gazed out into the trees, wondering what was out there waiting for us.

Chapter 30 The Trees

As we rode, the forest was still and eerie. Although we spotted the occasional wild animal and nothing seemed truly amiss, I couldn't help but glance over my shoulder occasionally.

"Do you feel that?" I asked quietly.

Hemsley nodded, scanning the trees. "It feels like something is watching us."

Chloe scooted closer to me, her grip on my cloak tightening.

We continued on our way although our senses remained on high alert. I saw movement out of the corner of my eye and turned sharply towards it but saw nothing aside from more trees. The hair stood up on the back of my neck and I brought magic to my palms.

Hemsley noticed and did the same. "What is it?"

I looked around, keeping my head on a swivel. "There's something out there."

A crack sounded from near Hemsley where he sat atop Cyrus and we all snapped our eyes over there. Our magic flared in response to our fear, but again we couldn't see anything. Chloe whimpered and pushed her head against my back. I guess she didn't know what it was either since she was all tapped out. The horses were getting skittish, stomping their feet and bobbing their heads.

"It's alright," I said, more to myself than Chloe. I patted Celeste reassuringly although I swear I saw something move again. Suddenly a flash of movement struck Hemsley, knocking him flat on the ground. Cyrus reared up and I saw that vines were wrapping up his legs. It was then that I felt something slither up my leg and I screamed, trying to kick it off. It was another vine encircling my leg as well as Celeste's. She reared as well and I heard Chloe scream as she fell off the back. I gasped and turned to see the vines gripping Chloe's ankles and dragging her off.

"No!" I let a stream of fire loose from my palm and it burned the vines pulling Chloe to a crisp. Celeste reared again in fright and this time the vine on my leg tightened and pulled me down, causing me to fall painfully on my hip. I cried out and looked around for Hemsley. I gasped as I saw him also being dragged off by the vines- no, they were tree roots I realized. But Hemsley wasn't fighting back. His head hung back, his eyes closed. He must have been knocked unconscious when he fell.

"Hemsley!" I screamed. They were taking him away. I blasted more fire at the root trying to drag me away and clambered to my feet to run after him. As soon as I did, a tree branch whipped out and struck me in the chest, knocking me down again.

"No! Hemsley, wake up!" I yelled, but he was getting further away. I tried to stand again, blasting more fire at my feet at the approaching roots but then I heard Chloe scream again.

"Vivienne, help!" she cried. I looked over to see her ensnared by the roots. They were tangling around her legs and arms and pulled her to the ground again. She had no way to defend herself and physically was no match for the sentient trees. I looked back and forth between Chloe and the direction Hemsley had disappeared to for a split second, conflicted between helping my unconscious mentor and helping the child who had joined us. I let out an anguished cry and blasted my concentrated white core magic at the vines holding Chloe. It cut through them easily, but more replaced them. The horses took off and I couldn't blame them. I couldn't protect all of us. Hemsley was gone. I had to find him. But more tree roots were snaking up my legs and I couldn't keep up. They pulled me to the ground and began latching onto my arms. I could hear Chloe screaming but I couldn't see her. I was too busy trying to free my own limbs. Her cries became more distant and I flailed wildly. I was losing them. My magic arced out erratically, cutting through roots and tree limbs. But I couldn't keep them off me and Chloe at the same time. I was being dragged away by my ankles, my skirt pulling up around my legs and I yelled in fear and frustration. Chloe's voice was so far away now. I'd failed her. The thought cut something open inside me and I screamed in defiance, my core magic ripping out of me. I sliced through the roots again and scrambled to my feet. A branch swept down at me again, trying to knock me to the floor, but I was faster this time. I swiped my arm across my body and my magic followed suit, a glowing white blade of my concentrated magic cut through the branch and it dropped to the ground.

"No!" I screamed at the trees. They reached for my ankles again and I opened my palms causing a ring of core magic to appear around my feet. It cut through the approaching roots, protecting me from their reach. "No!" I yelled again. "I decide where I go, not you!" I was angry now and my magic arced around me in sharp spinning rings. More branches reached for me and in a rage I spun, whipping my magic around. It sliced through the nearest tree trunks sending their long lengths plunging to the forest floor. The roots and branches fell away and I was left standing in a small clearing, five or so trees lying around me. I huffed heavily, energy pumping through me. I dismissed the circle of magic around me and ran back in the direction I'd been pulled from.

"Chloe! Hemsley!" I spun around, looking for any sign of them. They were nowhere in sight. "Chloe! Hemsley!" I ran my hands over my head in a panic. How would I find them? What if something happened to them?

At that moment a raven descended and perched in a nearby tree.

"Nox?" I asked hopefully. He flew over and landed on my extended arm. "It is you!" I exclaimed. "Will you help me? I need to find my friends." He looked at me with his beady eyes and then took off, staying low enough for me to see him. I followed quickly, clambering over the thick tree roots and uneven ground. Apparently the trees had decided to leave me alone now that I'd decapitated a few of them. Nox flew a little ways and would stop and wait for me to catch up before flying further again. As we went, the trees thinned out a bit and sunlight streamed through. It cast the air in a golden glow that seemed too beautiful for the distressed state I was in. Hemsley was hurt. Chloe was just a child. They were both alone and defenseless somewhere out there. I had to find them. Nox led me on until he came to a stop before a clearing. When I caught up he took off, leaving me to take in the sight before me. A spacious meadow of wildflowers. At the center stood an overgrown, ancient looking structure carved from white marble. I approached in awe, wondering how such a thing had come to be in the Wildlands. As I drew closer, I realized what it was. A temple. A place of worship. But who had constructed it? After all, nobody lived in the Wildlands, right?

Chapter 31 The Bridge
Chloe

The vines drug me across the forest floor, not heeding my screams. I had no idea where they were taking me when all of a sudden they released me and retreated. I scrambled to my feet. My wispy blond hair was full of leaves and debris. My worn dress was filthy and I clutched my cloak around me, looking around fearfully. I was all alone in the woods and my heart thundered in my chest.

"Vivienne?" I called out. "Hemsley?" I sniffled and wiped my eyes. I had known we'd end up separated. I had seen it in the jumble of visions that had assaulted my mind when I took the princess's hands. But I hadn't seen exactly how it would happen. Nor did I anticipate being dragged on my backside for half a mile. Blast it all. I rubbed my face more fiercely. Now was not the time to cry. I was essential to this quest. I needed to stay calm and find my way back to the group. I pulled the compass from the pocket of my cloak and lined it up. I had lost all sense of direction thanks to the magical trees, but I knew Alana was northeast. If I just headed in that direction, I'd have to run into somebody. I urged my power out a little bit to guide me despite feeling quite depleted, and felt confirmation that staying here when it got dark was a bad idea. I saw a flash of teeth and blood in my mind and shuddered. Nope, that was not the path I wanted. I searched a little further, my pale blue magic swirling in front of my eyes. To the northeast I saw... Cyrus? Well that was a good start, I thought to myself. Cyrus was a loyal beast. Perhaps he could lead me back to Hemsley.

My magic felt drained from my encounter with the princess and I dispersed it with a tired sigh. Vivienne's truths were bursting at the seams. There were too many things I had seen but not understood. Things I couldn't say. Things she wasn't ready to hear. And things she wouldn't like. From past experiences, I knew that the tangle of truths I'd seen would become more clear the more time I spent in her presence. All truths would see the light eventually. Whether I revealed them or not.

I pulled my hood up, and started walking. It was all I could really do. I clasped the compass between my hands and followed it faithfully. Hopefully I could find the others before I ran into anything else. I heard the sound of running water up ahead and as I came closer I saw a creek, engorged with melted snow from the nearby mountains. Lucky for me, there was a bridge that crossed it. It looked old and was covered in moss, but the structure appeared sound. I glanced at the compass again and then stepped up onto the bridge. As soon as I did, a rumble shook the bridge. I gasped as a huge, mottled green arm reached up from under the bridge to grab the railing. I stumbled backward, not believing my eyes. A huge creature crawled out from under the bridge. It was humanoid and stood eight feet tall. Its face featured beady black eyes, an upturned nose, and pointed ears. Though I had little experience in the world, I had seen such a creature illustrated in a children's book and knew it must be a troll.

"Well what have we here?" It said with a sinister grin that revealed two rows of crooked teeth.

My legs wobbled and I stepped back further in fright.

"A tasty little thing has wandered onto my bridge, hm?" it taunted me.

"I- I'm sorry! I didn't know it was your bridge. I need to get across to find my friends!" I stuttered.

"I'll let you cross my bridge, but first you must answer three riddles!"

"Riddles?" I asked in surprise.

"It's boring out here," it complained, "I need a bit of clever conversation. Answer them right and you can pass. Answer them wrong and I'll eat you for lunch." It grinned at me again and I swallowed thickly. But I was a Clarity mage, and I was very good at riddles.

"Okay. I accept," I answered in a slightly stronger voice.

The troll chuckled in a low voice. "This will be fun, here's riddle number one: I come in one color, but many sizes. I'm always around, but there's no surprises. I play in the sun, but disappear in the rain. I do no harm, and feel no pain. What am I?"

I knew this one. "Are you a shadow?"

"Ah! Very good! Let's do another! You have me today. Tomorrow you'll have more. As your time passes, I'm not easy to store. I don't take up space, but I'm only in one place. I am what you saw, but not what you see. What am I?"

I tilted my head and pondered for a moment. "Memories," I answered.

The troll peered at me suspiciously. "Clever girl. One more and you may go. Slayer of regrets, old and new. Sought by many, found by few. A type of death and a birth too. What am I?"

I closed my eyes for a moment, turning the words over in my head. A vision from my first encounter with the princess came to mind and I smiled to myself. I opened my eyes and pinned them on the troll. "Redemption," I said.

"Impressive," spoke the troll. "You may cross this bridge." The troll moved aside to let me pass and I considered the beast for a moment.

"Actually, I have a riddle for you Mr. Troll."

The troll spun on me. "A riddle? For me?"

I nodded with a conspiratory glint in my eye. "What do you say?"

The troll grinned, "I would very much like that, I accept."

I peered back at him. "I speak with a silver tongue, age but remain young. I keep my word when truths are heard and extend grace when losing face. Who am I?"

The troll rubbed its chin thoughtfully. He began to pace, muttering to himself.

He pondered for some time and scratched his head. "I speak with a silver tongue, age but remain young. I keep my word when truths are heard and extend grace when losing face," he repeated back to me. "I give up!" he exclaimed, sitting with a thud on the bridge. "What am I?"

I looked into his black eyes. "Not a troll."

His eyes widened in surprise and then he grinned. A shower of silver magic suddenly swept around him and the troll disappeared. In its place stood a young boy. Not just a boy, but a fae boy with iridescent wings protruding from his back. He smiled at me, thoroughly pleased with himself.

"Who are you?" I asked curiously.

His green eyes glinted at me and he ruffled the mop of sandy hair on his head. "My name's Puck. Who are you?"

"I'm Chloe," I answered.

He bounded over to me and I realized I was a few inches taller than him. "How'd you know I wasn't a troll?"

I smiled, "I'm a Clarity mage, I can see the truth."

"Is that how you answered my riddles? That's cheating!" he exclaimed.

I shook my head. "I didn't use my magic to answer your riddles. Discernment is just in my nature."

He looked at me with a pout. "Hm, okay."

"What are you doing here?" I asked, "I thought faeries didn't live in this world?"

He gave me a mischievous smile. "We don't. But I was awfully bored, and humans are fun to mess with. I used a faerie circle to get here."

I frowned. "That's not very nice."

He shrugged nonchalantly. "Hey! Since you figured it out, I'll give you a prize. How's that?"

"What kind of prize?" I asked.

"Hmm. Well, what do you want? I have lots of magic tricks!" he offered, bouncing on the balls of his feet.

I thought for a moment and then spoke slowly, "I have done and seen so little in my life. I fear my remaining years may pass and I will still have experienced so little. Do you have something to help with that?"

Puck rubbed his chin. "Human lives are rather short. I can't help you with that."

My shoulders slumped a little in disappointment.

"But!" Puck continued, pointing his finger in the air, "I have something that could help you see all sorts of exciting things!"

"You do?" I asked hopefully.

"Watch this!" He dropped to one knee on the bridge and pressed his palm to the wood. I knelt down too, curious to see what he would do. Silver magic circled his hand and a ring of tiny toadstools popped up.

"A faerie ring?" I asked in confusion.

"Just wait and see," said Puck. Under the toadstools grew moss and tiny vines that interconnected. Interspersed in the ring bloomed white flowers smaller than my pinky nail. I realized that it was no longer attached to the ground, but had formed a circlet of flora. Puck scooped it up between his hands and the connecting vines tightened, shrinking the circle down until it was maybe four inches in diameter.

"Give me your arm," he instructed and I extended my left arm to him. "You've got to push your sleeve up," he said.

I wasn't sure what he was doing but I did as he said and pushed my sleeve up above my elbow. He took my wrist, placed the faerie circle over my hand and brought it up just below my elbow. The circle shrunk again until it was flush with my skin. Then Puck waved his hand over it and silver sparkles rained down on the circlet. The little mushrooms and flowers shrunk away and melded into my skin. Then Puck released my arm and stepped back. I looked at it in wonder. There, just below my elbow was a circle made of the silhouettes of tiny toadstools, flowers, and vines. They looked as though they'd been painted onto my skin, but when I rubbed it with my thumb it was clear that the pigments were one with my flesh.

"It's beautiful. What is it?" I breathed.

Puck puffed up his chest with pride. "It's your very own faerie circle. Every night, while your body sleeps, your mind and spirit will travel to the faerie realm via this circle. There you can run, fly, swim- whatever you want."

I gaped at him. "I can see the faerie realm?"

He nodded, bouncing up and down. "Yeah, maybe we can play together sometime!"

I nodded, blinking back tears. "Thank you. You don't know how much this means to me."

"Enough to earn me a kiss?" he asked.

I balked. "What?"

"I've never had a kiss from a girl. Can I have one?" he was still bouncing up and down, his wings twitching like he was about to take off.

I frowned and tucked my hair back self-consciously. "Mm, just a little one on the cheek. Okay?"

He bobbed his head, causing his hair to bounce, and offered me his cheek.

I pulled my sleeve back down and inched closer nervously. Then I leaned forward to give him a peck on the cheek, but suddenly he turned his head and pressed his lips to mine for a split second. I gasped and jerked my head back but he had already taken off and was flying away.

"Hey!" I shouted in indignation.

He looked back at me with a laugh. "See you later, Chloe!" And then he was gone.

My cheeks heated in embarrassment and I huffed. What a cheeky fae boy.

Chapter 32 The Skeleton
Hemsley

I groaned and rubbed the knot on the back of my head. What happened? One minute I was sitting on Cyrus and the next… I sat up and looked around. Where was I? Trees stretched up into the sky above me, telling me I was still in the forest. But somehow I was now lying beside a creek. Where were the others? I stood and stumbled over to the creek where I kneeled for a drink of water. The cool river water helped clear my head and I began using it to wash my face when something caught my eye. I lifted my face from my cupped hands and saw little glowing lights skipping across the water's surface. Glowbugs? No, they were brighter and had a bluish hue.

"Will o the wisps?" I muttered out loud in fascination. Whatever they were, they seemed to notice me and bounced towards me across the surface of the water.

"That is one name we are known by." spoke a small, soft voice.

My eyebrows raised in surprise. As one little light came closer I saw that it was actually a tiny glowing being with pointy ears and wings like a dragonfly's.

"You look a bit like a pixie," I said, leaning in to get a closer look.

"Pixies are born from the first blooms of spring. We are born from the first drops of melting snow," spoke the little being before me.

"What are you?" I asked in wonder.

"We are sprites. Who are you?" asked the curious sprite.

"My name is Hemsley. Did you happen to see where my friends went?"

The glowing sprite shook its head and batted large, dark eyes at me. "What are you seeking here in the woods?"

"To get out," I said with a chuckle.

"Everyone wants something. Otherwise they wouldn't end up here. Tell me your truest desire and I will lead you to the answer."

I frowned. "There once was a witch who pried that answer from me. She made me stand before a magic mirror which showed her my greatest desires. Then she took away any chance of me ever attaining one of those things that I desired. Why should I trust you?"

The little sprite cocked its head at me and shrugged. "What else are you going to do? You're welcome to wander around. Maybe you'll run into your friends eventually."

I scowled at the mischievous creature. The others were bobbing around excitedly.

"Tell us! Tell us!" they chorused. "We love secrets!" said another.

"If you don't know what I want, how do you know you can help me?" I asked suspiciously.

"We know this forest very well. There are many magics here. Tell us what the witch took and we'll lead you to something good." urged the sprite.

I clicked my tongue. Maybe they really could help? It was worth the chance. "The witch saw that I desired a companion. A chance to have a family of my own. So she cursed me to be alone forever."

"Aww." cooed one of the sprites. "The mage wants to fall in love!"

I glared at him. This is exactly why I wasn't telling anyone. Apparently not wanting to be a bachelor forever was laughable. Vivienne certainly wouldn't want to go near me if she discovered the details of this curse. Rhiannon was cruel and had played her cards well.

The nearest sprite giggled. "Tis a noble desire, truly."

I rolled my eyes and moved to stand but another sprite jumped towards me, "Wait! Don't go! We can't break the curse but we know of something good!"

"Oooh, yes. Something powerful." said another. "Something to protect yourself. Something to protect those you love."

"So you won't get cursed again!" chimed another.

I paused. That certainly sounded good. They noticed my hesitation and latched on.

"Follow us! Follow us!" they chanted.

I stood. "Alright, let's see what you've got."

The sprites cheered and began bouncing off into the forest, forming a line of glowing orbs that led the way. I shook my head and hoped I wasn't walking into a trap. But I didn't have many options, and with a glance at my compass, I saw that they were leading me in the direction I needed to go. So I tucked the compass away and let out a sigh before following the little blue lights.

I trekked through the trees as the sprites ushered me along, bouncing and singing.

"You'll like it a lot!"

"No one's used this magic in ages!"

This part of the forest was darker and denser. I began to notice large webs strung between the trees and felt a prickle of unease.

"Guys… where are you taking me?"

"We're nearly there!" urged the sprites.

Finally, we came to a clearing formed by a circle of trees. The bases of the trees were coated in a thick layer of spider webs and I noticed suspicious looking masses amongst the sticky layers.

"What is this?" I hissed.

"There! There!" they said, pointing to the base of one of the trees.

My eyes shot around, looking for threats, but aside from the sprites and I, there was nothing else around. I approached the tree they had indicated and realized there was a large bundle at its base. I looked closer and then jumped back. It was a skeleton! Clearly it had become prey and succumbed to whatever arachnid had formed these webs.

"You've tricked me!" I hissed angrily.

"No!" cried the sprites. "Look! Look at his arms!"

I looked back at the ancient remains and saw that his arms were indeed sticking out. Hanging loosely from the arm bones were a pair of leather bracers. I gingerly reached out and pulled one and then the other from the skeleton, tugging slightly as the strands of spider silk. Upon closer inspection, I saw that each was embedded with a brilliant red jewel that shone when I wiped the dust from it. They were beautifully crafted from thick black leather and engraved with magic runes.

"What are these?" I whispered. But just then a crack sounded from the trees and my head whipped up. More cracks sounded as something large approached through the underbrush.

"They're returning!" squealed the sprites.

"Quick! Put them on!" another cried before they turned and flew away, floating through the forest. Blast it all. I hurriedly pulled the bracers onto my forearms. To my surprise, the red jewels glinted with light and the leather cinched itself down to fit my arms. I felt the presence of magic in them, but before I could wonder about it any further, a massive spider crashed into the clearing. It was twice my height and covered in black, bristly hair.

"Oh my-" The spider leapt at me and I instinctively threw my hands out. I shot water at its numerous eyes and then froze it solid. The spider writhed around furiously, but my moment of triumph was interrupted by another two spiders breaking through the underbrush. Oh boy. I was terrible with combat magic. My real power was in my healing abilities, but that wasn't going to help me right now. I felt the magic in the bracers reaching to join with mine, and with nothing to lose, I allowed my magic to greet and meld with the magic of the mysterious artifacts. All three spiders ran towards me with their long, hairy legs. Hisses of anger came from their nightmarish mouths. Without a second thought, I raised my hands and unleashed the power of the bracers. A wave of red energy erupted from my palms forming a shield that bashed into the creatures, sending them tumbling backwards.

I looked at the bracers in awe and then smirked at the recovering spiders. I bounced on the balls of my feet, ready for another round.

"Alright you ugly beasts, let's see what you've got!" They came at me again, squealing in rage. This time I hit them with another magic shield and then quickly followed it up with a mass of writhing vines that wrapped around their legs, anchoring them to the ground. They writhed and fought against the restraints and I quickly tried to think of a way to slay the beasts. A glint amongst the webs caught my eye and I ran over to pry what turned out to be a spear from the sticky trap. A few strands of dark hair had fallen into my face and I whipped my head to swing them aside. The spiders were breaking free, but before they could, I launched the spear through the air. It landed with a thunk into the nearest spider which screamed and writhed before falling still. One of the remaining two broke loose and came for me again. I released another red shield and sent more vines to ensnare its limbs. Then I shot a small blast of fire at it and watched it quickly engulf in flames. Who knew spiders were so flammable? The third and final spider broke free and this time I put all my energy into blasting it with the magic shield. When the shield struck the spider it was sent flying up into the trunk of a tree with a satisfying crunch before falling to the ground in a lifeless heap. I stood there for a minute, trying to catch my breath. I wiped my hand across my forehead, pushing my hair aside, and examined the bracers. The sprites were right. These would help me protect myself. And my loved ones. It would have been nice if they'd mentioned the spiders though.

Chapter 33 The Temple
Vivienne

I approached the temple cautiously. Though the overgrowth of flora and the antiquity of the structure suggested it was abandoned, I couldn't help the sense of reverence I felt. I paused and squinted. Was that a statue? Standing in the grand doorway stood a figure draped in white, but when a breeze blew through, the fabric of her robes shifted in the wind.

"Hello?" I called out.

"Welcome," she responded. "We've been expecting you."

I looked at her quizzically, but at this point, I was getting used to being surprised. She peered down at me from the top of the white marble steps. Her eyes were black and matched her hair. Her skin was the darkest I'd ever seen and contrasted starkly with the white robes she wore.

"What is this place? Who are you?" I asked in awe.

"I am Nephele, and this is a house of worship for our creator, Oma." she responded.

"Oma?" I asked with confusion. The name was vaguely familiar and I recalled reading it in the magic book from the tower, though it meant nothing to me.

"It is time for you to learn the origin story of our world. Come, you must bathe and change before entering the holy sanctum." She gestured for me to follow her through the door but I hesitated.

"I have to find my friends. They're in trouble." I called up to her.

"There is more for you to save than just your friends. There are things you must know if you wish to save your people." Nephele said with authority.

"How do you know that?" I asked uncertainly.

She turned to me with her piercing gaze and began descending the steps. "Princess, prisoner, wanderer, slave," she came closer and my breath caught, "servant, vengeful witch, villain. You don't even know who you are and you dare to question the knowledge of Oma?"

I stepped back with wide eyes and her gaze softened. "You are lost, child. Not just here," she gestured around us at the meadow, "but here." She touched her fingertips to my chest, above my heart. I felt tears prick at my eyes and I swallowed thickly.

"Can you help me?" I asked in a small voice.

"The Great Mother can help you. Come," she replied.

Inside, at the front of the building there was a bathing chamber where I was instructed to undress and wash myself. When I finished scrubbing myself I pulled on the white dress that had been laid out for me. It was an odd sort of flowy dress- not a style I'd seen before. It was baggy around the bust and tied around the middle with a sash that was embroidered with golden thread. It was probably the most comfortable thing I'd ever worn aside from the silk nightgowns I'd worn back at the palace. I emerged feeling a bit self conscious in the foreign gown. Nephele was waiting for me and nodded approvingly when I entered.

"I know you have many questions," she said, "and there is too much to learn in just the time that we have today. But have patience, Oma gifts knowledge to those who truly seek it."

I nodded and cocked my head. "Who is Oma?"

She turned and began walking down a grand hall where the walls depicted unfamiliar stories. "Oma is the Goddess. The Kind Spirit. The Great Mother. She and her spouse, Ome, are the creators of this realm. Long ago, Oma and Ome came together as husband and wife. Following their union, a great life force grew in Oma's womb. In preparation for this new life, Ome took clay and water and sculpted our world. He carved the mountains and valleys, he filled the oceans and streams. And when he was done, Oma birthed life into it."

I gazed at the beautiful paintings depicting the story she'd just told. "Why have I never heard this before?"

She shook her head sadly. "Oma and Ome gifted a portion of their power to humankind creating what you now call mages. When the monarch of Gotland rejected magic all those years ago, he also rejected Oma and her gift. She is worshiped in one form or another in every other region but yours."

I considered that. How had Gotland come to fall so far behind? They were missing out on the beauty of magic. They had rejected this ancient religion. They were suffering all alone, not allowing anyone to help them.

"But what does this have to do with me? How does this help me save Gotland and my friends?" I asked, not understanding.

"You will see in time. We will go in and pray before Oma." She opened another door and we entered a large room which featured an altar. Behind the altar was a tall stained glass window depicting a celestial woman in white robes. She had one hand over her heart, and the other over her womb, with rays of sun shining down around her.

"Do as I do," Nephele instructed. She knelt before the altar and then pulled the veil that lay over her head forward so that it hung over her face, all the way down to her sternum. I didn't have a veil, but as if on command, another priestess entered the chamber and draped a thin white veil over my head. It hung down just past my shoulders and was so fine I could see through it. I glanced over at Nephele and saw that she had placed her hands on her knees, palms up, and had her eyes closed. I copied her and then sat there in the darkness behind my own eyelids. What now? I'd never done this sort of thing, though it felt a bit like the early magic exercises I had done.

"Speak to Oma in your mind and she will listen. If you are earnest and true, she may even speak back to you." Nephele said reverently.

I scrunched my eyebrows. I wasn't even sure I believed in this deity or creation story. How had such a tale been kept from me for so long? But… if this was true, and she did have answers for me, I had to at least try. My brother, my friends, my people. They deserved that much. So I took a deep breath and reached out in my mind.

'Oma, I am not the girl I once was. I understand if you don't care to speak to me. I've never known you, so I don't expect you to know me. But if you're really there and you're listening, I could really use some help.'

Silence filled my head. Was I doing this right? I didn't hear any powerful, godly voices. I didn't feel any different. Maybe a little dizzy. Was I falling asleep? Heaviness pulled at my eyes. I could no longer feel the cool, hard floor on my knees. I couldn't tell which way was up or down. It was as if I were floating in space. Then suddenly I felt a prickly feeling on my back and sunlight on my face. I opened my eyes to see blue sky and sat up abruptly. The veil fell from my head as I did so and I looked around in surprise. I was in a field of wildflowers. A gentle breeze blowing them softly. No more than ten feet away stood a woman. She had bronze skin and dark hair down to her hips. She smiled at me warmly.

"Hello Vivienne."

I got up to my feet and looked around in bewilderment. "Where am I? Who are you?"

"I've come to give you a message," she said, "but first you must renounce your transgressions."

My eyebrows shot up. "Transgressions?"

She nodded patiently.

"You mean the curse I cast?" I asked.

She nodded again. "Do you admit that your rage was unchecked and your actions harmful? Do you vow to correct your errors and become who you were meant to be?"

I frowned and clasped my arms, suddenly feeling defensive. "Transgression seems a bit exaggerated. I didn't mean to do it, but I don't exactly regret it."

The woman cocked her head curiously. "Why?"

I rubbed my arms uncomfortably, running my hands over my scars. "He deserved it. He abandoned me. They all just went on partying while I was suffering."

"Ah, I see. You think you're the victim."

My head shot up and I glared at her. "Of course I'm the victim! I didn't do anything wrong and yet, here is the hand I've been dealt! Prison, isolation, disfigurement, pain. I don't deserve any of that, it's not fair!"

"Life isn't fair," she responded sternly. "Is it fair that an entire country suffers from plague because of a line of foolish kings? Is it fair that some are born into royalty while others are born into slavery? Is it fair to punish an entire kingdom, for the actions of one man?"

I withered at her words and tears began to spill. "If I'm not the victim, why does it hurt so much?" I choked.

Her voice softened, "You will always be the victim until you believe otherwise. There are two paths you may take. You may follow the path of rage and vengeance, or you may follow the path of forgiveness and mercy. Only one will give you the healing you seek."

I sobbed into my hands, my heart completely exposed. "But I'm still so angry. How am I supposed to let go of this anger?"

The messenger came closer and put her warm hands on my shoulders. "Look at everything you've accomplished. How far you've come. Rise above. There is so much more in store for you. It will take time, and it won't be easy. But the work to forgive is well worth it. I promise."

I looked up at her through teary eyes. "Do they deserve it? To be forgiven?"

She nodded with a gentle smile. "They do. And so do you."

That brought on a fresh wave of tears and I bowed my head, overwhelmed with emotion. "Okay, I'll try. You were right. I was out of control and I regret it. I don't want to feel like that anymore," I choked out.

She rubbed my shoulder approvingly and gave me a minute to gather myself. "Come. I have something to show you."

I followed her up a gently sloping hillside and came to a halt at the top. She gestured to the bottom of the other side of the hill and I looked to see a herd of brilliant white creatures grazing.

"Unicorns," I breathed.

"They are a sacred animal. Blessed by Oma," the messenger explained.

"I received a unicorn blessing once," I said sadly. "Though I am sure I am no longer worthy of such a thing."

"Why don't you go and see?" she asked.

"What?" I asked in surprise.

"This is my message child: Redemption is within your reach."

I looked at her wide eyed and she looked back at me, confident and slightly amused. Then I turned back to the magical herd, contemplating what she'd said. Redemption. Was it really possible? I couldn't go back to being who I'd been. But maybe I could become someone better. I took a few steps down the hill, towards the herd. It suddenly occurred to me that I hadn't gotten the messenger's name, or thanked her for her words. I turned back to speak to her, but when I did, she was gone. Leaving behind an empty hilltop. I blinked in surprise and then turned back to the herd and did my best to muster my courage. Then I released my breath and started down the hill once more.

Chapter 34 The Sword

I walked amongst the unicorn herd hesitantly. I didn't want to startle them, but they didn't seem to pay me much attention. I stopped in the middle of the grazing creatures and started to feel foolish. What exactly was supposed to happen here? I didn't know where I was though, and my compass was with the clothes I'd left at the temple which was… somewhere else. As I pondered my predicament, a unicorn took notice of me and approached. It was a magnificent stallion and he walked towards me with his head held high. The leader of this group, no doubt. We considered each other for a moment and I noticed he emanated a powerful aura. I had not felt such an aura in my first unicorn encounter, though perhaps that was because my magic had not yet been awakened. But what about Celeste? Perhaps her injuries had harmed her magic?

Whatever the case, the presence of the beast's magic was palpable as it stood before me.

"I once received a blessing from your kin. I still don't really understand what it was, or if I still have it. I'm not even really sure I still deserve it," I said to him.

He bobbed his head at me, brushing my forehead with his nose and I felt that same warmth flow through me. A single tear slid down my cheek. The blessing had been there all the time. I had never really lost it. Despite my mistakes, they still deemed me worthy.

The stallion then turned and walked to the edge of the meadow, towards the tree line. He looked back at me and whinnied and I got the distinct impression that he wanted me to follow him. I lifted my skirt and padded after him on my bare feet. When I reached the tree line he continued into the forest and I wondered where he was taking me. Maybe he knew where Hemsley and Chloe were? As we walked, squirrels darted to and fro along the unmarked path. They almost seemed to be following us. Birds were flitting about the tree branches and then a bunny joined us, hopping alongside me. They *were* following us. Our little animal entourage grew in number as foxes, deer, and mice joined us. I looked around in wonder at the excited animals. Why did the wild animals seem to like me? I had never noticed such a thing when I had lived at the palace. Then something occurred to me and I looked at the unicorn with its long, shimmering horn.

"This is the blessing, isn't it?" I murmured. This is why the animals helped me when I was lost. This is why they were so friendly with me, and why such things had never happened prior to my first meeting with the unicorn in the Gotland forest. I smiled at the answer which had been right in front of me the whole time. Wait till I tell Hemsley about this, I thought.

As we walked further into the woods, I heard a river running up ahead. The rushing waters grew louder and we drew nearer. Finally, when we emerged from the dense forest onto the river bank, the animals suddenly scattered. They dispersed quickly, leaving the stallion and I alone. I looked around, wondering why they had left so suddenly. The unicorn bobbed his head and I followed his gaze to the middle of the river. There, atop an exposed boulder, was a sword. It was embedded, point first, as if someone had driven it down into the rock. The large outcrop of rock was in the center of a round swimming hole where the engorged river slowed to a peaceful eddy.

"This is what you brought me here for?" I asked the unicorn. He snorted at me and I suppose that meant yes. I stepped to the edge of the swimming hole and peered into the water. My eyes widened in alarm. Filling the bottom of the deep swimming hole were hundreds of bones. Some formed intact skeletons of deer and other creatures, but below that lay a bed composed of hundreds of white bones. It was clear that these dangerous waters had been claiming lives for a long time. How would I get to the sword? I didn't know how to swim, and considering what I was seeing, I probably didn't want to anyway. I'd have to use magic.

I knelt by the water and extended my hand. I began freezing the water, creating a bridge to the island of rock. The ice branched out from my hand in swirling patterns, reaching for the rock in the middle of the water. When I was satisfied with the bridge I stood and gingerly stepped one foot out onto the ice. The cold bit at my bare foot, but as I transferred my weight, the ice held true. I ever so slowly made my way across the bridge, cautiously placing one foot in front of the other. There didn't seem to be any life in these waters, nor within a ten foot radius around the pool. The only movement here was the gently eddying water which made for an eerie scene. Finally, I stepped onto the little island and released a breath of relief. I approached the sword in the stone and knelt while I examined it curiously. It was a large, beautifully forged weapon. The silver glinted in the sunlight and embedded in the hilt was a gem, black as obsidian. To my awe, a drop of black liquid dripped from the gem. I watched as it ran down the length of the blade and onto the rock bed where it then trickled down into the water and dispersed. Right after it came another and another. The magic stone in the sword continually dripped inky drops down into the water. The substance was not one that I recognized and I observed as the drips dissipated in the water. Through the swirling darkness I saw the multitude of bones below and it seemed apparent that whatever it was, it was contaminating the water and turning it into a deadly poison. In the presence of the sword, I felt my magic pulling towards it. I stood and allowed my magic to run between my fingers. It quickly morphed into my core power, white flashes of light flaring from my hands. I planted my bare foot at the base of the sword where it met the rock, careful of its sharp edges, and gripped the hilt with both hands. My magic multiplied as my skin contacted the weapon. Flares of white energy ran down the length of the blade and up my arms to my shoulders. I felt my core magic penetrating into the cursed blade, burning through the corrupted steel. I tightened my grip, pushing more magic into it. I didn't know what exactly it was doing, but somehow it felt right. Then I tensed the muscles in my arms and with all my might I pulled the sword from the stone. I gasped as I looked upon the sword, my magic expanding to surround the entire rock island in rings of light. Its glow illuminated the entire clearing, as if a piece of the sun itself were present beneath the canopy of trees. As I watched, the inky black stone began to clear, revealing a pale purple amethyst in its stead. The sword was much too heavy for me and my muscles strained under its weight, but even as I thought it the sword began to shrink down. The hilt shrunk to match my hands, the blade shortened and narrowed until before my eyes I held a blade perfectly matched for me. I gazed at the beautiful creation, taking in the workmanship. Across the hilt and trailing a few inches onto the blade, crafted from the steel itself were perfect little thorny vines with tiny roses blooming from them. The corner of my mouth turned up at the irony of the brambles wrapped around this custom blade. Maybe, instead of inciting haunted memories, the thorns that reminded me of so much pain could become my power.

Chapter 35 The Reunion

When I returned to the riverbank with my prize in tow, the stallion was still waiting for me. We exchanged a look and then he turned and headed back in the direction of his herd. I wondered if I should follow, but at that moment Nox flew down from the trees and I extended an arm for him to land on.

"Hello Nox," I said with a smile. It was then that I noticed he had my compass hanging from a chain, clasped in his claw. I fumbled with the sword for a moment before tucking it into my sash and then took the compass from him. He cawed loudly and then took off again, leaving me alone on the river bank. I opened the compass and lined it up. Studying it, I frowned. The river I stood by ran south which meant… it ran directly into Gotland. All that poisoned water had been running into my homeland. Could it be that this was the cause of the plague? I looked down at the sword once more. Someone had planted this cursed sword here. But who would do such a thing? With this removed, maybe the sickness could be stopped. I looked back at the river and said a silent thank you for all the guidance I'd received. Then I returned to the task of finding Hemsley and Chloe.

I thought about everything I'd learned over the last day as I walked. There was so much I was struggling to process it all. People were living in the Wildlands. There was a deity the rest of the world was supposedly worshiping. Somehow I'd been magically transported from one place to another. A mysterious messenger had visited me. I'd discovered what the unicorn blessing was. I'd removed a poisoned sword. Not just removed it I'd... purified it. I halted abruptly at that realization, turning it over in my mind. What exactly did that mean? I shook my head and carried on. I needed to focus on finding my friends. Hopefully, they were okay and were also following their compasses in the northeast direction.

The sun dipped low as I hiked on. My bare feet were dirty and sore. I was faced with a choice I didn't want to make. It was going to be dark soon and I could either keep walking and hope to run into the others, or I could stop and try to make shelter before nightfall. The thought of any of us being alone in the woods at night was a grim one. At that moment a flash of white caught my eye and I did a double take. There to my left, a hundred feet or so away, was Celeste. She was trodding along, parallel to me, and beside her-

"HEMSLEY!" I shouted at the top of my lungs. His head shot up, his eyes locking on me and in an instant we were racing towards each other. I practically flew across the forest floor, arms pumping, my dress wrapping around my legs. He leapt over a fallen tree, crashing through the underbrush, his hair blowing wildly. The moment lasted only a matter of seconds before we crashed into each other. I wrapped my arms around his neck and he wrapped his around my back, lifting me off the ground. We held each other tightly for a minute before he set me down and held my face. I placed my hands over his and looked into his eyes as we panted from the sprint.

"Are you alright?" He managed to get out.

I nodded breathlessly. It was then that he noticed my change in wardrobe and the sword.

"What's all this?" he asked incredulously.

I laughed, "It's a long story."

He gave me a crooked grin. "I bet."

"Chloe," I gasped, "have you seen any sign of her?" I asked.

Hemsley shook his head with furrowed brows.

I ran my hands over my hair fretfully. "She's all alone. It's going to be dark soon."

"We've got to find her," he said determinedly.

"Isn't there some spell we can use?" I asked hopefully.

Hemsley shook his head apologetically. "I'm sure there are such spells, but I am not familiar with them."

I looked around into the darkening woods and rubbed my bare arms as I began to feel the growing chill. Then an idea occurred to me. "If we can't cast a spell to help us find her, maybe we can cast a spell to help her find us."

Hemsley raised an eyebrow in intrigue. "We could make a beacon- make it easy to see us. I can also use wind magic to carry my voice."

I nodded excitedly, magic already curling between my fingers. Hemsley cupped his hands around his mouth and called out into the forest.

"CHLOE!" His voice boomed and carried through the trees.

I summoned my core power and raised my hands above my head. With both hands encircled in bands of white light, I let it burn brightly. I may not have been a light mage, but this was certainly a useful alternative way of wielding my core magic. The light would be bright enough to catch anyone's eye if they were in the vicinity. Hemsley continued to walk in a circle, calling out into the woods in different directions. We continued at this for ten or so minutes when a crashing sounded from off in the woods. It was coming straight for us at a fast rate and we both stopped what we were doing.

"I'm afraid we might have caught the attention of something much larger and more dangerous than Chloe," Hemsley said apprehensively. We both lowered into defensive stances with hands at the ready. It occurred to me that I could use the sword, but the truth was I had no idea how to use it with any skill. I was likely better off just using magic. We searched the underbrush tensely, wondering what new danger approached when Hemsley suddenly straightened in surprise. I too squinted my eyes at the approaching creature.

"Is that-?"

"Cyrus!" Hemsley exclaimed. The beast was racing towards its master, loyalty driving him on. I squinted again and saw that on his back was a small form…

"Chloe!" I exclaimed. They crashed into the clearing, Cyrus prancing in excitement and Chloe holding on for dear life. I leapt forward to calm Cyrus and Hemsley reached up to pluck Chloe off his back. As soon as Cyrus was sufficiently calmed, I grabbed Chloe up into a hug. Hemsley joined us, wrapping his arms around us both in a protective bear hug.

"I'm so glad you're okay!" I croaked. The thought of losing the little mage so soon after meeting her had been tearing me apart on the inside. I felt responsible for her. I pulled back to see her blushing shyly at our response.

"I'm so sorry," I apologized. "I tried to stop them. I tried to save you, both of you," I said, looking at both Hemsley and Chloe.

"It's okay," Chloe said quietly, "I think- I think we needed to get split up. We each needed to find something different."

I looked at her in surprise and then at Hemsley who was nodding thoughtfully.

"Let's make camp and then we can exchange stories," he suggested.

"Yes," I agreed, "There's a lot to talk about."

We were glad to find that all our camping gear was safe on Cyrus' back and we quickly set up camp and were sitting before a crackling fire in no time. We devoured bread and dried meat ravenously. None of us had eaten since breakfast and clearly it had been a long day for everyone. Finally, with our bellies satisfied, we exchanged looks over the fire.

"Alright Viv," Hemsley said, "I'm dying to hear where you've been. Where did all this come from?" he asked, gesturing broadly to the dress and sword sitting beside me.

Chloe nodded eagerly, "Yes, you first Vivienne!"

I gave a half laugh and spread my hands before the fire. "Where do I even start? I'm still trying to process everything that happened." I said.

"Start with where you got the new gown, it's quite lovely," he said with a humorous tone.

I laughed and rubbed my bare arms again. "Well first I had no idea how to find you guys, but then Nox appeared and he guided me to this temple in the woods. Oh, um, Nox is a raven who became my friend while I was in captivity," I added.

"That's that bird you had in my study isn't it?!" Hemsley exclaimed.

I grinned sheepishly.

"The bird is not the most important part of this story," Chloe chided.

"Oh, right. Carry on," Hemsley said.

"In the temple there were priestesses worshiping Oma. They gave me new clothes and took me in to pray for guidance," I continued.

Chloe cocked her head to the side. "There are people living in the Wildlands?"

I nodded vigorously. "Yes, I was surprised too. I'd always been told the Wildlands were uninhabitable for humans. It seems more and more I'm finding the things I've been taught to be false," I said in a perturbed tone.

"Well go on," Hemsley urged, "how about the sword?"

I laughed, "Hold your horses, I'm getting there. So I went to pray with them, but then I went into some sort of trance, and when I opened my eyes I was in a field. There was a messenger there who spoke to me and gave me guidance. She brought me to a herd of unicorns."

Chloe and Hemsley were both wide-eyed, sitting on the edge of their seats.

"There was a stallion in the herd who led me to a river and- oh wait, I have to tell you- I figured out what the unicorn blessing is!" I exclaimed.

Hemsley was enthralled. "What? What is it?"

"It makes the animals trust and help me. That's why the birds always seem to like me," I explained.

Hemsley smacked his palm to his forehead. "No way! It was right in front of us the whole time! That's why the wolves didn't eat us! That makes so much sense. I knew it didn't have to do with your core power!"

I nodded with a grin and Chloe smiled softly, resting her chin in her hands.

I continued on and told them about the poisoned sword and how I'd pulled it from the stone. I shared my theory about it being the cause of the plague and Hemsley frowned as everybody tried to digest what I'd told them.

"May I see it?" Chloe asked quietly.

I raised my eyebrows but obliged and handed the sword over to her. She set it across her knees and ran her hand along the flat of the blade. She closed her eyes and took a deep breath as tendrils of her core power snaked around her hand and head. We watched expectantly and after a moment she opened her eyes again.

"The blade was once tainted with its master's desire for revenge. It is pure now though, and loyal to you," Chloe said, meeting my eyes.

I took the blade back from her outstretched hands and frowned. "How can a sword be loyal?" I asked in confusion.

"It must be enchanted. Forged by a mage," Hemsley said in awe.

Chloe nodded. "Forged by one of your ancestors actually," she said.

I gaped. "My ancestor? How can that be?"

She shook her head, "The past is convoluted with secrets. I sense that more will reveal itself when the time is right."

I frowned. That was about as vague as it gets. After an awkward silence, Hemsley launched into his tale of spiders and sprites. He showed us his new bracers and we inspected them curiously.

"Care to do a reading on these?" Hemsley asked Chloe.

She shrugged and obliged, running her hands over the bracers. "You found them on the arms of a thief who didn't know how to wield them. He stole them from a mage who hid his magic from the world in order to protect the woman he loved."

Hemsley and I gaped.

"Now there's a story I'd like to hear," I commented. Hemsley nodded in agreement.

"So much history hidden in these lands," he said quietly.

"How about you Chloe?" I asked her.

She shrugged again, "I met a troll who made me answer his riddles. Turns out he was actually a faerie. Then I found Cyrus."

We blinked at her brief story. She was all wordy when it came to her Clarity readings, but learning anything about her was like pulling teeth. Was she the only one who hadn't received anything?

"Well, we're glad you're safe," Hemsley said and I nodded in agreement. It was good to have the group back together and somehow our time apart made us feel closer than ever.

Chapter 36 The Desert

In the morning we packed up camp and I stopped to look at my scraped up bare feet.

"Hemsley? Can I use healing magic on myself?" I asked.

He looked up from his open pack in surprise and shook his head. "No, healing magic is a giving magic and you can't give yourself magic. Are you hurt?"

I shrugged a little. "I've just been running around with no shoes and my feet are a little beat up is all."

"Well why didn't you say something sooner? Come over here, I'll fix them up." He clapped his hands on his knees from where he sat on a log and I went and sat beside him feeling a little sheepish.

"Hang on a second, didn't you hit your head when you fell off Cyrus?" I suddenly recalled.

Hemsley reached back and touched his head gingerly. “Now that you mention it,” he said with a grimace.

I stood quickly and moved behind him. “You’ve healed me plenty of times, you ought to tell me when you’re hurt so I can return the favor.” I summoned my magic and did as he had taught me, guiding it into the skin. Hemsley let out a sigh of relief and I lowered my hands as I felt the damage repair itself.

“You did well. Now come give me your feet,” Hemsley urged.

I grinned, feeling pleased with myself, and returned to sit beside my mentor. He held his hand out expectantly and I lifted a foot up in offering, biting my cheek. He grasped my bare foot in his hands and began tenderly healing the many scrapes and bruises. There was something awfully intimate about having someone touch your feet. I couldn’t actually remember anyone touching my feet since I was a child. He had that intense focused face that he always made when he was healing and I found myself blushing to the tips of my ears. I hoped he wouldn’t notice, but when he was done with the first foot he glanced up at me and froze for a second. We stared into each other’s eyes for a minute and I felt my blush deepening. The contrast against my white gown was stark, there was no way he didn’t notice. I saw his Adam’s apple bob as he swallowed and then gently released my foot and took the next one. Hemsley was moving slower now though. Taking his time to brush his fingers along every scrape as he healed it. It tickled but simultaneously felt amazing on my sore feet. I was suddenly self-conscious of my dirty, probably smelly feet. He finished with the second foot but didn't release it. He had one hand on my heel and the other resting over my ankle. I got the distinct impression there was something he wanted to say but it was then that I glanced sideways and jumped an inch as I realized Chloe was standing across the fire pit, watching us with raised eyebrows. Hemsley abruptly cleared his throat and released my ankle.

"All done!" he announced.

I rubbed my arms awkwardly. "Thanks."

Chloe sucked her lips in to hide a teasing grin and turned away with a feigned 'I didn't see anything' sort of look.

I blew out a breath, trying to release some of the tension, and asked, "I don't suppose you can use magic to make some shoes?"

Hemsley perked up. "No, but you can alter existing clothing. Shrink, stretch, redesign it, and such."

I pondered on the implications of that. No more waiting on the tailor? No more growing out of clothes? Seemed a useful skill indeed.

"That's the next thing I want to learn!" I decided.

Hemsley chuckled, "It is similar to what you've already been learning about changing the forms of elements."

Chloe sighed. "I'll get there someday. I'm still figuring out how to manipulate basic elements."

I grinned at her. "Cheer up Chloe, I didn't start learning that until I was sixteen. In terms of age, you're years ahead of me."

She smiled back and we finished loading up our packs on the horses.

We covered a lot of ground that day and saw the landscape change as we went. The trees thinned and fell away. It grew warmer and the others shed layers under the sun. The rich forest floor was replaced by hard, dry dirt and the trees were replaced with hardy shrubs.

"I think we're out of the Wildlands," Hemsley said.

"So this is Alana?" I asked.

He nodded. "The outskirts of Alana, but yes. It'll still be some time before we reach civilization."

We traveled on until the sun grew low and then we stopped for the night. I was showing Chloe how to start the fire while Hemsley peered into the dusk.

"What do you see?" I asked.

"Rabbits," he said with a grin.

I cocked my head and laughed, "Do you fancy a pet?"

"No, he fancies a stew," Chloe called out from where she was crouched before the fire.

My eyebrows shot up. "You intend to hunt?"

Hemsley was already rummaging through his pack. "I'm tired of dried meat. I want a hot meal."

I couldn't disagree with that. He pulled out a long bow I hadn't even noticed stashed in the packs and set to work stringing it. "I carved this bow myself." He said as he worked.

"Oh, it's very nice. Though I can't say I know much about bows," I said.

He grinned and stood up, swinging a quiver of arrows over his back. "I'll be back ladies. Prepare the stew and I'll bring the meat." With that he was off, running out into the desert.

I shook my head a little in amusement as I watched him energetically hop over bushes, eager for a hot meal.

"We haven't even got a pot," I said to Chloe. She shrugged and shook her head.

An hour later, a very crude clay pot sat over the fire. I had used water and earth magic to make it and though it wasn't pretty, it would get the job done. Chloe was practicing water magic, filling the pot, and I was digging some tubers from a plant I recognized from my days in the tower. The pixies had brought me many such roots with the green tops still attached. Hemsley returned, carrying two rabbits by their ears. He set about bleeding and skinning them, but I chose not to watch beyond that as I found it rather repulsive. When the meat was added to the pot though along with some salt from the dry goods bag, the smell had us all drooling.

"I'll get more material for the fire," Chloe volunteered. She was quite proud of the fire she'd built and had been tending to it with a close eye. I smiled at her as she left. She was kind of cute. Made me wish I had a younger sibling.

I leaned over the fire, adding the tubers to the pot and stirring them in. I could feel Hemsley's eyes on me as I worked and I cast him a sideways look. He was gazing at my face and I straightened and met his eyes. I raised a self-conscious hand to my face, feeling the scar that ran through my upper lip.

"What?" I asked.

He gave me a half smile, his eyes not straying from my face. "You don't know, do you?"

"Know what?" I demanded.

"How beautiful you are."

A deep blush instantly heated my cheeks and I clamped my mouth shut in surprise. How could he say that so casually? He didn't even look embarrassed! He was just staring at me with that same deep look in his eyes.

"I-", but I was interrupted by Chloe returning to the clearing. I bent over the pot again quickly, letting my hair hide my face. I stole a glance over at him after a minute and saw that he had returned to his carving, with a cheeky half-grin on his face. This man. Was he flirty like this with every woman? Or did he mean it- that he thought I was beautiful? His face looked honest. But if he liked me, why hadn't he kissed me at the springs like I thought he was going to? The moment was so… right. But what did I know? Maybe my social skills were stunted from spending two years in isolation and I was misinterpreting everything. Yes, that was quite possible. I rubbed my eyes and shook off the awkwardness. We had more important things at hand.

Chapter 37 The Circus

We arrived in the capital of Alana midday the next day and found a bustling marketplace filled with bright colors and strange smells. The noon sun was blazing overhead and I noticed everyone here wore head coverings of some sort. Scarves, turbans, veils. Hemsley's dark skin was glistening with a sheen of sweat despite only wearing a loose white shirt. Still, with his dark riding pants and boots, the heat was getting to him. My loose white dress was much more appropriate for the weather but my skin was not accustomed to so much sun and I knew I'd burn if I didn't cover up soon.. I quickly tried out using magic to alter Chloe's cloak. From it I managed to make two scarves for us to cover our pale complexions. They were crude and not pretty like many of the ones I saw the local women wearing, but they did the job. I shifted mine to cover my shoulders and then adjusted Chloe's for her.

"Is there some sort of event going on?" I asked in wonder.

Hemsley shook his head, "No, this is how it is every day."

"Oh right, I forgot you studied here for two years," I recalled.

Chloe, who was riding behind me, shifted uncomfortably.

"There's so many people. He could be anywhere," I lamented. "What do you think Chloe? Where should we start looking for Damien?"

She looked around, scanning the crowd. "I think we should go further into the city," she said. Hemsley nodded and led the way through the crowded street. The further we went, the larger the buildings got. Hemsley began pointing things out and telling us about them, like a tour guide.

"At the center of the city lies the Alanian palace. Around it are the homes of the upper class interspersed with skilled tradespeople. Though it's very dry here, there is a wide river that runs further east. They use a series of aqueducts to carry the water here and to the northern plains where crops are grown," he explained.

"Fascinating," I murmured, taking it all in. I still didn't understand why or how Damien had come to be here. He'd be able to explain everything when we were reunited though. There would be much to catch up on. We rode until we could see the palace more clearly, towering over the surrounding city. Its construction was strange and beautiful with tall towers and arched windows. It was painted with many bright colors and trimmed with gold that glinted in the sun.

"How about now, Chloe? Any leads?" Hemsley called over.

Chloe closed her eyes for a moment and when she opened them, her pale blue magic floated in front of them in wisps. After a moment she blinked them away and peered at a series of large covered wagons heading towards the palace.

"I think… we should join the circus."

Hemsley pulled up short and balked. "What?"

"I think we should join the circus," Chloe said again more firmly.

I looked back at her in surprise and then exchanged a look with Hemsley.

"We brought the Clarity mage with us for a reason," I said with a shrug.

Hemsley let out a breath like he couldn't believe what we were about to do. "Okay, let's go join the circus."

At Chloe's direction, we approached the wagon at the rear of the caravan and lashed our horses to it before slipping inside. With the three of us crammed inside we observed the contents of the wagon curiously.

"It's all costumes," I whispered excitedly. The driver of the wagon didn't seem to notice us with all the surrounding noise so we rummaged around, grabbing various costume pieces. Hemsley ducked out with a bundle of clothes and left Chloe and I to change. Chloe finished first and climbed out onto Celeste's back, wearing a midnight blue ensemble that was stitched with fine golden threads that formed constellations. It was much too long on her but I had taken a knife and cut it short for her. She had taken the excess material and wrapped it over her head like a scarf. I fumbled with the costume I had snatched and then peered out the back of the wagon just as Hemsley rejoined us on Cyrus. He wore no shirt, just a black vest with gold embroidery that lay over his bare chest. His black pants were loose and baggy with a fiery red sash tied at the waist. His feet were clad in simple black slippers. My eyes were drawn to his bare arms and chest. The outfit put his dark skin and toned physique on display. It was a good look for him. As he drew up alongside Chloe, I emerged and his eyes widened. The costume was one of the less-revealing ones stocked in the wagon- I had given the full-coverage dress to Chloe, but it still showed more skin than I was used to. The ensemble was blood red and consisted of two pieces; a flowy, ankle length skirt, and a matching long sleeve fitted top that ended at my sternum leaving my stomach and back exposed. I had also donned some gold anklets with tiny tinkling bells that had been placed with the costume and a gold headpiece with an attached sheer veil that I left down for the time being. As I stood at the back of the wagon a wind blew through and swept my hair and skirt dramatically.

Hemsley was openly staring at this point and I shyly tucked my hair back as his words from the other night echoed in my head. *You don't know, do you? How beautiful you are.*

A grin broke out across his face. "You look fantastic. Both of you."

Chloe was smirking a little with one eyebrow cocked. "Thanks," she said dryly.

I ducked my head and hopped down from the wagon to mount Celeste. I had strapped my sword to the saddle bag using the sash from the temple. There was no way I could carry it on my person without drawing excess attention. The caravan was moving again and we followed behind the last wagon as it rolled towards the grand palace. I pulled my veil across my face and tensed as our turn came to pass through the iron gates, but the guards simply poked around the costume wagon and waved us all through. We were brought around back to the stables where the wagons were unhitched and the horses fed and cared for. We took Celeste and Cyrus in with the other horses and stashed our saddles and supplies in the back of their stall. No one would be able to get to our belongings without getting past Cyrus who was not to be trifled with. The circus performers and animal handlers began carrying things into the palace and we snuck in alongside them, hidden in plain sight.

"What now?" I whispered to Hemsley and Chloe as we walked amongst the performers preparing for their acts.

Chloe shrugged. "We're getting closer, just play along!"

A man with an outrageous mustache was unloading props from a crate and caught sight of us. He pulled a large glass orb from the box and gestured towards Chloe with it. "This is for your act isn't it?"

I raised a surprised eyebrow but Chloe didn't falter.

"Yes," she said firmly and stepped forward to accept it from the man. She seemed surprised by its weight and heaved it to her chest with both arms. The orb appeared to be filled with water and colored glitter. Chloe gave it a little shake and the orb swirled with dark purple glitter. She grinned and I couldn't help but think she was having a little too much fun with this.

"Hey!" A girl was waving at me and my heart sank as I took in her costume which matched mine exactly. "Come warm up with us!" she called, waving me over. I looked over and sure enough, there was a group of eight or so girls in matching red costumes stretching and practicing a sequence of dance moves. Oh no. I looked at Chloe and Hemsley in a panic as the girl ran over and linked arms with me, pulling me towards their group. Hemsley gave me a wide eyed look and shrugged and Chloe grinned and mouthed, "Just go along with it!"

I turned back towards the group of dancers we were approaching and tried to calm my racing heart. It appeared I really had just joined the circus.

Chapter 38 The Prince

The dance troop welcomed me warmly into their group and I looked around nervously as a girl raised her foot up over her head in a show of impressive flexibility.

"You must be the one they got to replace Sierra," said the girl who had dragged me over.

"Oh, um, yeah," I said. Play along. Right.

"It's too bad she got hurt," said another girl as she bent over backwards, "she was really good. Are you a fire mage too?"

"Um, no I'm a uh, light mage," I lied.

"Oooh, that'll be interesting," cooed another girl.

"Well don't worry about us, we'll do our thing and give you plenty of space to do your light show in the middle," said the first girl.

What? In the middle? "So, what exactly did Sierra do, when she did it?" I asked.

"She'd do like, rings of fire and dance around a bit. Sometimes she'd get bored of the routine and she'd just improvise the whole thing." said a dancer.

"Really?" I asked.

"Yeah, it didn't really bother us because we just do our dance routine, you know? As long as she kept the flames in real tight so they didn't get us- she could pretty much do whatever she wanted."

Some of the girls were practicing a series of dance moves now and I watched in trepidation. The dance was fast and fluid, their red skirts sweeping out as they moved. I glanced around for Chloe and Hemsley, but didn't see them. We needed to find Damien- before I made a fool of myself on stage. A gong sounded and the girls hurriedly stood and fixed their veils in place.

"We're on in five! Let's go girls!" called one of the dancers.

What? Five minutes? I broke out in a sweat as I was hustled along with the dance troop as they made their way down a hall. If I revealed I wasn't actually the new dancer or even a part of the circus, they could have guards dragging me away in an instant. And that would seriously hinder my plans to find Damien. No, I needed to blend in for now. We approached a large doorway and I spotted Chloe poking her head through it into the room beyond.

"Chloe!" I hissed.

She turned in my direction and waved me over. "He's here," she whispered.

"Where?" I looked up sharply and tried to step into the grand room she'd been looking in but she grabbed my arm and pulled me back.

"You can't just barge in there! They're performing for the royal family! You'll cause a scene!" she whisper-yelled at me. "I haven't actually spotted him. I just know he's somewhere in there."

"We need to find him or else I'm gonna be dragged out there for the next performance!"

"Good," said Chloe, "if you're out there you can get a good look around!"

"What? No, Chloe, they're expecting me to dance and put on some sort of light show!" I protested.

"Vivienne." Chloe stared into my eyes. "Is this really the worst thing you've faced?"

I gaped at her.

"Go out there, put on a show, and while you're at it, look around for your brother," she commanded.

I straightened and clenched my fists in determination. She was right. If this is what it took to save my brother and bring Gotland its rightful ruler- it really wasn't too much to ask.

"Also," Chloe added, "I think you'll enjoy this performance. Take a look."

I poked my head out to see a couple of acrobats juggling and balancing on balls. I frowned and Chloe smirked. "Not them, the musicians."

I turned where she had gestured to a group of musicians off to the side. There amongst them was

Hemsely looking very uncomfortable with some sort of flute. I clapped my hand over my mouth to stifle a laugh.

"He doesn't know how to play that, does he?" I asked.

"Nope," said Chloe.

I shook my head in disbelief at the situation we'd found ourselves in but my view of Hemsley was interrupted by the acrobats running towards the doorway as they finished their performance. The dance troop giggled excitedly as they moved forward.

"Looks like I'm up," I said in a strained voice.

"Knock 'em dead," Chloe encouraged me.

The dancers ran out into the room and I followed after. The room appeared to be a magnificent throne room with a collection of richly dressed people snacking and drinking at the head of the room. The dancers took up their poses at the center of the room, forming a circle and I moved to stand in the center where I assumed I was supposed to be. For a split second Hemsley and I's eyes met and I saw my fright mirrored in his face. I raised my arms into a pose that seemed complimentary to the other dancers and the first few notes of the music played out. The dancers began spinning and swaying around me and I summoned my magic to my hands. I took a deep breath and began improvising. I let my core magic surface and trail behind my hands in bands of white light as I swept my arms and feet in what I hoped looked like a choreographed dance. My only dance education was in ballroom so I wasn't familiar with dancing alone, but I did know how to move gracefully and with poise. I called on the muscle memory of hours of lessons to create a dance that showcased my glowing magic. Once I was in a rhythm I began searching the faces of the audience and their servants. I just needed to see that familiar face. His dark hair, his charming smile. Then I could take him home and he could- I stumbled and did a double take. There at the head of the room, amongst the royal family, was Damien. Wearing fine clothes and sipping a dark red wine, he looked perfectly content beside a beautiful woman who was hanging on to his every word. What? My mind raced. What was going on? He wasn't trapped? Cursed? Enslaved? I tried to calm myself while fumbling through the dance. I was sure there was a logical explanation. Damien could explain. I just needed to speak to him without causing a scene. But how was I supposed to do that? I didn't want to wait for answers any longer. I wanted an explanation. Now. And causing a scene seemed like the perfect way to do that. Luckily I was experienced in crashing parties. I glanced over at Hemsley who gave me a thumbs up while pretending to play the flute and though I knew he had no idea what I was about to do, I took it as confirmation and turned my gaze back to Damien. I used one hand to call on my core power more deeply and let it encircle me in three rings that spun rapidly, crossing over one another in an intricate rhythm. I used my other hand to summon winds that whipped around me making my skirt snap around my ankles. The other dancers gasped and began backing away as my air magic gently but firmly pushed at them, warning them to get back. With the dancers out of my way, I approached the pedestal on which the royal family lounged. Their eyes were on me now, confused and wary. They could not yet tell if this was still part of the act, but as I drew even closer, not diminishing my magic at all, their eyes widened in fear. I reached up and removed my veil, revealing my identity as I stared them down.

"Guards!" yelled the king. The music stopped and guards ran towards me from every corner, but just then Damien's eyes met mine and lit in recognition.

"W-wait!" he choked out.

To my surprise, everyone actually stopped and listened to him. I extinguished my magic but for a few tendrils floating around my fingertips just in case. The room was perfectly still as he gaped at me in disbelief.

"Vivienne?"

I swallowed tightly. "In the flesh," I said in a rough voice, not allowing my face to betray any emotion.

Damien's mouth opened and closed several times. "How? I thought- we all thought you were dead. How are you here?"

Out of the corner of my eye I saw Hemsley and Chloe approaching to stand behind me in solidarity. Here I was, once again having no idea what was going on and it felt good to have them on my team. "I could ask you the same thing," I replied evenly.

He blinked a few times and the Alanian king grew impatient. "Damien, do you care to explain what is going on?"

Damien appeared visibly shaken but immediately turned to the king and announced, "My long-lost sister has returned! This is cause for celebration!"

The royal family and nobles erupted into applause and chatter, congratulating him. My frown deepened. None of this made any sense. Damien walked around the table with arms raised in welcome.

"Come! Join us in celebration, sister!" He invited me. He glanced at Hemsley and Chloe who had drawn even closer, "Bring your companions, there's room for all!"

He wrapped his arm around my shoulders to pull me forward but I drew back to look at him. "Damien, I need to speak with you," I said intently.

"Of course!" he said lightly, "We have much to catch up on! Let us celebrate and speak tomorrow."

"No, Damien," I said adamantly. "I want answers now. Things are not right in Gotland. We must speak."

His jaw ticked and he gave me a tight smile. "Fine." He turned back to the nobles and announced in a loud voice, "My sister and her friends are weary from their travels. They wish to retire for the night, so we will join you again tomorrow!" He led us from the room and the woman he'd been seated next to at the table got up to follow us out.

"Let us go to my receiving chambers while rooms are prepared for you," she suggested. She had the black hair and darker skin many of the Alanians had and soft, pretty features.

"That would be wonderful, thank you dear," Damien said warmly. She seemed to melt under his praise and I looked between them in confusion. I glanced back at Chloe and Hemsley. Chloe looked perfectly calm and Hemsley gave me a cocked eyebrow that said he was just as confused as I was. Damien and his lady friend brought us to a lavish room filled with low, plush seats, decorative cushions, and rich, red drapes. We were seated and servants rushed in at a signal from the woman. They placed before us pitchers of lemon water, bottles of wine, fresh bread, exotic fruits, creamy sauces, and all manner of delectable food. The smells hit me like a ton of bricks and my stomach growled. Chloe's jaw was on the floor and Hemsley looked like he was barely restraining himself. Damien sat across from us and the woman joined him. She had a handmaid that trailed behind her, hands clasped and head bowed.

"Please, help yourself," Damien encouraged us. Our troop didn't need to be told twice and we dug in, momentarily forgetting about what had brought us here. After we had spent several minutes devouring the delicious food, Damien spoke again.

"Alright Vivienne, tell me, where have you been these last few years? You've lost weight, and your face-what happened to it?"

I flinched at his words and looked at my hands for a moment, focusing in on the fine, silver scars that crisscrossed my fingers. I glanced over at my companions and saw Hemsley frowning, looking at Damien and then at me.

"Well," I began slowly, "it's sort of a long story." I began relating to him an abbreviated version of the events of the last two and a half years including my time in the tower, Hemsley purchasing me, my return to Gotland and the curse I'd cast, and then our journey here to find him. I described it all rather matter of factly, feeling detached from the incidents that made up the last several years of my life. By the end of my story Damien had his elbows on his knees and his hand over the lower half of his face.

"Vivienne," he said slowly, "I'm so sorry. I had no idea. We thought you must be dead. Father couldn't find you…"

I swallowed down the emotion I felt bubbling up and looked stoically out at the setting sun through the window. There was a buzzing in my head, like my magic was stirring with my emotion and I tried to clear it away.

"And you? Did Rhiannon come back to take you too?" I asked, looking back at him.

Damien sat back and ran his hands over his neck in discomfort. "Not exactly," he said with a grimace. "It's a long story, but after you disappeared I was working on improving our relationship with Alana. Father was very against it so I did so secretly, against his wishes. In the course of those discussions, I met Ishana." He took the hand of the woman seated beside him and she smiled at him in adoration. "We fell in love," he continued, "but being a princess of Alana, I knew Father would never approve. So, I ran away. Ishana's family has welcomed me with open arms and we are engaged to be married in a few months." The couple stared dotingly into each other's eyes while I tried to process his story.

"But, what about Gotland? They need their rightful king. Father is running the country into the ground. He's not fit," I said.

Damien nodded and furrowed his brows in distress. "I thought I could run away from my responsibilities, but it seems they've caught up with me." He turned back to me and looked at our small band again. "I will return to Gotland and fulfill my duty. But I also won't abandon Ishana. We will need time to discuss how we are to proceed and what the best route of action is."

I nodded, feeling a weight lifting off my shoulders. Damien would return. He would make everything right again.

Chapter 39 The Palace

That night we slept in luxurious guest quarters. It was strange to be away from Hemsley and Chloe after our time together, but the bounty of pillows and soft sheets beckoned me into a night of much needed sleep. In the morning I awoke to find clothes laid out for me. It was another two piece dress in the style worn by women in this country. This one was cream colored with golden beadwork embroidered into it. I took some time after dressing to stand on the balcony, taking in the view of the beautiful oasis that made up the palace grounds. A knock sounded at the door and I bid them to enter. Hemsley poked his head in and his gaze found me by the railing. My heart squeezed at the sight of him. He was wearing clothes similar in design to mine, though cut in the men's style. His hair was half tied back and the outfit suited him well. I recalled that his late mother was born in Alana and it made sense. His complexion and features were similar to those who abided here and he looked right at home in his own cream colored clothes. He strode over and leaned with his elbows on the railing beside me.

"How are you?" he asked quietly.

I let out a deep sigh and copied his pose, leaning against the railing. "I thought we were rescuing my brother from certain peril so that he in turn could rescue Gotland from its own doom. But instead, he's been living in royal grandeur with the love of his life. And I'm happy for him, it's just not what I expected."

Hemsley nodded, peering over at me. "You've been through a lot, Viv. You're not the same person you were when you last saw him."

I gazed out at the horizon. "I know. It feels… different."

"How so?" he asked.

I furrowed my eyebrows. "I feel different. He feels different. I guess we're just on different paths now. He's going to rule Gotland with his queen by his side and I… well I don't know anymore."

Hemsley fiddled with his hands and then turned to face me with one elbow on the rail. "I think you're a bigger part of this than you think Viv."

I frowned in confusion. "What do you mean?"

Hemsley straightened and pulled me gently towards him. My heart beat faster as he gazed down into my face and I wondered what he saw when he looked at me.

With one hand still around my upper arm he responded, “I’m not sure, I just know you’re important. Rhiannon still wants you and that has to mean something.”

I nodded and lowered my eyes to his chest but he lifted a hand to my chin and ever so gently raised my face up towards him again. “You’re important to me too, you know?” he said in a low voice. Looking into his face, I couldn’t breathe. The morning sun was golden on his skin and a gentle breeze softly lifted the free stands of his hair. The moment was perfect, like a dream. I leaned in towards him, drawn in by his intense gaze.

“You’re important to me too,” I whispered.

Emotion swept over his face. A mixture of joy and grief that confused me.

“What’s wrong? Please tell me,” I pleaded.

He reached up and brushed a strand of hair from my face. “I want to tell you so many things. I worry what you’ll think if you know the truth.”

I opened my mouth to respond but another knock sounded at the door followed by Damien striding cheerfully into the room with a slightly annoyed looking Chloe hot on his heels.

“Vivienne!” he called in greeting.

I clicked my tongue and turned back to Hemsley, pinning him down with my eyes. “We’re not done with this conversation,” I hissed. I said it both as a command and as reassurance. I wanted to hear what was weighing on him. I needed to know.

"I have so much to show you sister!" Damien exclaimed. "Let us gather for breakfast in the dining hall and then I can show you all the wonders of this place!"

I gave him a thin smile and followed his lead, falling into step with Chloe.

After another extravagant meal, Damien gave us a tour of the palace. There was a grand hall for celebrations, beautiful gardens with flowing fountains, and a bathhouse with steaming water. When lunchtime came around, Damien's fiancé joined us for the meal. She had her meek little handmaid in tow, it seemed they were never apart. Ishana hung on Damien's arm and looked at me curiously.

"What kind of mage are you?" she asked me.

I frowned. I had only barely started to piece together that answer for myself and I wasn't sure I was ready to divulge that information to a girl I'd just met.

"I'm not entirely sure yet," I answered.

"Ishana is a mage too," Damien said. "She's a travel mage and can make travel dust." He looked at her with pride and she beamed.

I raised my eyebrows. "That's… very interesting." The only travel dust I had seen had come from Rhiannon. "Do you sell it?" I asked.

"Mostly it stays within the family though we sometimes use it as currency between royalty of other kingdoms." Ishana answered.

"It's extremely expensive. Priceless really." Damien added.

I exchanged the briefest of glances with Hemsley who looked very guarded. Chloe on the other hand was happily licking pudding off her spoon. She'd gotten us this far, maybe she wasn't interested in looking into our problems anymore.

"I don't suppose you've ever given some to a witch called Rhiannon?" I asked darkly.

They both froze. Ishana looked nervously at Damien whose face was suddenly filled with concern. "Rhiannon? Is that the witch who took you? She used travel dust that day didn't she?"

I didn't speak, letting my silence answer for me.

"We would never do business with the likes of her. There are other travel mages. She must have procured it from one of them," Damien explained gently.

I grit my teeth at his patronizing tone. He clearly thought that I was still the same little girl he'd last seen at the castle on my sixteenth birthday. I wanted to snap at him but instead, I nodded stiffly and gave him a tight smile. "Of course."

"There's a great celebration planned for tonight. I think you'll all enjoy it," Damien said, changing the subject.

"A party? When do you plan to return to Gotland?" I asked.

"All in due time," Damien reassured me. "There are many preparations I must make before returning. I have responsibilities I've taken up here in Alana. In the meantime we might as well have a good time right?"

This did little to soothe my worries and I felt buzzing in my head again, like my magic was agitated. My displeasure must have shown on my face because he reached across the table to take my hand in an effort to comfort me. His hand felt foreign on mine and I fought the urge to pull away. This was my brother. The only living family who had not forsaken me.

"Try to enjoy yourself, Vivienne. This is the kind of life you should have been living all along. You belong here, in a palace. It'll feel even better once we're home in Gotland," Damien said.

Those words swirled in my head. I had thought that after cursing Gotland I would be banished for my crimes. But Damien did not mind that I was a mage. He was even engaged to a mage. Certainly things would change in Gotland with him as king. Magic would no longer be outlawed. Could I really return to live in Gotland? Was that even what I wanted? I didn't know anymore.

"I think I'd like to get some fresh air," I said hoarsely as I pulled away and stood from the table. I turned and left, striding quickly to the exit. My emotions felt suffocating and I needed to clear my head. I found myself at the stables and Celeste greeted me with a whinny. I gave her a pet and walked to our belongings still hidden in the hay. I reached into the hay and pulled out the magnificent sword. I held it up and admired it once more. This did not belong in the hands of some prim and proper princess. Yet it felt so right in my hands. I shook my head and tucked it away again. Celeste looked at me curiously and I gave her a half grin. A ride was just what I needed.

My hair whipped in the wind as Celeste galloped across the palace grounds and through the expansive orchard growing adjacent. I felt so free in that moment. It was just Celeste and I under the endless sky, the sun on our backs, wind in our hair. No expectations, no responsibilities. No conflict in my mind. I slowed as we came to one of the many aqueducts running towards the city. Celeste drank and I dismounted to splash water over my face. I tipped my head back to look at the sky and released a breath that felt like it came from my soul itself.

"I'm lost, Mother. I don't know who I am or what to do." I wasn't sure if I was speaking to the Great Mother or my own departed mother. Nor was I sure that either could hear me, but the forlorn feeling in my chest was too heavy to bear alone. I had found my brother. I should be happy. He wanted me to come home and there was a time that was all I wanted, but now… Now I wasn't sure. There was a part of me that did not want to return to my old life, and another part of me that felt guilty for even thinking that. I spun slowly, closing my eyes against the sun. "I don't know the way anymore." Hot tears started dripping down my cheeks as everything I'd been holding back started to break free. "I don't want to feel broken anymore, I just want to redeem-"

I stopped and opened my eyes as the words of the messenger rang in my ears. "Redemption is within your reach," I whispered. Maybe it was okay that I wasn't sure who I was or what I should do. Maybe I needed to stop trying to be just one thing. I had played so many roles, letting my circumstances define me. I thought of the sword and its curling silver rose brambles. My pain could become my power. Why should my scars prevent me from being a princess? Why should being a princess prevent me from being a mage? Maybe I would return to Gotland castle, maybe I wouldn't. It didn't really matter. Because my redemption did not lie in reclaiming a past version of myself. Redemption came with growing into a better version of myself.

Chapter 40 The Celebration

As I trotted back through the palace grounds I spotted Chloe sitting by a fountain. She had a scarf over her head to protect her face and scalp from the sun and was gazing into the crystal clear waters. I changed direction to approach her and dismounted before the fountain. She turned and smiled at me.

"Feel better?" she asked.

I nodded. "Yes."

"You seem different. Less conflicted. Have you decided what you're going to do?"

I didn't bother looking surprised she knew what was going on in my head. I was getting used to it, and I was starting to see that her insight didn't always come from her magic. "No," I responded with a shake of my head. Chloe raised her eyebrows and I continued, "But I feel… peace."

She gave me another smile. "That's good."

I smiled back at her. "It feels good. How about you Chloe? What do you want to do? We could take you back to the children's home, or if you like, you're welcome to stay with me. Though I can't say I know where I'm going next."

She turned and looked out at the horizon thoughtfully. "I think I'll wait to see where you decide to go," she said finally.

I nodded. "What have you been up to all afternoon?"

Chloe made a face. "I've been with Ishana and her handmaid actually."

"Really?" I asked in surprise. "What's she like? I can't say I'm especially fond of her. Her entire personality seems to be 'Damien's fiancé'"

Chloe snickered. "That's a pretty good assessment. Yes, she seems thoroughly obsessed with your brother. She did talk to me a lot about travel dust. Showed me all the bags of it. It was all very… interesting."

I looked at her quizzically. "What does that mean?"

"She's keeping secrets," Chloe said and I frowned. "I know it's frustrating when I don't reveal everything I see, but sometimes I don't see everything. Sometimes it's better to use my visions as guidance and let some things play out for the best result."

I nodded slowly. "Okay. So, be cautious with Ishana? And the whole truth will reveal itself at a more convenient time?"

Chloe nodded. "Exactly. I'm not trying to be difficult, I've just learned from experience that spilling other people's secrets can have unpleasant outcomes."

I cocked an eyebrow at her. "You know more about me than you let on, don't you?"

She gave me a mischievous grin. "I know a lot about everybody, but I'm not just a secret seer- I'm a secret keeper." She lifted her finger to her lips with a conspiratory smile and I couldn't help but laugh.

"Very well, secret keeper. Shall we get ready for this party tonight? Something tells me this will be the last one for a while." I said.

Chloe and I changed into fancier party dresses- hers a pastel purple with lots of beadwork and mine a navy blue two piece with tiny pearl beads sewn into it. We chatted while we fixed each other's hair and it reminded me a bit of getting ready with Eleanor in my days in the castle.

"So, what's going on with you and Hemsley?" Chloe asked slyly.

I blushed a little and bit my cheek. "Why don't you tell me?" I asked.

Chloe put her hands up in mock surrender. "Hey, I haven't pried into that. All I know is what I've seen- which is a lot."

I barked a laugh, throwing my head back. "Nothing's happened," I assured her.

"Suuuure," she teased. "You just gaze lovingly into each other's eyes because you're such good friends."

My face heated further and I chewed my lip. "I think, I think he likes me but… he keeps holding back. He's keeping secrets- hey wait a second! You know, don't you? You know what he's hiding!" I exclaimed.

Chloe looked unbothered. "Of course I know. But you don't want to hear it from me, you want to hear it from him."

I blinked. "Shoot, you're right. I do need to hear it from him." I furrowed my eyebrows and squinted in concentration as I finished up Chloe's hair. "I'll talk to him tonight. We've got to clear things up," I said in determination.

"Yes!" cheered Chloe.

Chloe and I entered the party together and I felt eyes turn towards us as we did so. I was reminded of how I loved that feeling when I was younger. I soaked up the attention gladly, letting it fuel my self-esteem. Now I felt self-conscious. What were they thinking? Were they looking at my scars? I mentally shook myself. Why did I care what these strangers thought anyway? From across the room, Hemsley spotted us and made his way over. A flutter of butterflies erupted in my stomach. Now there was a man whose opinion I cared about.

Hemsley smiled. "You ladies look great."

"Thanks. Where's the food?" Chloe asked bluntly. Hemsley gestured to some tables with an assortment of finger foods and Chloe made a beeline for them, only stopping to turn and wink at me from behind Hemsley's back. I bit my cheek and grinned back at her. Hemsley and I stood in silence for a minute awkwardly.

"Sorry, I kind of disappeared for a while," I said.

Hemsley nodded understandingly. "This is a lot for you." A new song started up and he tilted his head to listen. "Do you care to dance?" he asked.

I smiled shyly. "I don't know how to dance to this kind of music," I said. The musicians were playing flutes and drums and stringed instruments I didn't recognize. The music was beautiful but foreign to me.

"That's okay, I'll lead," Hemsley said. He extended his hand in offering and I accepted it graciously. He led me out onto the dance floor where others were already dancing and turned to face me.

"There's a lot of overlap between the partnered dances of Gotland and Alana. Plus you're a quick learner so you'll catch on," he reassured me. Then he took my hands and began guiding me through a series of steps. He was right, the steps were similar to another dance I knew and as soon as I'd caught on to the pattern, he introduced more steps, guiding me through spins and turns. The dance was lively and dynamic. At one point he turned to stand side by side with me, still holding my hands and then he quickly spun me out and back in again. This time we were closer though and his arm slid around my back, keeping me in tight. His other hand held mine and as the song came to a close, he dropped me into a dip and then pulled me up for one last spin, pulling me flush against him. His face was so close to mine I couldn't breathe. My chest was rising and falling rapidly against his which seemed to be doing the same. His eyes searched mine, but I wasn't sure what he was looking for.

Clapping sounded through the room and my eyes broke away from his to see Damien clapping loudly as others joined in.

"Well done Vivienne! You've always been an excellent dancer!" he called.

Hemsley and I pulled away from each other and I tried to collect myself as Damien came over to join us. I spotted Chloe at the dessert table, watching us with interest over a plate of sweets. She gave me a big thumbs up and I grimaced.

Damien wrapped an arm around my shoulders, pulling me to his side- and away from Hemsley. "I look forward to seeing you dance in Gotland's grand hall once again," he said.

"I don't know that parties will really be a top priority when we return," I said somewhat cautiously.

"Well we'll have to celebrate my coronation and your dramatic return from the dead of course!" Damien insisted. "Come! I want you to meet the king!" he said, pulling me along. I looked over my shoulder at Hemsley who was clearly displeased, though his dirty look was pointed not at me, but at my brother.

"We'll talk later!" I called back to him.

Damien guided me over to a middle aged man whose features resembled Ishana's.

"Hello, my son!" the king greeted Damien. I blinked in surprise at their familiarity as Damien embraced him.

"I want you to meet my sister, Vivienne," Damien said, gesturing to me.

I curtsied politely. "It's an honor to meet you, your highness."

The king bowed in return and smiled. "It's so good to meet a member of Damien's family. Ishana is about your age, perhaps you could be friends!"

I gave him a small smile. "I look forward to getting to know my future sister in law."

The king seemed pleased with this response and dismissed himself to sit with his wife who was lounging on a velvet couch and watching the festivities.

Damien grabbed two glasses of wine from a passing servant and handed one to me. "Isn't it wonderful? Gotland has not had relations with Alana since magic was banned. Now we have an opportunity to bring our kingdoms together."

I nodded, looking up at him. "It is wonderful Damien. You've always been good at winning people over. You'll make a great king."

Damien grinned. "It's good to hear you say that. I know you're in a hurry to get back home, but you've got to trust me that it will be worth it to take our time with this."

I frowned and fidgeted with the glass I'd yet to drink from. It didn't sit right with me that the people of Gotland were sleeping, frozen in time while we were here celebrating. Hemsley came over to join us and I relaxed a little, feeling relieved by his presence. Damien didn't acknowledge Hemsley and I had to wonder where the animosity between them came from. They had hardly interacted since we arrived in Alana so I wasn't sure how they could have come to dislike each other.

"You know Vivienne, you could be a great asset to Gotland," Damien said.

I looked at him confused. "What do you mean?"

"For the last 150 years, Gotland royalty has only wed non-mages. But with me in charge and you being a mage, a whole new realm of possibilities is opened up."

I blinked at him. "I'm sorry, I'm not following."

"Look," he said, "we both have a duty to do what's best for Gotland right?"

"Right..." I said hesitantly. Up until recently, I thought Gotland would be better off without me and I would not be welcome in court. I had planned to return with Hemsley. But if Damien wanted me there... I suppose I did have a duty to Gotland.

Damien continued, "You being a mage absolutely makes up for your disfigurement."

I flinched and saw Hemsely tense up out of the corner of my eye. He seemed to be holding his tongue in the presence of the future king of Gotland. Then it dawned on me what he was talking about.

"You're referring to my marriage potential," I said in realization.

"Yes, imagine all the wealthy men who would love to have mage children," Damien said with a gleam in his eye.

I felt a bit lightheaded and sick to my stomach. "I-"

"It will be so good for Gotland. You'll easily make up for the damage you've caused."

I blanched. My head buzzed and guilt swam around in my stomach. I had cursed my entire kingdom. Set them behind in trades and crops. I owed them whatever I had to offer. It was my duty.

"I-I suppose," I stuttered.

Hemsley slammed his drink down on the table. "I've had enough of this." He looked at Damien, radiating fury. "She's not just some animal you can barter with." He turned towards me. "And you, you should know better than this." With that he whipped around and stormed away, leaving us dumbfounded.

"He'd better watch his tongue," said Damien darkly.

"I have to go," I said abruptly. I set the glass down and hurried after Hemsley. He'd exited the room and was headed towards the guest wing. "Hemsley! Hemsley, wait!" I called after him. He stopped and turned towards me, anger emanating from him.

"How can you just roll over for him like that!" he exclaimed, gesturing angrily.

"That's not fair." I said in defense.

"You had plans! We had plans! But you're just going to let him guilt you into a lifetime of servitude?"

"I have a duty to my kingdom. You wouldn't understand," I said desperately.

"You don't owe your kingdom your misery. You owe them your best, and that's not it," Hemsley reprimanded me.

I clenched my jaw and gave him an angry scowl. He rolled his eyes and threw up his hands in exasperation.

"I'm leaving tomorrow morning," he said.

My lips parted in surprise. "What?"

"There's no point in me being here anymore. I have an estate to run and I've been away long enough," he said coldly.

I stood there, frozen in place. My heart twisted with a devastating pain, like someone had driven a dagger through it. I could find no words so I just stood there and watched him walk away. As soon as he was out of sight the tears started to spill over. I ran to my chambers and slammed the door behind me. In the privacy of my own room I gasped for air, pacing back and forth. I clenched and unclenched my hands repeatedly, needing an outlet for the storm of emotions I was feeling. He was leaving. He was leaving and he was taking a piece of my heart with him.

Chapter 41 The Cursed

I slept hard and woke early the next morning. My face was blotchy and swollen, my eyes puffy. I sat on the balcony with a throw blanket around my shoulders, watching as the sun rose. It was a glorious sunrise, yet I felt unaffected. A numbness had settled into my bones. It was better that way. The peaceful quiet was interrupted by my door slamming open. I startled but then relaxed as I saw it was just Chloe storming across the room to join me on the balcony.

"Hemsley is leaving!" she shouted.

I turned back to the horizon. "I know."

"He can't go! We're not done!" she exclaimed.

I shrugged dully. "He's done his part."

Chloe stood before me where I was sitting curled up. "No! We are not done until the curse is lifted and Gotland has its rightful ruler!"

I pulled my blanket tighter. "He wants to go home."

She looked at me in exasperation. "How can you just let him leave!"

I clenched my jaw. "Why would I fight to keep someone in my life who doesn't want to be there?"

Chloe stomped her foot and I looked at her a bit taken aback. "No! No more playing the victim! You fight for what you love, Vivienne!"

I swallowed as the emotion began to surface again, the numbness fading. "I can't keep being left alone, Chloe," I said, my voice cracking. I met her eyes with tears swimming though I was sure I'd cried myself dry last night.

"He needs you right now Vivienne. Ask him what Rhiannon took. Make him tell you."

I frowned. "I don't understand, I-"

"You can't let him leave Vivienne!" Chloe said urgently. "If you care about him then go! Go stop him!"

I stood, letting the blanket fall from my shoulders.

"GO!" yelled Chloe. And with that, I took off running. My dark, unbrushed hair floated behind me as I sprinted down halls and ran downstairs. What was I doing? My brain told me this was scary and stupid, but my heart held out hope. I ran out of the palace and towards the gates where I saw Hemsley sitting atop Cyrus.

"Wait!" I called to him. He turned and his eyes popped open in surprise. I didn't slow, still racing towards him. "Don't go!" I said breathlessly. He slid down off of Cyrus and walked a couple of steps toward me then stopped. I came to a halt ten feet before him and bent over for a moment, trying to catch my breath.

"Tell me," I panted, "tell me what Rhiannon took."

He frowned darkly and clenched his jaw.

"I told you everything. Now you tell me," I commanded, pointing a finger at him.

His jaw ticked and he looked around uncomfortably.

"She cursed me, Vivienne," he said in a defeated voice. " I'm cursed to be alone. To never find love. To never be able to be with them. To do so would be to harm them."

I scrunched my eyebrows, running that through my mind. So maybe all those times he'd hesitated or pulled away… "She took away your chance at love… with a curse?"

He nodded and rubbed the back of his neck. I suddenly knew what I needed to do. I strode towards him in determination, calling magic to my hands. His eyes widened and he took a step back. "What are you-" But I interrupted him as my magic shifted to my core power and I planted one hand on his chest and the other on the side of his face. Then, before I had a moment to doubt myself, I pulled his face down to meet mine and pressed my lips to his. My heart and magic thrummed together as I felt the warmth of his mouth on mine. It was only a few seconds but I felt my magic penetrate through him, finding the binds of the curse and burning through them. When it was done I pulled back to meet his utterly shocked eyes.

"I-how? But you're not a frog?" he stuttered.

"What?" I asked in bewilderment.

"The curse, she said if I kissed anyone they'd turn into a frog. How are you still human?" he asked in disbelief.

I blinked a few times and then grinned crookedly at him. "I'm a Purification mage. I broke the curse."

Hemsley gaped at me for a moment. "A Purification mage? That makes so much sense now. You did it ,Viv! You freed me from her curse!" He grabbed me up into a hug, lifting me off the ground and spinning.

I laughed and he set me down though as we slid apart we still held each other's arms.

"Rhiannon would have lifted the curse if you'd brought me to her. You were really going to give up true love to defy her?" I asked.

"I couldn't take you back to her," he said, shaking his head. "That'd kind of ruin my whole 'knight in shining armor' persona wouldn't it?"

I laughed and shook my head. "Still think I'm the damsel in distress, hm?"

Hemsley grinned a cheeky grin. "You are a damsel and you have been quite distressed."

I clicked my tongue. "That's fair."

"Speaking of," said Hemsely, "I should apologize for the way I spoke last night. It wasn't my place."

I sighed and released his arms to push my hair back. "No, you were right. I have more to offer Gotland than strategic marriage."

Hemsley grinned. “I’m glad you see that. So what are you going to do?”

I looked out at the palace gates determinedly. “I’m going back to Gotland.”

Hemsley raised his dark brows, “You’re going back with Damien?”

“No, I’m going now. Damien is taking too long. It’s not right that we are here, living in luxury while the people of Gotland are still cursed. I’m going back to lift the curse.”

Hemsley nodded slowly, “And then what?”

I blew out a breath. “I may not be the monarch of Gotland, but I can still help its people. I’ll start from the bottom up. My purification curse will have purged the plague, but I can go and heal the beggars. I can work at healing the crops and help my people rebuild. When Damien is ready he can come and take over. And, well, I could really use your help with all that if you’d come with me.”

Hemsley gave me a big smile. “That sounds like an excellent plan. I would be proud to help the princess of Gotland restore her kingdom.”

I returned his smile and pushed him playfully. “Hey, don’t call me that. I don’t really have a place in court anymore and I don’t think Damien will care to have me around once he realizes I don’t plan to participate in his political marriage schemes.”

Hemsley shrugged. “His loss. What will you tell him?” he asked.

I grimaced. "What I just told you I guess. I don't think he'll like it. He tends to want things his way."

"Yeah, I kinda picked up on that," said Hemsley.

"Let's see what Chloe wants to do," I said. Hemsley nodded and we walked back towards the palace.

"I feel a bit silly now, trying to run off like that," Hemsley admitted bashfully.

I bit back a smile. "You do have a flair for the dramatic, don't you? I guess that makes two of us. I've officially crashed two parties now. Also, I've been running around in my nightgown," I said, frowning as I suddenly remembered my appearance. I grabbed the skirt of the gown and did an altering spell, changing it into a simple day dress.

"Impressive. You're learning fast, as always," Hemsley praised me.

"Well I have a great mentor," I replied with a grin.

We stopped by the stables and I saddled up Celeste. Now that I knew what to do, I didn't want to wait any longer than necessary. Then we headed back to the dining hall where we found Chloe greedily consuming a hot quiche. She looked up excitedly when we entered and looked back and forth between us with a curious glint in her eye. I suddenly felt embarrassed, thinking about the kiss and rubbed my arms. Hemsley cleared his throat and looked at me expectantly.

"We've decided to return to Gotland and lift the curse. We're going to help build the kingdom back up while we wait for Damien to return."

Chloe lifted an eyebrow.

"And," I continued, "we'd like to invite you to join us."

Chloe fiddled with her fork and chewed thoughtfully. Then she grinned. "Sounds like an adventure. I'm in."

Chapter 42 The Conqueror

After a quick breakfast with Chloe, we headed to Damien's chambers. A servant opened the door for us and we entered into a large sitting room that was attached to Damien's bedchamber. He was sitting at a desk with various documents spread before him. Ishana sat perched on a chaise lounge, her dutiful handmaid close by. My brother looked surprised when we entered.

"What brings you all here?" he asked.

I stood before him with Hemsley on one side and Chloe on the other. "We've decided to return to Gotland. You may remain here until everything is in order, but it's time for me to lift the curse I cast and start repairing the damage our forefathers caused by banning magic."

Damien shook his head. "Vivienne, I thought you agreed to wait with me. You can't just wake everyone up with no monarch in place. The people need leadership, authority."

I had anticipated this answer and lifted my chin. "They've made it this long with poor leadership, they'll be okay without the bureaucracy while waiting for your return."

Damien smacked his hand on the desk and we all jumped, Ishana included. My brother rose up from the desk, bracing his hands against it.

"You don't get it, Vivienne. And I wouldn't expect you to. I was raised to be king, and you- well you were raised to be a pretty trophy."

I withdrew from his words like I'd been slapped and felt anger rolling off of Hemsley. The temptation to concede and let him have his way crawled up my throat, but I swallowed it down. In a level voice I replied, "It's my curse Damien, and I'm going to lift it. And when I am done helping Gotland I will leave. Because I have no interest in being a pretty trophy if that is all you see me as."

Damien glared at me and came around the desk. "You can't just leave!"

"You did," I replied.

"That's different!" he shouted.

"Is it?" My heart thundered, but I kept my voice cool. I'd never argued with Damien like this before. He could be pushy, but never like this.

"I am king and I say you must stay!" He was red in the face with anger. But why? Why did he care so much?

"You have no good reason for me to stay Damien. I'm going, and you can't stop me."

Damien froze and then stood and swept his hair back, his demeanor flipping like a coin. Chloe tensed beside me and she grabbed my arm to whisper, "Vivienne we should-"

"Actually I can," Damien answered. He nodded to Ishana who hurriedly exited the room with her maid. At the same time, a heavy thud sounded at the door and I realized with a sinking feeling that they'd just bolted the door.

"What are you doing?" Hemsley demanded.

"Shut up peasant," Damien snapped. "You have no place in this conversation."

I gaped at him. "Damien, what's going on? Why are you doing this?"

"I thought I could get you to join me Vivienne, but I can see that you're just as stubborn as always. I have plans, Vivienne. Big plans." He paced the room nonchalantly as our eyes followed him. "You see, with Rhiannon's help, I intend to unite the entire northern hemisphere."

I froze. "You're working with Rhiannon?"

"She's the most powerful sorceress of our time, Vivienne. It would be foolish not to side with her." He said it like it was obvious and I was ignorant.

Chloe crowded in closer to me, "Vivienne," she hissed.

But I couldn't turn away from my brother. "How could you side with her after what she did to me!" I shouted. "She's evil, Damien."

Damien rolled his eyes. "You were in the way Vivienne. Honestly, she did me a favor by removing you from the equation."

The betrayal sank through me like a rock. I felt my heart break all over again as the last of my family turned their back on me. My throat was tight and I wanted to cry but instead, I fisted my hands and brought magic to them. "I'm leaving," I said in a low, hoarse voice.

Damien chuckled, "Oh Vivienne, did you think you were the only mage in the family?" He raised his hands as magic swirled around them and my eyes widened in surprise.

Hemsley lifted his own hands, swirling with magic. "It's three against one, Damien," he said in a warning tone.

The traitorous prince studied the magic swirling at his fingertips. "Hm, is it though? Didn't you have a job to do, dog? Why don't you go ahead and finish the task Rhiannon gave you?"

His voice seemed to reverberate in my head and I winced. Hemsley's hands closed around my upper arms and I looked at him in surprise.

"What are you doing?" But when I looked at his face, he was expressionless and didn't respond. He began dragging me towards the door and I pulled against him. "Hemsley, what are you doing?"

"Vivienne, he's a Charisma mage!" Chloe shouted, "He can control people with his voice!" She started trying to pry Hemsley's hands off to no avail.

I looked at Damien as a dozen childhood memories fell into place. The way Damien always ordered me around, getting frustrated when I wouldn't do the ridiculous things he demanded. The way people flocked to him. The way our father listened to him. The way everybody listened to him. It all made sense. But I had a core power too. I called it to my palms and reached back to clap my hands over Hemsley's ears. He froze and then loosened his grip on my arms, looking around in surprise.

"I'm sorry, I didn't want to do that," he apologized.

I smiled in relief and turned back to my brother. "I'm immune to your powers. That's why I was in the way, wasn't it?"

He growled in frustration. "You never listened. Never obeyed. But if you won't bend, then you will break." He lifted his hands and Hemsley shouted in warning. A blast of fire shot towards us but Hemsley leapt in front of Chloe and I and activated his bracers. A red shield erupted from the magical relics and stopped the fire dead in its tracks.

"A little more warning next time would be great," I said to Chloe as we ducked despite the shield.

"Sorry," she said, "I can't look all the time and sometimes when I do it's too late!"

"It's okay, just find us a way out of here," I urged her.

Hemsley was still maintaining the shield while Damien hurled spells at it in a rage.

"Any ideas here?" Hemsley asked.

Chloe had her baby blue magic whirling around her eyes as she searched for a potential way out of the locked chamber and she didn't answer.

"If he calls the guards in here, we won't be able to take all of them," Hemsley said. Except Damien didn't seem interested in calling in the guards. He finally took a break from trying to break through Hemsley's shield and panted for a moment before brushing his hair back and collecting himself.

"You know, I had hoped to take care of this myself, but in this case I think you might enjoy a visit from your old friend Rhiannon."

My stomach dropped and Hemsley looked at me in a panic as Damien began casting some sort of communication spell, his rings glowing.

Just then Chloe popped out of her trance and grabbed my arm. "You can take him!"

"What?" I asked in confusion.

"You can take him. The only way out is through him," Chloe insisted.

I looked past Damien to the third story balcony behind him. A hundred reasons why that was a bad idea ran through my head- most importantly falling from three stories and the fact that I'd never fought another mage. I shook my head.

Hemsley looked back at me. "I think she's right, Viv. He's powerful but untrained and you've got natural talent for combat magic. I'll back you up."

I looked between my two friends who I'd grown to trust over the course of our journey and then set my jaw in determination. "Drop the shield."

Hemsley nodded and I called my core power to my hands just before he lowered his arms and dropped the shield. Damien looked up in surprise from the spell he was trying to focus on just as I released a bolt of magic right at his face. His head snapped back like he'd been punched in the face and he stumbled backward, his spell broken. He caught himself against the desk and looked at me in bewilderment. The stupid look on his face would have been a lot more satisfying if my heart wasn't absolutely broken over his betrayal.

His expression hardened into a snarl, "You little bit-" I threw my magic at him again, sending him careening over the desk. I didn't feel as bad about it this time. Damien rose up from the other side of the desk and threw fire at me, but Hemsley stepped up beside me and raised his shield again. The fire scattered across its surface, causing no harm.

"You're too late, I've already called her here. She'll be here any minute," Damien taunted.

"Lower the shield," I commanded Hemsley. We needed to get out of here. Now. But as soon as the shield was lowered, Damien spoke.

"Come here, little one."

His voice was laced with power and I realized too late what he'd done as Chloe crossed the room obediently. Hemsley and I both reached for her, but Damien leapt over the desk, blasting fire in our direction, and snatched Chloe. He held her against his chest, her dazed eyes facing us. In his other hand, he held another ball of fire near her face.

"Don't hurt her!" I cried.

Damien sneered triumphantly. "You are weak. Your friends are weak. You were never a match for me. Rhiannon will take you all and use you as she pleases."

I panted as panic started to set in. I could not go with Rhiannon again. I would not. Hemsley took my hand and I saw my fear reflected in his eyes. I looked again at Chloe and an idea formulated in my mind. As it did, I saw Chloe's eyes clear and meet with mine- her core power activated.

"*Do it,*" she mouthed.

Between our joined hands I pressed water magic into Hemsley's palm- the only clue I could give him to my plan without giving it away. He squeezed my hand in response.

"Maybe I am weak," I called back to Damien, "but I do have something you don't."

"And what would that be?" he sneered.

"Desperation."

In unison Hemsley and I shot water at Damien and Chloe. It doused Damien's fire and he flew back, releasing his hostage, but Chloe knew what was coming and had held her breath- bracing herself against the onslaught. We ran forward and Chloe turned to run with us as we leapt over the desk and Damien. Not waiting for him to recover, we ran side by side towards the balcony, stepped up onto the railing, and jumped off the edge.

Chapter 43 The Handmaid

For a minute we were free falling and I felt panic rise up as my mind went back to that dreadful fall from the tower. I had but a split second to glance down at the ground before us and take a breath before we plummeted down into a pool of crystal clear water with a tremendous splash. For a moment I thought we were very lucky to have Chloe to see a way out, but then I remembered I did not know how to swim. Instinctually I swept my arms and legs, trying to push myself to the surface, but my movements were awkward and inefficient. I saw Hemsley and Chloe rise up to the surface and then Hemsley ducked back down to drag me up with him. If I'd had any clarity of mind, I would have thought to use water magic to propel myself up, but Hemsley had already grabbed hold of me by the time I thought of it and he quickly pulled me to the edge of the pool. Chloe was already hauling herself out of the pool and her wet hair swung as she turned back to us.

"We've got to get out of here before Rhiannon arrives!" she hurried us along.

We stumbled out of what appeared to be a private swimming pool and ran through the palace grounds towards the stables. I was glad we'd thought to saddle Celeste beforehand as it would certainly save us time now. I picked up Chloe's pack, the only one we hadn't loaded up yet and turned to meet Hemsley's eyes. He looked at me and his eyes widened, his mouth slightly agape.

"What?"

He cleared his throat and gave me a very unconvincing, "Nothing!"

I looked at Chloe who sucked in her lips and raised her eyebrows, then gave a pointed look at my dress. I looked down and gasped a little as I realized my soaking wet, white dress was very much clinging to my hips and thighs. Suddenly I was very grateful for Chloe's pack which I was holding in front of my chest. I blushed deep red and couldn't help but look back at Hemsley who also looked a shade darker now, though he still didn't tear his eyes away. I quickly summoned wind magic which whipped around me, leaving me mostly dry. I then did the same for Chloe while Hemsley also dried himself. We mounted our horses with Chloe behind me and headed for the stable door, but stopped dead in our tracks at the sight of a figure in the doorway. Ishana's handmaid?

"Step aside. We don't want to hurt you," Hemsley commanded.

She stepped forward nervously. "I can help you! You'll never get away in time!"

Hemsley and I exchanged a glance.

"Lift my curse and I'll help you escape!" the handmaid urged us.

I glanced back at Chloe who was already nodding. I quickly dismounted and approached the woman. Standing before her, I lifted my hands and summoned my core power.

"Give me your hands," I instructed. She willingly placed her hands in mine and I closed my eyes for a moment as I pushed my magic into her. I felt it flood through her body, seeking out the curse and then burning it up when it found the binds that held her. I opened my eyes and watched in surprise as what appeared to be an illusion burned away with bright, white light.

Standing before me was not a middle aged woman, but a young boy, maybe a few years older than Chloe with dark skin and tightly curled black hair. He withdrew his hands and looked at them in wonder.

"You've freed me!" he exclaimed.

All I could do was blink at him in surprise. The shouting of the palace guards sounded in the distance and we all jumped.

"Let's go!" exclaimed the boy, "we don't have much time!"

Hemsley came around and pulled him up onto Cyrus while I climbed back up.

The boy pointed towards the palace gates, "Hurry! Once we're beyond the wards I can transport us out of here!"

We urged the horses into a gallop towards the palace gates which were, for the moment, open for the day. However, the guards quickly caught sight of us and shouted for us to stop. Ahead of us, they began pushing the iron gates closed and we drove the horses harder. But we weren't fast enough, the gates were already halfway closed and we weren't going to cover the distance in time. I stood a little taller in the stirrups and threw a blast of concentrated magic in the direction of one of the guards pushing the gate closed. Though I'd only intended to cast him out of the way, the blast instead slammed squarely into the gate- bending the tall doors outwards and throwing the two guards several feet beyond. Oops. I guess I needed to scale it down a bit. We barrelled through the mangled gates and didn't stop to look back as we took off through the city.

"We've got to stop so I can transport us!" called the boy we'd collected. Hemsley nodded and led us into a sharp turn that landed us in an alley. I pulled up alongside him and we all watched as the boy began to spin orange colored magic between his hands. Hemsley and I exchanged a surprised look. When he had said he could transport us I had assumed that meant he had stolen travel dust from Ishana, the travel mage. The sound of the palace guards was drawing nearer and we watched the boy with bated breath. His spell grew and just as the guards caught sight of us once more, he threw it over our group and we were once again sucked into the darkness.

Chapter 44 The Harpies

My gut clenched at the breathtaking sensation of the travel dust and I tried to calm my mind knowing that this time I was escaping an evil witch- not being kidnapped by one. My vision rushed back and I was suddenly aware of Chloe gripping me tightly from behind.

"You okay?" I asked her. She nodded and I turned my attention back to the mysterious boy who'd helped us escape. He hopped off the horse, stumbling a little as he hit the ground. Hemsley looked down at him in surprise.

"You helped us escape, but why? Who are you?" Hemsley asked, voicing the question we were all wondering.

The boy dusted himself off and stood resolutely. "My name is Ejiro. The princess captured me and forced upon me that magical disguise when she discovered my magic."

"Why would she do that?" I asked in alarm.

"She forced me to stay by her side and pretended that my magic was her own. It gave her status and value in her culture and she used it to entice your brother." Ejiro explained. "She has no magic of her own but she is clever and conniving. She bound me to her using another witch's spell, but I watched through the keyhole as you fought the prince and I knew my chance at escape had come."

Hemsley and I exchanged shocked expressions. We would not have guessed that the princess, with her quiet and demure manner, could be capable of such things.

"We owe you a great thanks, Ejiro," Hemsley said, bowing at the middle in respect.

"Will you come with us to Gotland?" I asked. "We could provide a bed and food. It's the least we could do."

Ejiro bowed in return and looked at me with his bright eyes. "I appreciate the offer, but I have not seen my family in nearly three years. I fear Ishana will come for them when she discovers my escape. I must get them to safety, but I believe we will meet again."

"Thank you, Ejiro," I said. "Travel safely."

Ejiro nodded and seemed to take a deep breath in preparation to see his family again. He summoned magic to his fingers but before he cast his spell, Chloe spoke up.

"When you get there, take care of the driver first. He reports back to Ishana."

Ejiro raised his eyebrows in surprise and then nodded in understanding. Then he cast his spell over himself and disappeared in a scattering of magic. Our trio looked at each other for a moment and then we turned our attention to our surroundings. We were just outside the border nearest the mountain range that separated Gotland from the Wildlands. The castle was not far from this side of the border. The wards seemed to have prevented us from transporting in which was probably a good thing since Rhiannon and Damien both had access to travel dust. I dismounted and approached the nearly invisible shield on foot, but just as I reached out to it, a screech sounded in the distance. We all whipped around to see a black cloud of flying creatures advancing quickly.

"What is that?" I asked in dismay.

"Harpies," Hemsley replied, gritting his jaw. "Courtesy of Rhiannon no doubt."

"Let's go then!" I urged, walking through the ward. But Hemsley shook his head solemnly and pressed his hand to the shield, reminding me that only I could pass through.

"Shoot! We'll have to fight them." I cursed.

Chloe shook her head. "No. You've got to go to the ward and give us access."

Hemsley nodded in agreement. "She's right. We're sitting ducks, backed up against this shield and the harpies will just keep us busy until Rhiannon arrives. Then we're all doomed."

The harpies were drawing closer, their bodies becoming more defined as they came into view. I clenched and unclenched my hands in frustration.

"I can't leave you!" I cried.

"You don't have a choice, Viv. You've got to get to that ward and give us entrance," Hemsley pushed. He dismounted and stood before me. Gently, he pushed me back till I stood on the other side of the shield and his hands lay flat against the surface. His eyes bore into mine. "We'll be okay. I'll protect Chloe, but you've got to hurry."

I nodded finally and Chloe appeared, passing Celeste to me. Her eyes were clear and sure which gave me some comfort so I heaved myself up into the saddle just as the harpies landed. I looked at them fearfully, but Hemsley smacked Celeste's hindquarters and yelled, "Go!"

I took off, racing towards the heart of the city where the castle stood. I glanced back to see Hemsley's red shield holding back the monsters. I urged Celeste to go faster and faster, the city drawing nearer. I didn't know how long Hemsley could hold his shield, nor when Rhiannon would arrive. Once in the city, Celeste's hooves clacked against the cobblestone road, echoing in the silent streets. My hair and dress blew behind me as we raced on, through the palace gates which had been left ajar and we pulled up to a halt in the front courtyard. I slid off Celeste's back and flew up the palace steps, taking them two at a time. I sprinted down the hall and past the ballroom, my Alanian slippers sliding on the marble floors. I ran down the dungeon stairs, nearly tripping and rammed my shoulder into the wall of the narrow staircase. I pushed off the wall with a grunt of pain and continued through the dungeon to the chamber Hemsley and I had uncovered. Bursting into the room, I came to an abrupt stop before the enchanted pedestal.

"Let them in!" I bellowed at it. Nothing happened. "Give my friends passage!" I commanded. Still nothing. I slapped my hands down on the stone relic, "I command you to let my friends in!" The ward lit up in response and from the center of the ring of runes rose up a tiny pedestal on which sat a silver bracelet embedded with a clear stone. I picked it up in confusion and placed it around my wrist as that seemed to be what the ward intended. The bracelet was wide with intricate runes that matched the ward. As it touched my skin it shrunk to fit and the clear stone turned amethyst purple, the same way my sword had. I looked at it and then on a hunch spoke to it, "Passage for Hemsley and Chloe." It flashed and I took that as an indication that my request had been fulfilled.

I ran back up the stairs, retracing my footsteps and returning to Celeste in the courtyard. I considered riding her back to the border, but she looked tired and gave me a side eye that said, "Absolutely not." So I grabbed my sword from the pack and took off towards the border.

It wasn't long though before I spotted Hemsley and Chloe in the distance, riding on Cyrus. I stopped and bent over with my hands on my knees to catch my breath. Then, I raised my hands over my head in victory and whooped loudly. They spotted me and Chloe waved back enthusiastically. I couldn't help but laugh as they clambered to a stop before me. The past 24 hours had been wild and a manic laugh seemed appropriate at this point. Hemsley grinned at me, though he also looked a little concerned for my mental state. After I'd caught my breath I waved them on, "Alright, let's go. I've got a curse to lift."

Hemsley hopped down and caught my arm. "Hold up."

I looked at him in surprise and he shook his head. "First things first, you are not walking all the way back." He guided me to the horse and lifted me up to sit in front of Chloe who grinned at me. He then took the reins and began walking us through the city towards the palace.

"Second, I know we were in a hurry to get here and all, but now that we are safe behind the ward, do you think it might not be so terrible to let everyone sleep just one more night?" He looked at me in question and I frowned. "Plus," he continued, "there's going to be a lot to deal with when you wake everyone up, right?"

My frown deepened. He was right. "Shoot," I said, rubbing my eyes. "I didn't even think about that. We can't let my father rule, and we definitely can't let Damien rule. What am I going to do?" I groaned into my hands. My companions were quiet. When I lowered my hands Hemsley glanced back at me.

"There is another option…" Chloe said.

I looked back at her. She looked like she was barely containing herself, her eyes sparkling. I frowned and looked back at Hemsley who was looking at me pointedly. My eyes popped open in understanding and I shook my head vigorously. "No. No way."

"I think you'd be good at it," said Hemsley with a cheeky grin.

"I just cursed the entire kingdom! They're not going to follow me!" I protested.

Hemsley shrugged. "They'll get over it."

"You don't get it. The royal court is terrified of magic," I said.

"Then fire them. You make the rules," Hemsley said nonchalantly.

I rubbed my forehead in incredulity.

"You are the only viable option, Vivienne," said Chloe quietly.

I shook my head in refusal, not able to put into words all the reasons why that was a bad idea.

"Let's sleep on it," suggested Hemsley gently. "You can think about it in the morning."

"Sleep sounds good," I relented. I couldn't think clearly. My mind was spinning and I could only hope that morning would bring clarity.

Chapter 45 The Queen

I woke early the next morning and watched the sunrise from the terrace of one of the guest chambers. Having spent some time in the Alanian palace, we had opted to help ourselves to the comfortable beds found in the palace rather than the stiff beds at the inn. After watching the sunrise, I padded down the long halls of the palace I'd grown up in. My bare feet didn't make a sound as I wandered around in a soft dressing robe. I realized I'd never walked these halls barefoot- let alone in my nightgown and dressing robe. It wasn't considered proper. I avoided the ballroom where I knew everyone still lay sleeping. I wasn't ready to go in there just yet. I found myself standing in the doorway of my old bedchamber. The curtains were drawn, keeping the room dark, but when I pulled them wide open I found that the room was exactly as I'd left it. My hairbrush still sat on the vanity, my cloak still hung on its hook, and… sure enough, my grass stained slippers were still hidden under the bed. It seemed that the room had been kept clean, but nothing had been disturbed. I moved to the closet and looked over the rows and rows of elegant gowns.

"Are you going to wear one?"

I jumped a little and turned to see Hemsley standing several feet behind me. He had helped himself to a white dress shirt, black vest, and black pants. He looked much more like how I remembered seeing him at his estate. I huffed a laugh, "No, I don't think so."

He grinned, coming closer to peer in at the many shades of pink, purple, yellow, and white. Tufts of tulle stuck out and tiny sparkly beads shone back at us. "Why not?"

I ran my hand over the pretty fabrics nostalgically, taking in the bubbly designs. "I don't feel this way anymore."

Hemsley gazed at me and leaned against the door frame. "How do you feel?"

I let out a heavy sigh. That was a loaded question. "Damaged," I whispered.

Hemsley caught my hand and placed his other hand lightly on the side of my face, "We're all damaged, but no less valuable."

I swallowed thickly and met his eyes, seeing the sincerity there. "They think I'm a villain."

He gave me a mischievous smile. "I've always had a thing for villains."

I threw back my head, laughing and gently pushed him away. "You're insufferable!"

That only made his smile stretch wider and he backed out of the closet. "I'll see you in the ballroom in an hour?"

I nodded, an unspoken agreement there.

"Maybe you can find something in there to wear for the occasion," he said with an amused look.

I shook my head with another laugh as he left the room and then I turned back to the closet. My thoughts began to click into place as I fiddled with a gown. I was not the naive princess I had once been, nor could I play the role of the perfect girl they expected me to be, but maybe I could invent a new role. One that better suited my purposes. One that would demand the respect and loyalty I would need in order to radically change Gotland for the better. I snatched a dress off the rack and set to work as an idea took shape in my mind.

An hour later I stood in one of the doorways leading to the ballroom. Chloe and Hemsley were waiting for me and Hemsley froze as he took in my appearance. I wore a long, black velvet gown that didn't remotely resemble the gown it had once been. It had a low, open back that revealed my shoulder blades and the scar that ran across them. The sleeves fit my arms snugly and came to points on the backs of my hands. Chloe was grinning a wicked grin, like she'd seen this before, but somehow it was better in person. Hemsley's gaping mouth slowly turned into a crooked grin and he bowed deeply before offering me his arm.

"May I?"

The corner of my mouth curled up and I took his arm. The three of us walked to the middle of the room, stepping over the slumbering party guests. I dropped Hemsley's arm and put some distance between my companions and myself.

"Thank you," I said. "For standing with me today. For going on this crazy adventure to fix my misdeeds. The pain of the past is still with me, but had those things not happened, I would never have had my eyes opened to the suffering of these people. My people. And I never would have met you two. So, in some ways, I am grateful for where my suffering has brought me, and who it has brought me to."

Chloe was still smiling way too much and I narrowed my eyes playfully at her. "I suspect you've known this would happen." She shrugged and I had to laugh.

I met Hemsley's eyes and he looked at me with a tinge of sadness. "I'm proud of you, Viv."

I smiled a shaky smile and turned to face the rest of the room. "Time to wake up my kingdom now." I summoned my magic, but instead of casting it, I drew in the coat of purification magic I sensed lay draped over the inhabitants of the kingdom. It returned to me from every corner of the kingdom as I beckoned it and grew into a fierce storm of glowing magic that whipped around me.

The magic was so intense, that it hummed audibly. Finally, the last of it returned to me and I began to quiet the storm with each exhale until the room stood silent once more. I waited until I began to see twitching and stirring amongst the many bodies.

"Rise and shine everyone!" I called out in a singsong voice. All around me party guests and members of the court stirred from their deep sleep. As they raised their heads and looked around in confusion, I stood resolutely and captured all the attention in the room.

"You'll be happy to find that while you all were sleeping for the last few weeks, I saved the kingdom from certain destruction," I announced

Father gaped at me from the floor beside the throne while his wife quickly rose to grab up her child from the bassinet.

"You're welcome," I added. I climbed the steps to the throne, the train of my black velvet dress trailing behind me. My heels clicked on the marble steps and I held my chin high, exuding power. As I approached my father I lowered my voice, "And I intend to save it again, which means I'll be needing this," I plucked the crown from his head and climbed the last step before turning to face my terrified audience. Hemsley and Chloe stood in the center of it all, watching me proudly and I drew strength from their confidence. I paused as my magic wrapped around the crown in my hands causing it to shift and warp till I held something much more fearsome. A golden tiara with sharp golden spines that pointed upwards.

"There's a new queen in Gotland," I said as I placed the tiara on my head and smirked, "Me."

A collective gasp followed by fearful whispers broke out from the crowd. I soaked in their fear with satisfaction. Their horrified faces didn't bother me. Because if a villain is what Gotland needed, then that's what I would be.

What happens when the villain wins?
Find out in book two: Once There Was a Queen

Made in the USA
Las Vegas, NV
16 April 2024

88770011R00184